DAUGHTERS OF BAD MEN

A NOVEL

LAURA OLES

Unlocking New Worlds

Daughters of Bad Men
Copyright © 2017 by Laura Oles All rights reserved.
First Print Edition: October 2017

ISBN-13: 978-0-615-81631-9

Red Adept Publishing, LLC
104 Bugenfield Court
Garner, NC 27529
http://RedAdeptPublishing.com/

Cover and Formatting: Streetlight Graphics

The world breaks everyone, and afterward,
some are strong at the broken places.

—*Ernest Hemingway*

CHAPTER ONE

"**D**O YOU THINK YOU CAN get my money back?"

Jamie Rush was used to that question, just as she was accustomed to tempering her answers with hope while still remaining honest about the realities of such cases. As a skip tracer in the small town of Port Alene, Texas, Jamie had built a somewhat steady clientele of women just like Sarah Mathers.

Sarah, a single mother of two little boys, sat across from Jamie, her small frame almost folded in on itself. The weight of being in such a situation showed itself in her posture and in her eyes. It was as if she wore the shame of her circumstances like a blanket.

"I'm going to do everything I can," Jamie said. "Start from the beginning. Tell me about him."

Sarah avoided direct eye contact, glancing at the table, the ground, and her lap. "My mom warned me about him. Said he wasn't good for me, which was all I needed to stick with him long after I knew he was a loser."

"Don't beat yourself up too much," Jamie said. "I think we all have boyfriends in our past who we chose because our parents disapproved. It's like an aphrodisiac for teenage girls." Jamie pulled a chair next to Sarah and sat down. She didn't touch or hug the woman. She just sat close.

This was uncomfortable territory for Jamie, showing her softer side. Her closest friends joked that being close to her was like trying to hug a porcupine. But with these cases, Jamie was willing to dig a bit deeper, to let her compassion show.

"You going to be okay?" Jamie asked.

Sarah gave a slight nod, still avoiding eye contact. "I'll figure something out. Anything but going to my family. They won't lend me another cent." She reached to the corner of her eye to wipe away a forming tear. "And I can't blame them. I need to handle this on my own now."

Cookie Hinojosa, Jamie's partner and best friend, appeared, carrying three glasses of iced tea on a tray. He held out the tray with some fanfare, lowering it to eye level for Sarah and Jamie to see. He balanced the drinks on the tray like a pro. "Don't forget to tip your hot waitress," he joked as he placed the drinks on a nearby table. Cookie sported his daily uniform of Hawaiian shirt, cargo shorts with who-knows-what stashed in the pockets, and tan leather boat shoes. "I just told Marty to put it on your tab, okay?"

Jamie nodded. Their referral-only investigation business was run out of the studio loft atop Hemingway's Pier, a local restaurant and pub run by their friend and personal bartender Marty Scout. He'd named the place after Ernest Hemingway because he liked the way Hemingway lived his life. Jamie was pretty sure Marty hadn't read *A Moveable Feast,* although she had bought him a copy years ago for his birthday.

The term "studio loft" was a gracious term, although it was technically correct. The area was small, clean, and neat, but the furniture left much to be desired. An old black leatherette couch, non-matching recliner, and a weathered wood coffee table faced a small kitchenette on the opposite side of the room. In most situations, Jamie held her client meetings downstairs at Hemingway's at a table Marty kept reserved for her, but certain cases—more delicate cases—were better handled away from the ears of boisterous patrons.

Jamie gestured to the tea glass on the table, and Sarah reached for it. It was time to get back to business. "Let's go over what you know that can help me find Ricky."

Ricky, a.k.a. Ricky Finch, was a deadbeat father and a lousy boyfriend. In addition to owing money to care for his children, Ricky Finch also owed his bookie, Erin Clay, over ten thousand dollars. Erin had hired Jamie to track him down, but this time, she wanted the money he owed to go to Sarah, and she was willing to write off the debt if that happened.

"He mostly works off the books, doing construction, so he doesn't have a regular job that he shows up for. I know he does some work for a guy named Lenny, but I think it's been a few months since that job ended."

Jamie retrieved her small notebook and wrote down Lenny's name. "Okay, what else? Do you have photos of him so I know what he looks like? Does he do any social media?"

Social media had been a boon for skip tracers and investigators.

Countless cases had been closed because the debtor in question couldn't help but brag about something online or comment on a hot girl's photo. Yes, criminals were actually that stupid. In those instances, catching them was like fishing in a barrel.

Sarah scrolled through the camera app on her phone and pulled up an image. She handed the phone to Jamie, who studied the photo. Ricky didn't look like anything special. Shorter than average, he had the beginnings of a beer gut and was balding in the front. Next to him in the photo was Sarah, her arms around his waist, smiling for the camera. Clearly she saw something in the guy that compelled her to have two kids with him. The couple was resting on the front of a tangerine Dodge Charger, complete with racing stripe—an indicator that the man had not mentally left high school.

"Is this his car?" Jamie asked.

"Yes." Sarah said. "He didn't have money for rent, but he could make the payment on the car. He'd pay that bill first before anything else."

Jamie zoomed in on the photo, using her thumb and forefinger, so she could see the license plate number. She jotted down the number on her notepad.

Returning the phone to Sarah, she asked, "Anything else? Where does he like to hang out? Does he have a regular place?" Guys like Ricky always had a regular place.

"The Tarpon Taproom."

Jamie nodded. The Tarpon Taproom was a run-down bar and grill that would fail the scrutiny of even the laziest health inspector. No one much cared about the food. The draft specials, the opportunity to pick up work of a dubious nature, and the general sense of anonymity made the Tarpon Taproom an underground hit.

Sarah tucked a strand of hair behind her ear. "I know he's there a lot, but I also know he owes money on a tab, so he may not go back until he can pay. The owner doesn't like deadbeats. I know that because he's asked me to cover Ricky's tab."

Cookie interjected, "Well, he likes them, but they still have to pay up."

Sarah smiled for the first time since she had walked through their office door. Cookie had a way of making people feel comfortable.

As Sarah sipped from her tea glass, condensation ran down the side and dripped onto her leg. She wiped the water on her jean shorts and placed the glass down. "I know I shouldn't have, but I gave Ricky my paychecks because he's supposed to handle the bills, and now we're about to be evicted. And I'm close to having my own car repoed." Hints of tears started to form, but she wiped them away with the palm of her hand, sniffing as she turned her head to the side. She then looked at Jamie and shrugged. "I'm an idiot, I know."

"You're not an idiot." Jamie meant it. "And don't worry. You've given us a lot to work with here. Cookie and I are going to do our best to find Ricky and get things settled for you. You deserve a fresh start."

Cookie turned on his signature charm. "We'll hang him upside down and shake out every penny. Don't worry."

After Cookie escorted Sarah to the door, he closed it and sighed. He plopped down on the couch, the leatherette material rustling under his weight, and propped his feet up on the armrest. For a man pushing 270, his feet weren't proportional, maybe no more than a size ten. Jamie had landed far more jokes about that than he deserved.

He caught her staring at his shoes. "Not one word, Jamie."

She laughed. "We've been together too long if you're reading my mind now." She remained sitting in her chair but had pulled her laptop from her bag and waited for the operating system to load. "I'm going to run his license plate and see what I can find. Sounds like the address he uses is bogus, anyway, so we're going to need to catch him when he's out somewhere."

Cookie smiled. "Sounds like Danny's Den is our best bet. Guess we'll be doing some surveillance."

"With any luck, we'll tie this up in the next day or two and move on to some other cases."

"Hopefully cases that pay," Cookie added. "I'm happy to do freebie jobs too, but we need some money coming in. Our operating account has almost enough money to cover lunch at Taqueria San Juan."

Jamie cringed at the comment. "That's no bueno."

"*No bueno, mija,*" he agreed. "As the company finance manager, I'm ordering you not to take any more free cases until we book some divorce cases or surveillance or something else that pays solid."

Jamie knew her friend was right. Compassion was good for the soul but bad for business. She typed in Ricky Finch's license plate number and waited for the Investig8 database to load. Databases often helped put together the beginning pieces of a puzzle, but data had to be accurate and actionable. Turning facts into information required legwork. Lots of data wouldn't solve a case. Knowing how to use the tools and understanding how to take the data and make connections were the keys to finding Finch and his money.

The hunt had begun.

———————

Jamie Rush focused her attention on the man walking alone through the parking lot. Ricky Finch was smiling and comfortable. She peered above her tinted driver's side window—raised enough to shield most of her face—and watched him fumble in his pants pocket for his keys. He did not act like a man on the run.

He acted free.

She would fix that.

Cookie shifted his substantial weight in the passenger's seat. He filled the available space in the black Tahoe, leaving no room for so much as a stray thought. "I hate surveillance. My butt always falls asleep."

Jamie kept her attention on Ricky as he walked across the parking lot. "Thanks for canceling your evening with Netflix so you could keep me company by complaining," she joked.

Finch slipped into the driver's seat of the flashy tangerine Dodge Charger, which he had parked at the Tarpon Taproom.

Jamie handed her cell to Cookie. "Send Erin a text and let her know that we've got him at the cash-out location and we're following him. I'm expecting his payout was over 8K. He wouldn't be in there if he couldn't pay his tab."

Cookie placed his thumb on Jamie's phone, unlocking it with his fingerprint. His phone had the same function for her. She trusted only a few people, and Cookie was at the top of the list. Plus, if she were ever kidnapped and left her phone behind, Cookie wouldn't waste time hacking when he should be trying to rescue her.

Ricky started his engine, and Jamie did the same. "Okay, let's get this done. And I hope he's not a fighter."

"That's what I'm here for, remember?" Cookie's large thumbs navigated the text app on Jamie's phone. "Erin's good. We'll update her after we clear his take."

This was the best part of her job—the feeling that the mark was close and unaware of her presence. It brought her a sense of satisfaction she'd never experienced when she'd been on the other side of the law. But this guy didn't behave like a man on the run. He must have thought he'd slipped off the radar. He'd gotten sloppy and let his guard down.

Finch pulled out and turned right onto Island Main, the primary drag through the coastal town of Port Alene, Texas. The street was lined with countless seafood restaurants, souvenir shops offering shark necklaces for a dollar, and enough liquor stores to keep college students on a two-week bender. The lure of island luxury on a limited budget also attracted tourists and snowbirds in search of a charming island community.

Jamie remained fascinated by the secret side of Port Alene, known only to locals and people with colorful backgrounds. Just off Island Main existed a parallel universe of people her mother had warned her about—individuals with small-time rap sheets, bad daddy stories, and worse boyfriend stories. Those people lived from job to job—and not the kind they would put on a résumé. Some folks were damaged, some wanted to make a clean break, and others wanted only to fade into the background and simply get by.

Once Ricky turned his Charger off Island Main, Jamie dropped back a bit farther behind him. She didn't want to be too close on his tail, although Ricky didn't appear to be the overly observant type. Still, she didn't want to get sloppy. She had learned that it was always better to give a mark more credit than he deserved because underestimating anyone in her business could lead to things going bad in a hurry.

Jamie followed at a safe clip. She spent so much time in her car, she wondered why she paid rent to live above Hemingway's. Surveillance paid well, but it required patience and focus. Jamie tended to have more of the latter than the former, but she knew the ability to wait until the right time was pivotal in closing cases. Still, her last name was Rush. Cookie had a good time with that one.

Her Tahoe continued en route to Danny's Den, just as they had anticipated. Most people, even people in hiding, couldn't help but visit their regular favorite hangouts.

Cookie pointed out his side window. "There he goes."

Finch pulled into the parking lot, choosing a dark space that was close to the adjacent road.

He surveyed the lot then made his way to the side door of the bar. Jamie turned into the same lot, positioning the Tahoe a few rows behind Finch's Charger. He was on her radar, and she wanted to stay off his.

She considered following him inside and handling the confrontation in the bar, but she knew that was risky and stupid. She had often flirted with risky and stupid but knew never to pass second base with either one. Plus, her intel was solid that Ricky would receive the payout inside the bar. The last thing she needed were patrons—and she used that term loosely—recognizing her if she made a scene. Another unknown to consider was the possibility that Ricky's friends may have been hanging out by the bar, itching to jump in the middle of something.

She would wait. She hoped it would pay off.

She sent Erin another text:

He's at Danny's. Just went inside.

Cookie rolled down his window, and Jamie did the same before cutting the engine. The island breeze provided welcome relief from the oppressive humidity.

Ten minutes later, the bar's side door opened, and Finch tumbled to the pavement, thrown out by one of Danny's henchmen. Cookie moved to open his passenger's side door, but Jamie put her hand on his forearm. "Wait a minute. We don't need this other guy in the mix too."

Finch yelled at the bouncer, "I didn't know she was married! It was an honest mistake!"

The bouncer turned his back and went inside.

Finch got up and thrust his right hand in his pants pocket as he neared his midlife-crisis car.

Jamie gave Cookie the signal. "Now."

The pair quickly exited the Tahoe and positioned themselves on either side of Finch, blocking him from reaching his vehicle.

He stared at Jamie. "You look familiar."

Jamie closed the space between them. Her physical stature was smaller than his, but her stance was far bolder, letting Ricky know who was in charge. Dressed in a gray T-shirt and jeans, she could have been mistaken for a weekend tourist… except for her expression, which warned of the storm to come. Her eyes narrowed. "I'm a friend of Sarah's—you know, the mother of the children you never bother to see?"

Finch's grimace told her he'd connected the dots.

He turned to Cookie, who smiled. "I'm here for moral support."

Jamie kept her eyes on Finch. He shifted his weight from side to side, his hands fidgeting with his car keys. His body was rigid and on guard.

"I heard you hit it big tonight on the Packers game," Jamie said.

His eyes widened in surprise. "Where'd you hear that?"

"You've been dodging some serious child support, and your ex is working two jobs to pay for those kids you left behind. Seems to me she's got some money coming to her now that your luck has changed."

Ricky shrugged his shoulders, seemingly unconcerned with the fact that he had left his dependents... dependent. "Look, that whole family thing just wasn't for me."

"Maybe you should have thought about that before making those Irish twins with her."

"She'll find a new guy," Ricky replied. "He can cover it."

Jamie knew taking deadbeat-dad cases were her personal challenge, given her background with her own father. The reality of standing in front of Ricky with his flippant attitude about the chaotic wake he'd left behind was more than she could manage at that moment. Her anger blinded her more sensible side, and Jamie sucker-punched him with a left cross. Clutching his nose, he watched the blood drip between his fingers. He looked at her not with anger, but with surprise. She tried not to show her own surprise that she'd landed such a clean shot.

Ricky sniffed, using the front of his shirt to wipe the blood from his nose. His hand shook just enough to alert Jamie that the man might actually be scared.

"Here's how this is going to work. Hand over tonight's take, and I'll keep Cookie here from throwing you off the pier. You owe your ex-wife twice what you've got on you, but she'll take it. And don't tell me you don't have it on you because I already know you got paid on your bets tonight."

Cookie moved a few inches closer, scowling at the man.

Finch took the hand from his nose, reached inside his shirt, and pulled out a wad of cash, hundreds in a tight roll. He held the roll up with trepidation, and the neat wad of cash twitched from the shake in Finch's hand. "Here, take it. I don't want any trouble."

Cookie grabbed it, examining the cash. "How much?"

"Seventy-five hundred. I had to clear my tab at Danny's. Owed him for a while too."

A drop of blood marked the corner of one of the bills. Jamie reached over to pluck it from the roll Cookie held and threw it on the ground. "There's your gas money to help you get home. And make sure you keep making money because you still owe your kids." She nodded toward Cookie. "Cookie has a soft spot for babies, so you'd better keep paying on time, or else he's going to find you. Understand?"

Her glare must have convinced him because he nodded and reached down to pick up the bill. Cookie and Jamie strode back to the Tahoe and drove off, leaving Finch to process his options.

Cookie turned on the dash's satellite radio and settled on ZZ Top. "It's not like you to lose your cool like that. I mean, he deserved it, but damn, girl."

Jamie felt her anger dissipate, her shoulders relaxing from the tension they had held. "All I could see was Sarah's worried face as she agonized about how to feed her kids and having to take crap jobs. And Finch not giving a rat's ass about any of it." She stopped at a red light, her forefinger tapping the steering wheel in rhythm with the radio. "I shouldn't have hit him. If he'd been a brawler, I could have been in real trouble." She glanced at Cookie. "We both know I got lucky with that punch."

As they drove to Hemingway's Pier to celebrate the night's success, Jamie's cell phone pinged. "Can you check that?"

Cookie picked up her cell from the car's cup holder and glanced at the screen. "It's from some guy named Brian. Says it's urgent."

Jamie straightened up in her seat, her posture tight. "No, it's not."

Cookie pressed her. "So who's Brian?"

"Bad news, my friend. Bad news."

Another text alert sounded.

"Now what?"

Cookie checked again. "It says, 'Urgent. Kristen hasn't checked in. She's not returning my calls.' Who's Kristen? Who is this guy?"

Jamie pulled into Hemingway's parking lot and cut the engine. "Brian is my brother."

Cookie's expression quickly changed from lighthearted humor to full-blown confusion. "You have a brother?"

Jamie really didn't want to have this conversation. The topic of her sibling was one of the few things she had failed to share with her close friend. The tension returned to her shoulders.

"He's my half brother, from one of those affairs my dad liked to dabble in. Brian's ten years older than me. Kristen is his daughter, my niece." She took her keys from the ignition and stepped out of the car. She could feel the tightening in her chest and her breathing becoming shallower. "Can we not talk about this now? It's really complicated."

"Sounds like he needs help, Jamie." Cookie's pleading expression wasn't helping. He didn't understand what he was asking of her at that moment, couldn't possibly appreciate the strain of his request. Those people—her supposed family—were to be kept at a distance.

"He's done this before, Cookie." Jamie worked to keep her face from showing any emotion, from allowing any positive memories of Kristen to weaken her resolve. "Kristen's so good at disappearing that she could moonlight as a magician."

Cookie smiled and walked over to her. He put his arm around her, and she hesitantly leaned into his big-brother embrace. Her body was still rigid after receiving Brian's text message. Cookie brought out her softer side, and while she loved him, she also hated it a bit. Vulnerability was not a friend, not to her. It betrayed her every time.

Jamie wanted to avoid the conversation, avoid her family, and most of all, avoid being pulled into the latest Rush family drama. Each time she answered her family's siren call for help, the end result left her a bit more broken and a little less trusting, even with friends like Cookie. Her family got in her head and made her doubt herself in a way that harmed even her strongest relationships. It was self-preservation to stay out of it because they always worked it out, with her on the sidelines, feeling used and cast outside their circle.

She considered Cookie her best friend, had confided in him more than anyone else save for Erin. Still, she hadn't shared everything. The topic of Brian and Kristen still stung, even though three years had passed since she had last seen them. But she knew she owed Cookie an explanation. If she truly trusted him, she had to let him in a little.

Jamie gave Cookie a quick squeeze then retreated from his embrace. She patted him on the chest. "Let's go get Deuce settled, and then I'll tell you everything."

"Everything?" Cookie asked.

She nodded. "Every last awful detail."

CHAPTER TWO

"HOME SWEET HOME," JAMIE SAID to Cookie as she opened the door to Hemingway's. The crowd was just beginning to gather. The long bar was more populated with people who had tales to tell than it had been only hours before. She glanced around the place, taking note of the fact that several of the souls she spotted seemed to spend as much time at the establishment as she did, which said a great deal since she actually lived above the place.

Hemingway's Pier was a hidden jewel in Port Alene, a hangout off the beaten path of Tourist Row. The food was perfect, the ice-cold beer was a local brew, and the pub's frequenters were the eyes and ears of the island town's current events. The place also served as her office. Every person's office should include a bartender.

Jamie ducked through the crowd with Cookie on her six, not wanting to stop for fear of being pulled into a conversation with one of the patrons. She avoided eye contact and made her way to the back of the bar, to the steps that led to her place. She had someone very important waiting for her.

Cookie followed Jamie up the steps to the loft studio's door. Turning the key triggered a scratching noise on the other side. She opened the door and found her furry love tumbling toward her, all paws and drool, to greet her. Jamie bent at the knees and rubbed his round, wrinkled head with both hands. "How are you doing, Deuce? Did you have a good day?"

Deuce stomped his paws on the ground. His prancing brought to mind a pudgy reindeer getting ready to fly.

"I think he's ready for a night out." Cookie took his own turn at giving Deuce a pat. He scratched Deuce behind the ear, and the pup leaned into the attention full force. "I'm his favorite because of this move. No one gives behind-the-ear action like Uncle Cookie."

"True that," Jamie agreed. "Maggie texted me and told me that she took him for a long walk on the beach this afternoon. Said she wore him out." Maggie Clark ran Doggy Day Adventures, and she was, essentially, Deuce's doggy nanny. Jamie paid a pretty penny for Maggie's services, but with Jamie's unpredictable hours and the fact that Deuce hated surveillance work even more than Cookie, Jamie thought Maggie's services were a good investment.

Cookie remained standing at the door while Jamie hustled Deuce outside.

"Let's hit the road," he prompted. "I bet Deuce would like to hang out downstairs with Marty for a bit so we can go for a quick drive and talk." The car drive was a common tactic in getting potential clients and witnesses to open up, and Cookie and Jamie also used it on each other. Something about the open road combined with not having to make eye contact made the challenge of difficult conversations seem a bit easier. Jamie had heard the technique was also popular with mothers trying to reach their despondent teenagers, but she had no experience there.

The mention of Marty's name was enough to trigger Deuce to make his way to the stairs. He carefully navigated the steps one at a time, his top-heavy nature always a disadvantage during his descent. After making his way down, Deuce made a beeline for the bar, disappearing as he turned the corner to speak with Marty and the other bartenders on duty. Jamie watched as Marty's head bent below the bar, presumably to give Deuce a pat, before straightening.

Marty Scout, owner, proprietor, and head bouncer, enjoyed keeping company with Deuce. With his thick white hair and matching beard, Marty looked as if he could have stepped out of any sea-adventure novel. Though his face was wrinkled and weathered from decades of sun and wind, he remained youthful. Jamie assumed the daily shots of whiskey kept him smiling, but the steady stream of female companionship might have had something to do with it too.

"No stepping on our short barback down here," he called, smiling, as he cautioned the bartender next to him.

"Marty, we're going to go out for a few minutes, and then we'll be back, okay?"

"No problem. I'll keep an eye on him."

With that, Jamie and Cookie cut a path to the front door of

Hemingway's and went outside. Even with as stingy as Marty was with the air conditioning, the contrast between the inside of the bar and the humidity Port Alene served up each day couldn't be ignored. The humidity hung in the air, following them until they got inside Jamie's car.

Jamie backed out of the parking lot and turned toward town. She had no particular destination in mind; she just preferred to have this conversation away from the bustle and curious ears of Hemingway's evening crowd.

She and Cookie drove in silence for the first few minutes with nothing more than the wind blowing through the back window.

"So, you know about my family, right?" Jamie asked.

"Apparently not as much as I thought," Cookie huffed, his voice indicating disappointment that Jamie had kept some things from him. He didn't seem angry as much as hurt. Cookie had no poker face when it came to important topics, and for a very select few people, he wore his heart on his sleeve.

"I wasn't intentionally hiding it from you," Jamie responded, her eyes still focused on the narrow two-lane road ahead. "It's just something… It hurts to think about it, okay? And you know how I am about those things."

Cookie nodded in agreement and fiddled with the air-conditioning vents on the front dash. "You want to talk about it now?"

"Not really."

"You said you were going to tell me a story."

Jamie tightened her grip on the steering wheel, her eyes glancing at her rearview mirror from time to time, although the nearest car was a good quarter mile behind her. "Once upon a time, I had the chance to be an awesome aunt to a little girl named Kristen, and I got to do that for a while. And then I blew it."

She had Cookie's attention now, though she really didn't want it. She still didn't want to talk about her family. She had tucked her history away and had no interest in dragging it out for further inspection.

"So what happened between you two?"

Jamie fiddled with the air-conditioning vents, buying time, hoping to cut the conversation short. "It's just hard thinking about them, let alone talking about them," she confided.

"I know," Cookie said. "But I'm your partner, and you need to trust me. Think of me as your therapist." His face shone with his cheesy signature grin. Cookie could defuse any situation with humor. It was one of the things she loved about him.

She tried to suppress a smile but failed. "Good lord, if you were my therapist, we'd both be ruined." Jamie found herself at the intersection of Island Main and Avenue E. The light was red, and cars were lined up behind her. She glanced again at her rearview mirror, wondering if she recognized the car behind her. Nope, it was full of college students looking for a party. The light switched to green, and the arrow gave permission for Jamie to make a left turn.

"So, Brian is my half brother because my dad had a problem with fidelity, as you well know. Anyway, when Brian had a daughter, Kristen, we didn't meet her for a long time. We were moving around when my dad's cons were over, and you know how it is. New job, new move. But at some point, my dad wanted to settle down in Austin, and Brian followed. He moved there too."

"Sounds like he was trying to have a normal family," Cookie interjected.

"Normal by my family's standards, anyway." Jamie eased the pressure on the gas, noting the speed limit had dropped to thirty miles per hour. She knew the Port Alene police loved to hand out speeding tickets. She'd collected a couple over the last two years.

"Anyway, he started coming around with Kristen about five years ago—she was only sixteen then—and she was a great kid. Funny, a bit wild, but really smart. But she was running with a fast crowd, just like Brian, and she started getting a little out of control. She would do these disappearing acts, and Brian would always beg me to find her. And I would. I'd find her and talk to her, and it was great." Jamie tightened her smile, squashing the sadness into a footnote. "And then at some point, Brian thought I was too much of an influence on her, and he told her she had to choose—either me or him."

"Why?"

"Because he was using her for his own small-time cons, and I was trying to talk her out of it. She had so much potential. She could do something better with her life, but that's her dad, right? Every girl wants her dad's approval."

Jamie had now completed a loop through downtown and could once again see Hemingway's ahead. She returned to the parking spot she had left open, put the Tahoe in park, but left the engine running.

"So, she chose him, and she cut me off. Wouldn't answer my texts, my calls. I tried, Cookie, but she froze me out, so I just returned the favor. I cut them both off. She sent me a couple texts last year, and I just ignored them." She looked at her friend. "Mature, right?"

"You were hurt. I understand."

"I just stopped trusting both of them. I mean, I never trusted him, but when she told me she didn't want me in her life, that was it for me. She's just like the rest of my family now." Jamie held up her hands, palms to the sky. "And that's my sob story."

The two sat quietly for a moment, and Jamie was grateful for the silence. She didn't want to admit it, but telling Cookie about what had happened with her and her family had relieved a small burden. He glanced at her, and she could tell that he knew it too but was kind enough not to make her say it aloud.

"C'mon," Cookie said, coaxing her out of her car. "I'll buy you a beer."

Jamie pushed open Hemingway's heavy wooden door, and it creaked in response. The comforting scents of seafood and cigarettes welcomed her. She spotted Marty still behind the bar. "Hey, Marty."

Marty raised a beer glass, the light above the bar reflecting off it. "You need one?"

"Maybe more than one."

He observed Cookie. "You don't even have to ask."

"That's my man," Cookie said.

"Coming your way, hon." He winked at Cookie. "Her, not you." Marty pulled the beer tap and filled two steins with Shiner Blonde.

Jamie dropped her satchel on the wooden floor and wrapped the strap around the leg of the barstool. Lots of people with sticky fingers lived in Port Alene. If something was worth more than ten bucks and not nailed down, it disappeared. Jamie raised the beer glass with a nod of appreciation. "Thanks, Marty." She drained her glass more quickly than usual.

Cookie struck a sidelong glance but said nothing. He knew her well enough to keep his comments to himself, at least for tonight.

She tapped the bar to get Marty's attention. Her effort resulted in a second beer delivered with a cocked eyebrow. "Tough day?"

"Good things and bad things today." Jamie didn't need to explain the two-sided nature of the business to Marty. Three years of using his bar as her unofficial office space meant he probably knew more about her work than he should. He'd once said discretion was his superpower, and Jamie knew that to be true. His lips were sealed like a vault.

"You know what I say. A cold beer fixes everything." He wiped down the bar with a dingy rag. Unsanitary, yes, but also part of the charm.

"I'm getting tired of doing divorce cases. It's all surveillance, and I have a small bladder. But the sad truth is that cheating-spouse cases pay big, so I need to find more of them." She pointed to Cookie. "And I need to keep this guy in the style to which he has become accustomed. Those Hawaiian shirts are custom cut, expensive."

Cookie nodded. "It's true. I have an image to uphold." Cookie held a special place in Jamie's heart. She had never experienced such fierce loyalty from anyone... ever. They were equal partners in their referral-only private investigation venture, and he was closer to a brother than a buddy, one of only two people she trusted without question. Their partnership had started as a professional matchmaking session headed by Erin. She had told Jamie that she and Cookie were her two favorite people in the world and that theirs could be a great partnership if they gave it a chance. Looking back, Jamie knew she was lucky Cookie had given her a shot. He'd been the more experienced investigator at the time, while Jamie had relied upon her instinct and knowledge from being a con artist's kid. Somehow, they'd connected immediately, and that early bond had been cemented by three years of successfully working together and repeatedly pulling each other out of tight spots.

Marty stood in front of Jamie, rag in hand, and leaned in. "So, any football betting? Have you finally realized that America's team doesn't deserve your loyalty?"

Jamie peered into her glass, refusing to meet his gaze. He loved to tease her about betting on the Cowboys. "No thanks, I lost a grand on them last week."

Marty snickered. "Damn, really?"

"I don't want to talk about it." She glared at him, but after a moment, she couldn't help but smile. "And quit hating on the Cowboys. They have their eyes on some new players. Their time is coming."

"You should keep your cash in your pocket 'til that happens," Marty offered. "Save your money for my place."

Jamie glanced over her shoulder, grateful to see Erin Clay walk through the front door. Erin offered a half wave and made her way to the barstool. "Thanks for saving my spot." She reached over and gave Cookie a quick side hug. "How are you?"

He returned the affection a hair short of cracking her ribs. She groaned in his embrace, and he released her. "Sorry, I forget you're a skinny little thing."

Marty stood at the ready for her drink order.

She glanced at Jamie's draft beer.

"Shiner Blonde?" he asked.

"Better bring me two at a time," Erin said.

"You too, huh?" Marty asked as he placed a draft beer and a spare in front of Erin.

She held one up in a brief toast to Marty, who winked before turning to handle his other waiting patrons.

Erin turned to Jamie. "Congrats on closing down Ricky Finch," she said while simultaneously pulling the first beer close to her lips.

"Glad to help," Jamie replied. "Every time I think that married life might be nice, I take one of these cases, and it sucks the desire right out of me."

"I don't see any one of us walking down the aisle anytime soon," Erin said.

"Speak for yourself," Cookie chimed in. "My sugar mama is out there somewhere."

Jamie finished her second beer before Erin drank half of her first. "I hear you. I think I'll find myself some rich young boy toy with a trust fund."

"You'll find lots of those here in Port A," Erin joked.

"Yeah, I think I've now lowered my standards from rich, smart, and gorgeous to employed registered voter." Jamie grinned at her friend. "I think we should both stay single."

Erin lifted her beer in a mock toast. "Agreed."

Jamie slid an envelope on the bar to Erin. "Here's Finch's take. It's not everything he owes, but I think it's most of what he won tonight."

Erin tucked the envelope in her tote. "I wish I could have seen his face."

"Can't say I understand what Sarah ever saw in that loser, but it's not like I'm one to judge. Glass houses, stones, and all that."

Erin reached over and squeezed Jamie's hand. "I'll make sure she gets it all back. There's no way I can keep this—even though he owes me too—when she's in such bad shape right now. I hear kids are expensive."

Cookie held up his beer glass. "A bookie with a heart. That can't be good for business."

"You guys should talk," Erin said. "I know how much free work the two of you do. You pretend to be all salty, but you're big mush balls inside."

Jamie grinned. "Don't you dare ruin my reputation by spreading that nonsense."

Erin reached for her friend's hand and gave it a quick pat. "Between all your freebie cases and my debt forgiveness, we'll end up bartending for Marty to make ends meet."

Marty passed by and caught the tail end of the conversation. "Hey, I'm hiring. You interested?"

Jamie's cell phone buzzed, and she checked the screen. *Brian.* She ignored the call.

Erin noticed her friend's expression. "What's going on?"

Jamie ran her finger down the side of her beer mug, not much wanting to get into it. "It's Brian. He called a couple of times tonight. He thinks Kristen took off again. Wants me to help find her."

Erin was the only person in the Port Alene circle Jamie had known since childhood. She was also the only one who had seen firsthand the way the Rush family rolled. She knew better than to speak of them unless Jamie initiated the topic. "I know you've been down that road with them many times. Where is Brian"—she hesitated—"working now? Is he with the rest of your family?"

"No, he settled around Corpus, actually, but we've done a good job of keeping our distance."

"How did you manage that?"

Jamie traced a long scuff on the bar with her finger. "He reached out to me when he first moved to Corpus, tried to get me to help him with a job. I just blew up at him, told him he'd better not step foot in Port Alene or I would make things very difficult for him. And Corpus is a huge city compared to our island, so he should have plenty of work there without us ever needing to cross paths."

Erin nodded. "Kudos to you for setting boundaries. So what do you want to do now?"

Jamie shrugged. "I'm not sure. I'm guessing he wants some free skip tracing to get Kristen back in line with the family business. I'm not sure there's anything wrong, but…"

Her friend finished her sentence. "But you'd hate yourself if she was in trouble and you did nothing to help her." Erin wagged her finger in Jamie's direction. "I know you, Jamie. You want to help find Kristen even if it is some silly, attention-getting stunt."

Jamie signaled Marty for another draft. "Maybe, but I don't want to get pulled back into my family's mess." She grinned. "I'm using my skills for good, not evil now."

"Yeah, Wonder Woman striking another blow for justice," Cookie explained, pumping his fist in the air, bragging about her impressive fighting skills. "You should have seen her, Erin. Sucker-punched Ricky Finch right in the nose. She's on a roll. All she needs is a cape."

Jamie grinned at Cookie's animated description of the evening's events, even if they were a bit embellished. "Here's the main difference between us," Jamie explained. "I like doing things the mostly legal way. And I'm only bending the rules if I'm trying to help people." *Emphasis on "mostly."* She sipped the foam from the top of her beer and wiped a hint of froth from her top lip. "Brian, on the other hand, thrives on scams. He lives for the hustle, just like my dad. Can't wait to part a fool from his money. What's that famous quote? When someone shows you who they are, believe them? Which is why I should learn my lesson and bow out of their drama." Jamie straightened on her stool and turned the conversation to Erin's life. "So, what's going on with you? Give me some good news."

"Things are good. Making some decent money with my senior set. They like the idea of having bets with a bookie. It makes them feel like renegades."

"Hey, those winter Texans have money, or they wouldn't be on the Island," Jamie said. "So, bets are up?"

"Yeah, and they know just enough to be dangerous, so I'm making a nice return, but my success is getting some unwelcome attention."

Jamie's eyes narrowed. "What do you mean?"

Erin hesitated before answering. "Boxer is pushing for some of my action."

Jamie puffed up at the mention of Boxer's name. "Oh, hell no. His territory ends at Highway 77 before crossing over. The boundaries are set."

"He wants to renegotiate, and he's thinking that my territory looks pretty good."

"What are you going to do?"

"I don't know."

"You need to call your dad in on this?"

Erin shook her head. "No, I don't want to get him involved. It's like using a sledgehammer on a nail at this point. I'd get some protection, but you know how it is. My credibility would be shot if I have Dear Old Dad doing my heavy lifting. It would look like I can't stand on my own and protect my business. Can't go running to Daddy every time someone tries to shake me down."

"Yeah, well, your daddy isn't just anybody. He could make Boxer disappear like Hoffa."

Erin shrugged. "Maybe, but I need to make it on my own terms. Besides, I don't need to bring that kind of heat here. We're friendlier in the South. I need a little time to figure things out."

Jamie ran her finger around a small ring of condensation on the bar, evidence of her ale indulgence. Not wanting to push the topic, she knew she had to for Erin's sake. "You know that Boxer doesn't play, and if your bets are getting his attention, you need to have your guard up. He's bad news."

"I know it."

Jamie had said her piece, and Erin had heard her. She knew Erin took it seriously, but Jamie was still concerned for the rookie bookie's safety. She studied her friend, who was taking small sips from her beer glass. It would take Erin the entire weekend to finish that beverage.

"It's painful to watch you drink," Jamie said.

"I was going to say the same thing about you."

"At least I wouldn't leave a beer to get warm on Marty's bar. You better drink that second one, or he'll be pissed."

Jamie had placed her cell on the bar, and it vibrated against the wood. She glanced at the screen, and Erin did too. "It's him again, isn't it? I noticed you have his contact name as Brian the Loser. Hostile, much?"

Jamie groaned. "My dad has lots of people in his circle who could help. Why does Brian keep calling me?"

Erin put her arm around her friend's shoulder. "Because no one can find a missing person like you can. And you and Kristen were close once. That matters."

"I guess a childhood filled with running had some unexpected benefits."

Erin placed her hand on Jamie's forearm. "Kristen's pretty young, and she's your niece. What if you can save her from this life? What if she's running from the very same destiny you worked so hard to escape? Don't you want to be there to help her?"

Erin made a strong argument, though Jamie hated hearing it. She wanted nothing more than to flee from this latest family crisis, but Erin's plea confirmed what Jamie already knew.

She decided she wouldn't return Brian's call. Any advance warning of her considered support could easily have been used against her somehow.

She would do what she did best—track Brian down.

She had already run from the burning building known as her family, and now she was returning to it as flames shot from its roof.

CHAPTER THREE

JAMIE DEFTLY NAVIGATED HER TAHOE through the crowded, pulsing stop-and-start traffic along Corpus Christi's main highway. Corpus Christi was considered the "big city" by Port Alene standards, with its countless restaurants, shopping venues, and popular Ocean Drive, which was considered a crown jewel and boasted lavish seaside homes nestled next to the Performing Arts Center and other city attractions. On rare occasions, Jamie would cruise down Ocean Drive to take in a lighter, more glamorous version of island life.

But not today.

Today, Jamie had more pressing business.

As she turned off South Padre Island Drive, SPID for locals, she followed her GPS instructions as the automated voice commanded her to turn right, turn left, and go half a mile. After several minutes of back-road navigation, Jamie drove into an older neighborhood touting a faded sign that read Blanco Springs Estates. Its front acreage displayed the weary harshness of late summer, a sad brown hue withering from prolonged drought with bushes so dry they might break in a gentle wind. Passing the sign, Jamie drove along a main road that led to rows of similar-sized houses—single story for the most part, nothing particularly distinguishing. Several real estate signs advertised foreclosure status.

After two more turns, Jamie's GPS announced, "You have arrived."

If this was arriving, it was quite a disappointment.

She made sure not to park too close to the car next to her in the driveway, a newer sky-blue Mercedes that seemed distinctly out of place in this faded neighborhood. The second vehicle parked in front of the house, a black older-model Toyota, seemed a better fit—nice, practical, and understated.

Jamie opened her car door into the welcoming path of a warm, humid breeze. She glanced around and noticed almost no activity on the quiet street. A couple of cars were parked in driveways and on the street, but there wasn't much in the way of people, although in the middle of the day, most were likely at work. The lawn of the home in front of her was neatly trimmed, though also brown, and two wooden chairs decorated the small front porch.

Through the open front blinds, Jamie noticed two men and a woman standing in the living room. The woman wore a floral sundress and held a baby in her arms. Jamie knew one of the men all too well, the other not at all.

Jamie grabbed the doorknob and opened the front door. Brian turned and, for a moment, seemed surprised, an expression which disappeared quickly into confidence, like smoothly flipping a switch.

"Ah, perfect timing." Brian's eyes stayed on Jamie as she closed the door behind her. He extended his hand toward her and, without missing a beat, introduced Jamie, immediately pulling her into his performance. "This is my assistant, Anne Kramer. She was willing to come in on her well-deserved day off to see if we needed anything."

Jamie gave Brian a slight raise of her eyebrows before turning to the couple. She extended her hand to the man, who couldn't have been more than twenty-five. Like Jamie, he was dressed casually, and if he noticed the extreme disparity between Brian's tailored pants and pressed shirt and his "assistant's" jeans and T-shirt, he kept it to himself.

"Nice to meet you both," Jamie offered, shaking his hand. Then she turned to the young mother. "You look like you have your hands full."

The woman smiled, but her pretty features couldn't mask her fatigue. Dark circles under her eyes and a distracted disposition colored her expression.

"Sorry if I don't shake your hand. She isn't sleeping much right now, and if I put her down, she'll scream up a storm."

Jamie felt a surge of compassion for the exhausted mother, who had no idea that she had added to her troubles by crossing paths with Brian. If he had his way, he would leave her both weary and broke.

Brian redirected the conversation back to his own priority. "I was just showing them around since they're going to be moving in soon on a year lease." His eyes locked with the woman's. "You know, we got several other calls on this property in the last week since it's one of the few that has an extra half bath and a back porch. You're lucky you got here first."

Jamie said nothing, not wanting to aid in whatever scam Brian was currently running on this innocent-looking couple. She simply stood next to him, her arms crossed, leaving him to handle her surprise visit.

"But we do have the place, right?" the husband asked.

Brian nodded and put his hand on the man's shoulder. "The owner said you've passed the background check, so we'll just need a money order for the first and last month's rent plus the cleaning deposit. You should be able to get in by the end of the month."

The wife's fog of tiredness broke for a momentary smile. She turned to her husband. "That's great news. I don't think we can handle your mom's place much longer."

Brian clapped his hands together and pointed Jamie's way. "My assistant and I have a few things to take care of with paperwork and getting everything properly cleaned before you move in. I'll call you when we have everything finished, okay?"

Brian strode to the front door to show them out, and when the baby began fussing, the couple followed, hurrying out of the house. Jamie followed them. "I'm going to walk them out," she told Brian, "to answer any questions they have about the move-in process."

Jamie closed the door behind her and followed the couple to their Toyota. The wife busied herself with placing the baby in the car seat. The husband extended his hand to Jamie. "Thanks for all your help."

Jamie held onto his hand for a moment. "Don't give this man any money. He runs this scam all the time, and he doesn't represent this house. Don't ask me any questions. Just leave. Trust me, you won't be moving in here."

The man's thankful smile slipped from his face, replaced by stunned confusion. Jamie left him to process the news that he'd just dodged a financial bullet. She returned to the house and closed the door.

Jamie hoped her warning had been enough. She didn't want to linger outside for fear Brian would come out and smooth-talk his way around anything his "assistant" might have said.

Brian stood in the living room and kept his head down, his eyes focused on the floor and his hands on his hips. "You told them, didn't you?"

Jamie smiled, enjoying the satisfaction of crushing his con. "Of course. You don't think I'd let you screw over that nice couple, do you? I just wanted to see your whole spiel first. It's rather convincing. I'm sure you do pretty well with it."

"I can't believe you ruined that one for me." He made eye contact. "On second thought, yes I can."

Jamie scoffed at his comment. "Unfortunately, I'm sure you have plenty of other unsuspecting families on the hook." She stared at him, her face solemn. "And *you* called *me* for help, remember?"

She watched him switch gears as he morphed into Mr. Nice Guy. Years of studying him, his tactics, and his behaviors had proven beneficial. She had seen most of his cards and could observe him trying on personas the way teenage girls tried on clothes at the mall.

"I know, you're right. I just didn't expect you to be here so quickly." He smiled in a way that almost felt genuine.

Jamie reminded herself to keep her guard strong. "You mean you didn't expect me to crash one of your scams?"

Brian barely made eye contact. "Okay, yeah. How did you find me?" He touched his forefinger to his lips, contemplating the answer. "It was Monroe, wasn't it? He's always had a thing for you."

Jamie shook her head. She peered past her brother, noticing a small bird fly past the outside kitchen window. "You're still using that ridiculous Dexter Hutchinson alias. I just had to search that and call the bogus number to speak to your bogus secretary."

"Tiffany," he interjected.

Jamie rolled her eyes at his correction. "Of course that's her name. Yes, I told Tiffany I needed to get a check to you for a deposit, but…"

"You misplaced the address."

"Yep."

"That transparent, huh?" He ran his hands through his coiffed hair and smiled. "Well played, Jamie."

She had expected more of an outburst. "You're not mad?"

"No. Truth is, I sometimes feel a little guilty when they have kids. Scamming arrogant bachelors is way easier. And I guess I got sloppy with my business since you found me so easily."

"Skip tracing's easier if you know your subject."

Brian exhaled. "I hope that works with Kristen, then."

Jamie surveyed the living room with its fresh-paint smell and new carpet. "If Kristen's really missing…"

Brian walked to the back sliding glass door off the breakfast nook and opened it. "Want to go outside for a minute? The paint fumes are giving me a headache."

Jamie followed, and the two stood sheltered by the wooden porch cover, which offered a sliver of shade. The decent-sized backyard appeared suitable enough for a dog or two if anyone bothered to fix the gaping hole in the run-down fence.

"What do I need to know?"

Brian exhaled so audibly that his breath might have rustled leaves on a tree. "You know we're pretty close, right? She's good about checking in with me. But this time, she's not answering her phone. No texts. Nothing. And she's not answering her friends, either."

"At least the friends you know."

He conceded the point. "True, but we've been working together for a long time now, so I think I know who she's spending time with."

Jamie tilted her head as she considered his point. "Maybe so, maybe not. Young women can be notoriously clever when it comes to keeping secrets. Maybe even more so in our family." His expression told her that she had struck a nerve. "Or Kristen dropped off the grid after a big party bender and is staying with someone you don't know. That's not so unusual. At least not from what I remember."

"Maybe. Pretty sad, right?" He waited for her to say something in response, but she remained silent. "Anyway, we could always track down someone that knew something, and even if she isn't answering her phone, she might be online, checking in."

Jamie thought for a moment. "She knows how to disappear if she wants to. I'm sure you and her dear granddad taught her all the tricks of the trade. Maybe she just needs to dry out or something."

Brian shook his head again. "I thought that too at first. But this feels different. Her friends don't seem like they're covering for her. They really don't know where she is. You know what a talker she is. She hasn't called anyone."

"Does she have a boyfriend?"

Brian nodded. "There was this one guy she was seeing named Dylan. They worked together some."

Jamie raised an eyebrow. "Worked together? Without you? I'm guessing that they weren't operating a convenience store."

"Small-time stuff." Brian rubbed his eyes, the bags underneath them a sign that sleep had not visited him recently. "Dylan's actually a pretty enterprising young man. He's got a network of guys faking injuries and getting pain meds. He buys the pills off them and sells them on the street. Kristen said he also has a few kids with doctor parents, so he buys script pads, uses fake IDs, and gets them filled for hydrocodone, oxy. Impressive monthly cash flow for a small-timer, really."

"What was Kristen's role in all this?"

Brian beamed, such a proud father. "She's a jack-of-all-trades. She got pretty good at forging scripts and built a nice clientele on the street. She could always drum up business and knew how to sell without attracting attention. That girl could show up at a high school and talk those boys into anything. Made a lot of money with her charm."

Jamie bit her bottom lip in an effort to keep her mouth shut. The fact that his daughter was dating a drug dealer—and that he seemed proud of that—ousted him from any father-of-the-year award.

But she couldn't help herself. "So you were fine with your daughter trading on her looks to make money on drugs? You should put that in the next Christmas newsletter. I'm sure Dad shares your pride in her work skills." It saddened Jamie to be reminded that any father would be proud to have his daughter act in such a way. Then she recalled her own father's parenting skills and realized it shouldn't come as much of a surprise.

Brian straightened his posture. "This is the way the world works, and you know it. Pretty girls get ahead, and it would be stupid not to use that as an advantage. You know our family motto—"

Jamie finished his sentiment. "Trade on your assets, I know."

It was hard to argue with Brian's logic. They were each products of their upbringing, and Jamie had fought long and hard to shed her family's imprint. Deception was part of their DNA. How angry could she be at her brother and his daughter for being who they were raised to be? Jamie's gut told her Kristen could possibly be in real trouble.

Right now, she hated her gut.

Though she didn't want to get involved, if Kristen truly were in over her head, how could she walk away? This was her niece, and maybe after she was found and safe, the door would be open for her and Jamie to rebuild their relationship. As much as Jamie kept her family at a distance, the truth was that a part of her still longed to have some connection. Kristen was a wild one, but she had a good heart—that much Jamie remembered. A fresh start seemed worth the risk. It was the only possible outcome that seemed worth the risk.

"What about her mom?" Jamie asked. "Would she go to her?"

Brian looked away and shook his head. "No. Vickie kicked her out a long time ago and told her not to come back. She's got a new guy, and she always chooses the boyfriend over her daughter. Sad. They haven't talked in forever."

It was Jamie's turn to shake her head. No wonder Kristen ran away.

Jamie stood quietly for a moment before she spoke again. "Okay, Brian, I'll help you. Once I find her and make sure she's fine, I'll let you know. I can't guarantee she'll come back, but I'll make sure she's safe." She added one caveat. "And if she says she doesn't want you to know where she is, I'm not telling you. That's up to her."

"Thanks, Jamie. I mean it."

She almost believed him. "You had better be straight with me about whatever I ask you, Brian. No bullshit, no lying, no keeping things from me. If she's really in trouble, you need to tell me everything, even if you think I don't want to hear it. Surprises are for birthday parties, get it?"

Brian put his arms up as if to protest. "Of course. Anything you want to know."

CHAPTER FOUR

AFTER MEETING WITH BRIAN, JAMIE needed the half-hour drive to Pier 5 to sort her thoughts and get her mind right. She'd considered waiting until the next morning to follow the lead Brian had provided, but her experience with missing cases had taught her that time was always the enemy. *Chase the lead the moment it lands in your lap.*

Pier 5 was nestled between Port Alene and Corpus Christi, a small fishing venue connecting the two towns. The pier was frequented by an eclectic mix of retired winter Texans, freelance artists, fishermen, and kids skipping school. Pier 5 attracted a small network of street kids because they could hide in plain sight among locals and tourists and make deals with side-glances and simple handshakes. Those exchanges were easy to spot if a person knew what to look for.

Jamie sat on a bench at the far end of the pier. It was a busy spot, even on a Tuesday afternoon, and she felt a momentary chill run through her from the ocean breeze. She appeared relaxed, much as a tourist would, with a book in her lap and sunglasses shielding her gaze. A Corpus Christi Hooks baseball cap protected her skin from the sun and from identification. Her tote concealed her tools of the trade, including her firearm, a much-loved SIG Sauer, a taser, and recording devices cleverly hidden in pen casings and other everyday items. A meticulous note taker, Jamie kept her surveillance journal with her at all times. Tucked among back pages were the latest bets she'd placed with Erin. Each page attested to her private encryption method, all but indecipherable to anyone who attempted to read it. Even her surveillance notes appeared to be nothing more than messy mental ramblings. She combined betting jargon, past events from her parents' cons, and landmarks from different places she loved to represent the details of who she was watching and why.

Each client received a code name derived from characters in her favorite books and movies. Jamie had assigned Ricky Finch the code name Biff, named after the bully in *Back to the Future*. When one spent as much time on surveillance as Jamie did, pretending to read books, sometimes she actually ended up reading them. In fact, being a closet reader was a bit of a problem in this regard. She really wanted to lose herself in a book but couldn't—her attention needed to remain on her subject. The only way to thwart temptation was to start carrying books she knew she wouldn't like. Today's selection was a self-help book. She knew she needed all kinds of help but couldn't imagine getting it from an author guru with a ten-point plan for success.

At that moment, Dylan Luna topped her surveillance list. She'd received a solid description of him from Brian, who remained a bit ticked off by not being allowed to tag along with her. Although he might have been helpful in spotting Dylan, she believed that was where his aid ended. Besides, she didn't want to spend any more time in his company. Jamie pretended to read her book, pausing at times to admire the ocean. The daily *Corpus Christi Caller Times* crossword puzzle, neatly folded, peeked out from the top of her tote. A crossword offered another way to make surveillance notes, each square filled with observations.

Her eyes glanced down at her book for a few moments, then she rechecked the pier. Her bench sat close to restaurant row, which was augmented by several food vendors selling their culinary creations from trailers. Pedestrians could choose from fish tacos, burgers, hot dogs, and ice cream cones. There were several cuisine options within a few hundred feet, from one end of the trailers to the other.

Jamie spent almost half an hour observing, getting a feel for the people and activity around her, and becoming part of the environment. She had witnessed little more than a stream of tourists strolling along the pier, eating, fishing, and enjoying the day. Jamie spotted at least three drug buys, but none of the buyers or sellers resembled Dylan's description. Sadly, two of the kids didn't look old enough to drive, let alone deal, and the third dealer tipped the age scale on the far end, appearing to be about sixty. Drugs added years to a person in the same way a television camera added pounds. Neither was particularly kind.

Jamie's stomach rumbled with ravenous force, likely stimulated by the mix of food smells wafting through the air, or it could have been because she'd only had a cup of coffee for breakfast and skipped lunch altogether. Concentration proved difficult. She tucked her book and crossword puzzle back in her tote, stood, and wandered leisurely over to the taco stand. She knew the owner, Gilley Morales, but they always pretended to be strangers since he regularly served as extra eyes for her. She had met him a year ago while working another case, and he had proven both useful and discreet. Plus, he had mad cooking skills in that food truck. No one else waited in line or stood within earshot when she arrived because she'd timed it that way.

"Can I get two fish tacos and a side of fries, please?"

Gilley winked. "Coming right up." He went to work preparing the tortillas and lining them with lettuce, tomatoes, fried fish, and a special sauce that resembled Thousand Island dressing.

Jamie leaned forward and inhaled. "That smells so good. I'm starving."

"Well, I guarantee this will be the best meal you've had all day."

She lowered her voice to just above a whisper. "I'm looking for my friend Dylan. You know, early twenties, likes to share script meds with his friends?"

"Oh yeah, Dylan," Gilley replied. "He likes my fish tacos, too. He usually hangs out farther down the pier where the locals fish. Sometimes they work by that grove of trees past the sidewalk. Lots of great shade and some camouflage from nosy people."

"Hmm," Jamie mused. "Anyplace for nosy people to sit?"

"Yeah, but you won't hear them talk." He handed her a cardboard serving container piled high with fish tacos and fries. "Don't forget the ketchup." He handed her two small plastic containers of red condiment.

"Great, thanks." Jamie handed him two folded twenties and left. Their arrangement provided each of them with tips, but Jamie also benefited from the bonus of a grab-and-go lunch. She nibbled on her fish tacos while strolling down the pier toward the area where she hoped Dylan had set up shop for the day. She passed men carrying buckets, coolers, and fishing poles, and more teenagers than she could count. *Shouldn't these kids be in school?* Thinking of her own childhood, she knew she could have been one of those kids roaming the pier. Her dad had often let her skip school if she was willing to play a role in a con. For a thirteen-year-old who'd found middle school to be hell on earth, her choice had been an easy one. She'd skipped every time.

After downing one taco and most of the fries, she tossed the remaining food in a nearby trash can. The farther she walked, the quieter her surroundings became. The crowd thinned, and her pace slowed.

She tucked her tote closer to her body, considering how to best approach Dylan should they cross paths. Twenty feet ahead, she spotted the trees Gilley had mentioned. Four or five boys were hanging out, all similarly dressed in jeans, knit hoodies, and tennis shoes—the normal core fashion for the pill-pushing crowd. As she approached, the boys noticed her and ceased talking. Two of them put their heads together, whispering and snickering, while one kept his gaze locked on hers. The two with their heads together stepped apart. Only one seemed confident in the space he claimed.

"You Dylan?" she asked.

"It depends. Who are you?"

"I'm Kristen's"—the next words stuck in her throat—"Aunt Jamie."

He appeared genuinely surprised at her claim. "Her aunt? You must not be her favorite. She never mentioned you."

Jamie's stomach fluttered in response to his comment. The words he spoke stung, and she hated herself for feeling hurt. She brushed off his observation with a quick hand gesture. "It's complicated."

"Everything's complicated with that girl." Dylan threw a nod to the other boys. "Gimme a minute." They disappeared into the trees like small creatures into the night. It seemed as though they knew the drill.

"Tell me about you and Kristen. You two get in a fight?"

The young man shifted his weight while her question hung in the air. "Why would you ask that?" he asked after a minute.

"I heard she went off the grid for a bit. She hasn't texted or anything lately?"

Dylan shook his head. "Nope, nothing, but she gets moody sometimes. She never knows what she wants, you know? Anyway, we haven't really been together in a while. Sometimes we fight, and she ends up hanging at Beth's apartment. She came by a few days ago to get some stuff she left at my place."

"What did you two fight about?"

"All kinds of stuff. Small stuff. Big stuff. We got along fine when we were working or"—he looked down at the ground and grinned—"or doing other things, but the rest of the time, it wasn't so much fun."

"So you didn't help Brian much when he called looking for her?"

"Who?"

"Her dad."

He huffed, straightening his baseball cap so it was perfectly off center. "Her dad? He's slick, like glass. Haven't seen him in a long time." He shoved his right hand in his jeans pocket and withdrew a piece of gum. He unwrapped the silver wrapping paper and folded the gum into his mouth, shrugging. "I thought she was gonna work with him on a job that was supposed to have a big payday, but I don't think it went anywhere. If it did, she didn't tell me about it."

Jamie felt a flush of familiar anger in her stomach. Of course Brian wouldn't have been completely straight with her. Why would this time be any different?

"What kind of job?" she asked.

"Kristen didn't say much about that gig, but she worked for him sometimes, doing different stuff. Nothing major. Between her dad and me, she did fine. She was always working."

I bet she was. But what was she doing?

"Anyway, she lived with me for a few months, and then it was going wrong so she just sort of bounced around."

"Sounds like she was looking for a home."

"Well, she didn't have one at her mom's place."

Jamie knew something about complicated mother-daughter relationships. "That must've been hard for her."

Dylan straightened his cap. "She said it didn't matter, but I know it did. Kristen was always dreaming of doing something big, and she talked big. She wanted to be someone else, live another life, have another family, turn into somebody different."

Jamie understood, remembering those very same dreams as a teen, wishing she could have traded her parents for Erin's. Erin's dad, a big-time gambling icon with nefarious business dealings, was far from being the perfect parent, but it was clear he did what he did out of love for his family. Jamie's dad? Not so much. Maybe she and her niece had more in common than she'd thought.

"Look, Dylan, Kristen's been gone for a few days now, and no one knows where she is. Can you tell me anything that might help?"

Dylan shook his head. "She was real moody the last few days, but hey, in my business, I'm used to that, you know? They're up, they're down." He laughed at his own joke. "Maybe Kristen got a lead on a new job. Maybe it was her time to jump."

Dylan seemed somewhat insightful for a small-time dealer who was making money two twenties at a time. Perhaps that was what drew Kristen to him. He had a confidence in how he saw the world around him. Jamie understood that a young woman could find such self-assurance appealing, even comforting.

Jamie handed Dylan her card. She had printed them in a short run for leads only. "Call me if you hear from her, okay? Her dad is worried about her."

Dylan looked unconvinced but said, "Awright. I'll ask around." Then he added, "You need to see Beth Whitland. If anybody would know anything, she would. She doesn't dally in my products, so we don't hang out much. I don't really know her, but she seems okay."

Jamie didn't remember seeing Beth's name on Brian's list of contacts. She wondered if that was an intentional omission or simply a part of his daughter's life that he knew little about.

"Can you tell me where to find her?"

"Sure. She works at the Port A Youth Center. Tutoring."

The revelation surprised Jamie. Someone in Kristen's circle was interested in something other than a street education?

Jamie nodded and turned away, not sure what to make of her interaction with Dylan. A charismatic, self-aware, prescription-pill pusher?

She'd seen stranger things, and the day was still young.

CHAPTER FIVE

Jamie checked the time on her phone. Just past two in the afternoon. She had already received some actionable intel from Kristen's script-dealing boyfriend. Finding Beth was next on her list, but she still had one thing to do first.

Jamie drove to Hemingway's and pulled into the parking lot close to the side door. Cookie stood outside in the grass, and his sizeable fist dangled a leash attached to Jamie's only true love, her bulldog Deuce.

She got out of the car and bent to give her dog's skin-folded face a rub. "Thank you for taking him out while I was tracking down Dylan," she said to Cookie while her attention lay fully on her pup.

"No, don't go trying to make up to him now," Cookie joked with her. "He loves me more. He just lives with you."

Jamie reached down and nuzzled her face to Deuce's. "Did you have a good time with Uncle Cookie while I was out?"

He snorted in response and rubbed his face against her leg.

"He can smell the beach on you," Cookie chided. "He knows you went out without him." He grinned at her, making his digs. The two were always in a battle for Deuce's affections, which in truth, could be bought with a belly rub and almost any food product.

Jamie continued rubbing Deuce's wrinkles while addressing Cookie's comment. "As you know, I was at Pier 5, which isn't the beach, and Deuce knows I can't take him in those situations. He's too cute, and he attracts too much attention. He's an asset for diversionary tactics, but I needed to be discreet." She gave him a final pat on the head. "I'll take you the next time I need to create a scene, okay?"

Deuce sat between Jamie and Cookie, a fur baby sandwiched between two doting parents. He snorted, encouraging a laugh from Jamie. "I'm sorry, buddy. I'll take you out again soon. Promise." She signaled to Cookie to go back inside. "Let's get him settled with Marty so we can get on the road."

"Go where?" Cookie asked.

"I've got a lead on Kristen from her on-again-off-again boyfriend."

"So you're taking the case?"

Jamie hadn't really thought of Kristen as a case, but rather a family problem that needed solving. "I'll fill you in on the drive. Let me get Deuce something to eat."

"I already fed him."

Jamie's eyes narrowed. "You didn't give him more leftover rice and beans, did you? It gives him gas."

Cookie smiled, his ornery side showing through. He gave Jamie a playful push and took over the important task of giving Deuce some attention by rubbing his jowls. "You tell her, Deuce. Tell her that you love your Uncle Cookie more."

"Take him back inside and see if Marty will let him hang out behind the bar for a while. The ladies love him. He's good for tips."

Cookie nodded and opened the side door to Hemingway's, an excited Deuce following him. Jamie called after her friend, "Don't let Marty give my dog any jalapeno poppers. It's not funny anymore!"

Jamie waited for Cookie to return from dropping off Deuce to be overrun with attention from the local bar crowd. She stood outside and replayed the conversation with Dylan in her mind, wondering how to best approach the lead he had provided.

Cookie emerged from the bar and followed Jamie to the Tahoe. He snapped his fingers. "Oh, we need to stop by and see Erin on the way to wherever we're going next."

"Everything okay?" Jamie asked. "Nothing new on the Finch case?"

Cookie shook his head. "Nothing like that. She just said she had a problem she wanted to discuss with us. I told her I'd tell you."

Jamie filled Cookie in on her surprise meeting with Brian and her discussion with Dylan, including Dylan's news about Kristen mentioning an upcoming job with her dad.

"Dylan told me about a friend of Kristen's. Her name is Beth, and she works at the Youth Activity Center. We call it the YAC. Hopefully, she can tell me where Kristen is so that I can close this case and stop worrying about her."

"Feeling some responsibility here?" Cookie asked.

"I could claim Catholic guilt, except that I'm not Catholic... so there's that."

Cookie lowered the passenger's window halfway. "My mom is the road-trip master of the guilt trip. Hers travels cross country."

Jamie cracked a small smile but kept her focus on the road.

Jamie parked outside the YAC, and after she turned off the engine, the pair surveyed the landscape. Like almost every other building in Port Alene, the center's façade showcased an island design with seafoam-green and sky-blue shells embedded in textured stucco. Several tables were positioned to the right of the building, each holding a deep-blue shade umbrella. Every table had a chess set placed in its center. Two of the tables were occupied. One group was engaged in a match, while the other simply used the table as a place to chat.

As she and Cookie stepped out of her vehicle, Jamie slipped her keys into her bag. At the entrance to the center, Cookie pulled the door open to let Jamie go first, and the burst of cold air momentarily startled her. *You could hang meat in here.*

The pair approached the young man seated behind a tall, rounded reception desk. "Hi, I'm here to see Beth. I understand she's a tutor here."

The man eyed the couple with slight suspicion. "And your name is?"

"Jamie Rush." She signaled to Cookie, who gave his best nonthreatening expression. "This is Cookie Hinojosa. Beth is friends with my niece. I need to talk with her for just a few minutes." Jamie smiled to put the young man at ease, and he seemed satisfied.

"Beth's in the back," he said. "I'll walk you in."

"We can find it."

He was insistent. "No, really. I'll walk you in." His tone told her that was not up for discussion.

Jamie decided not to press it. "Lead the way."

They followed their uptight escort down a wide hallway awash with light from numerous skylights. The walls showcased many paintings of ocean life and the sea. All seemed painted not by teenagers but by the same person as part of a series because each piece was painted using similar colors and brush strokes.

The hallway opened to a larger room segmented into several meeting spaces. The room was full but not crowded. Twenty or so teenagers, more girls than boys, sat with their attention focused mostly on their phones, with a few in the mix reading books. Jamie was happy to see that a couple of teenagers still enjoyed losing themselves in a good story.

Their escort pointed to the back room, where several kids sat, writing on notepads. "Beth is the one in the blue shirt."

Jamie nodded her thanks and walked to the group.

Beth appeared to be giving her students an assignment. As soon as she noticed Jamie and Cookie, she moved to greet them. "Can I help you?" She smiled at Cookie but didn't extend the warmth to Jamie, who figured Beth must like heavyset men wearing Hawaiian shirts.

Jamie nodded and stepped forward. "Yes, I hope I'm not interrupting." She extended her hand, noting that she needed to change her approach since Beth didn't appear to be much of a girl's girl. "I'm Jamie." She had considered posing as someone else, using her tracing skills to try to extract the truth, but from what she had gleaned about Beth from Dylan, it was best to play this one straight. She waited to share anything further about the reason for her visit.

Jamie's openness seemed to work because Beth's shoulders softened. "You're not interrupting. They're working on a short-story assignment. Writing fiction is always a good way to indulge some angry fantasies without a trip to juvie. Good therapy, and their imaginations go wild."

"I'm sure. I'd hate to go back and read some of my old teenage journals." Jamie studied Beth's face. She was young, likely mid-twenties, but seemed in possession of a mature soul. "You seem to know an awful lot about keeping kids out of trouble, considering you're not much more than a kid yourself."

Beth smiled. "Well, most of my family serves as a warning for bad behavior, and I got in some trouble not so long ago. I've watched this movie play out ten different ways. All the endings suck."

"I'm with you on that one."

"So, what can I help you with?"

Jamie clasped her hands together before speaking. "I hear that you're close to Kristen."

Beth's demeanor changed as soon as Kristen's name left Jamie's lips. The girl tensed, looking uneasy. "I haven't talked to Kristen in a few days."

"I know. Her father thinks there's something wrong."

Beth's eyes remained focused on the ground. "I'm surprised her father noticed. He only calls her when he needs something."

Jamie couldn't help but grin. "Sounds like my own dad."

"How do you know Kristen's dad? Do you work for him?"

Jamie waved off her question. "Oh, lord no. Brian's my half brother, but we aren't close." She leaned in a bit for emphasis. "At all." She felt the need to establish as much distance as possible between her and Brian. "In fact, I usually ignore his calls, but with Kristen not answering her phone…"

"So you're Kristen's family?"

Jamie tried to shrug off the connection, wondering if Kristen did the same thing.

Cookie chimed in. "Yes, Jamie is her aunt."

"Apparently, she's been gone almost four days now without contacting anyone," Jamie added.

"She drops off sometimes. It happens."

"You aren't worried about her?"

Beth sighed. "Look, I used to worry every single time it happened. She'd do this little routine before and after a job. It's like she needed to regroup, get herself in character, or think things through."

Jamie didn't want to ask the question, but she knew she had to. "So she doesn't hide out to get high?"

Beth looked at the ground. "Well, I didn't say that. But she's been clean for a while. I really think she wanted to stay away from that stuff. That was the problem she had with Dylan. Once she was clean, she wasn't much fun to be around. Or so he said."

"I take it you don't like the guy?"

She smiled a bit. "I hate to admit it, but I actually do like him. He's a drug dealer and not an ideal boyfriend for her, but he treated her okay. They had a good time, but I think she got tired of it. He was always happy with where he was. Live-in-the-moment kind of guy. She always had a plan."

Jamie thought for a moment. "What was she working on lately?"

"Not sure. She wouldn't say." Beth shrugged it off. "It doesn't surprise me, though. She always kept a part of herself secret." Then Beth hedged. "There was… never mind."

Jamie gently placed her hand on Beth's forearm, careful with her touch.

"Tell me, Beth." She could see the indecision on the woman's face. "What if she's not okay? This isn't the time to hold back."

Beth shook her head. "It's not that simple. She swore me to secrecy."

"I won't tell her you said anything."

Cookie put his hand on his heart in mock solidarity. "Cross my heart."

Jamie leaned slightly toward Beth, not to be combative but to foster a feeling of quiet collaboration. "We'll be discreet. I promise." Jamie stood close enough to simulate pressure but far enough back to respect the young woman's personal space. Cookie positioned himself on the other side of her. Jamie took great care with such things because she knew the power of uncomfortable silence. She refused to fill the space herself so the other person had to—a tactic she'd often used to get people talking. *Skip Tracing 101.*

"She had a friend whose dad is a local real estate agent," Beth began. "This guy set her up in a foreclosure so she could crash when she needs to. It's her private hideaway. Her dad doesn't know about it, not that I think he'd care unless he wanted to use it for a scam. Kristen said she needed someplace where she could be alone, away from people wanting something from her."

Jamie couldn't help but smile. That sounded like Kristen. "Where is this place?"

"It's on Kensington in that old subdivision by the ferry. It's a blue single-story. Nothing fancy, but it's a place to crash. There's a Seaside Escapes Realty sign out front. We would joke that it could be our own escape."

Jamie extended her hand. "Thanks, Beth. I promise that if she's there, I'll tell Brian only that she's fine and she'll be in touch whenever she feels like it. I won't tell him where she is."

Beth nodded but said nothing else. She glanced back at her students. "I need to get them going on the next project, or else I'll lose them." She rolled her eyes. "Short attention spans."

"We'll call you if we need anything else," Jamie said.

The pair said a brief goodbye, and Beth returned her attention to her students, who were entertaining their restlessness by playing a game of paper dodge ball.

Once outside the front door, Cookie put his arm around Jamie and squeezed. "Sounds like you found Kristen's hideout."

Jamie pushed the key fob to unlock her car and reached to open the door. "Looks that way." She checked her watch. "I promised Erin I would stop by and pay off the last Cowboys game. You want to ride along?"

"Always," Cookie said.

Jamie smiled, grateful for his friendship. Even if she didn't tell him enough, he knew. She started the Tahoe and pulled out of the parking lot, glancing at the kids still sitting at the game tables in front of the Youth Activity Center. She tried to picture Kristen there among them, but somehow, the idea seemed too carefree for Kristen's taste.

"Okay, let's visit your favorite bookie, and then we can put Kristen's case to rest."

Jamie smiled at the idea. Reconciling with Kristen wasn't completely out of reach, was it?

CHAPTER SIX

J AMIE AND COOKIE ARRIVED AT Senior Seaside Adventures and were greeted by a parking lot hosting more golf carts than automobiles. It was official—they were deep in the heart of winter Texan land.

Cookie held open the door for Jamie, gesturing with his outstretched arm. "After you."

They stepped inside, and Jamie immediately spotted Erin greeting her guests. Jamie walked over and hugged her friend. "What's shakin', bacon? Any big plans for your silver-haired high rollers I should know about?"

Erin returned the hug but laughed Jamie off. She hurried to greet one of her regulars, a frail but spunky woman pushing eighty... and a walker.

Erin helped the woman maneuver her walker through the front door. "Ready for an evening of high-stakes bingo?"

"I'm on a roll this week," Mrs. Kramer said. "I'm going to kick some gray-haired butt tonight!"

Jamie had heard stories from Erin about Mrs. Kramer. The woman had a competitive streak that ran deep and mean. Recently, she had started sprint-walking on the seniors' circuit. That sweet face masked her ability to throw a wrinkly elbow when least expected. No one got between that woman and the finish line.

"What's with the walker?" Jamie asked, noting the spry woman had not needed one before.

"Sprained my ankle in my last race. Can't manage crutches so this is easier. I hate it. Makes me look old." As if the gray hair, wrinkles, and orthopedic shoes played no part.

Erin helped the woman to her chair at the bingo table, and Mrs. Kramer whispered to her, "Put fifty on the Cowboys for me this weekend. I have a feeling that our losing streak is over."

"Will do." Erin patted her back. "I'll take care of it for you."

"You're a dear. Now let's hope this new quarterback can hold it together."

"I'd sit on your bets until you have some wins under your belt," Jamie interjected. "Your guy may have talent, but he gets injured every time he gets the ball."

Mrs. Kramer nodded. "His bones are worse than mine are these days. Poor guy breaks a collarbone every time he steps on the field."

Erin smiled, feigned a salute, acknowledging her orders, and returned to her greeting duties.

Jamie and Cookie stood back, eavesdropping on the bet requests taking place. Mr. Dorsey wanted a hundred on the Steelers game, the widow Martin decided to go against her favorite team—something to cause her long-departed husband to roll over in his grave, she was sure—and take the spread on the Broncos. The Carnole twins placed identical bets on the Packers. They explained they were die-hard fans of their home state of Wisconsin except when it came to the climate, which was why they'd moved to Texas. Even they couldn't resist the lure of temperate winters.

Erin executed her bookie duties with skill and smiles, managing the active band of winter Texans with a warmth Jamie admired. Jamie not only appreciated her friend's openness but also her business acumen. Erin had established Senior Seaside Adventures as the perfect cover for her fledgling bookie business, and it also fostered her cultivation of well-heeled gamblers over the last couple of years.

Erin had purchased the building as an investment as well as a cover for her betting business. Real estate prices had soared during the last five years in Port Alene, and she'd known enough to get in before the boom. She understood that a business catering to snowbirds would generate cash and clientele. The property would only continue to increase in value, but what it housed was where the true treasure flourished.

Erin signaled to Jamie and Cookie to follow her down the hallway. Cookie stopped and greeted several senior citizens along the way. Jamie overheard two older ladies complimenting Cookie on his Hawaiian shirt. They gushed over him, and Jamie rolled her eyes, knowing her friend just ate it up.

"You running for office?" Jamie asked. "I haven't seen that much glad-handing since Mayor Vicentes stopped in before the last election."

"I'm kind of a big deal with the over-sixty set," Cookie responded, his deadpan expression begging for a response.

"He really is," Erin said. "Betting goes up when Cookie comes and works the room. I may need to start giving him a cut."

Jamie grinned. "Don't encourage him, or I'll have to listen to him brag all the way home."

Erin ushered her friends into her office. Unlike the sterile environment of the main game hall, with its gray plastic chairs and long white nondescript banquet tables, Erin's office could have come straight out of Vegas.

Her phone rang, and she instinctively reached to answer it but stopped before picking up the receiver.

"What's wrong?" Jamie asked.

"It's Boxer's guy Reggie."

Jamie gestured to the phone. "Go ahead. Put it on speaker. We'll be quiet."

Erin couldn't run from Boxer's crew. She had to deal with him head-on.

"This is Erin Clay." Her voice had none of the lovely lift it normally had. Her tone was lower, stronger, and all business.

"How are you, Erin?" The man's voice had an edge of gravel to it, hinting at a lifelong smoking habit. Jamie glanced at Erin, noticing her posture.

She folded her arms as she stood over the phone. "I'm working, Reggie. What are you doing? Besides harassing me?"

"No harassing. Just a friendly call to check on the competition, that's all."

"You're not the competition, and you're about as friendly as a pit bull."

"Pit bulls get a bad rap."

"I'm busy, Reggie."

"Boxer heard you're picking up some customers north of the bridge, and he isn't too happy about that."

Erin glanced at Jamie, and Jamie rolled her eyes. Boxer was a rival bookie and had a reputation for breaking bones. Erin had discussed her growing worry about Boxer and his intentions several times over the last few months. Boxer scared the seniors. He told them he could make it look as though they had fallen in the bathtub, and the cops would be none the wiser. The seniors had started pulling their bets back in favor of friendlier company—one reason of many that contributed to Erin's success. Erin had recognized a market opportunity and seized it, knowing her softer approach would bring better benefits than the stereotypical strong-arm tactics so common in her industry.

Erin employed her own muscle but often relied upon other methods of persuasion to keep payments arriving on time. She preferred to keep her customers in the nonthreatening category. She believed that hurting anyone—especially the elderly—brought bad karma. It simply went against her nature to bring such harm, even when her own money was involved. She remained particularly protective of her older clients, and they knew it.

"Not that I owe you any explanations, Reggie, because Boxer can't claim any territory just because he says so, but I get lots of clients on referral, friends of friends. Doesn't matter where they live. They want to book with me because I don't threaten to push them down the stairs and make it look like an accident. That's all."

"Well, he don't see it that way."

"It doesn't matter. You tell Boxer to mind his own business."

"I don't think he's going to like that much."

"I don't care what Boxer wants," Erin shot back. "He's got his business, and I've got mine. Coming in and threatening my clients would be a mistake."

Erin stabbed the end call button on the console. "What am I going to do about him? Boxer has already chased off two bookies. I'm the last man standing in the area."

"What about Big Charlie?" Jamie asked.

"No one's heard from him for a while. Rumor is he's taken up permanent residence at the bottom of the Gulf."

Jamie moved behind Erin, who was still sitting at her desk, and hugged her around the shoulders. "Cookie and I can do some research to see if we can figure out what Boxer's up to."

Erin tilted her head backward to look at her friend. "I'd really appreciate that. Thanks."

"Anything for you," Jamie replied.

"You know, you still owe me two hundred from last week's game."

"No family discount?" Jamie joked.

Erin patted her friend's arm, which rested on her shoulder. "If you look into Boxer, we'll call it a hundred."

"Done."

Jamie released her embrace and reached into her bag for her wallet. She selected the cash and dropped it on Erin's desk. "There you go, fresh from the bank. And don't let me place any more bets this month. I can't afford it."

"Okay," Erin agreed. "But don't get upset with me if you have your latest sure thing and I turn you down."

"I'm a witness," Cookie said. "No more betting this month."

Erin snapped her fingers as though she had just remembered something. She leaned toward her open front door. "Becky!" she called out. "Can you come here for a minute?"

At over 250 pounds, with the haircut of a marine and a sense of humor to match, Becky could enforce almost anything without pulling a weapon. Rumor had it she once left a convicted felon in tears, although no one was sure how she'd done it.

Becky stepped through the open door of Erin's office. "One down on the completion sheet, two to go today," she reported.

"If you can close both today, that would be great," Erin said.

"Working on it," she replied. "I only had one dodge my call so far, but you know who he is."

Jamie interjected herself into the conversation. "Hey, Becky, what do you know about Boxer?"

She shrugged. "Enough that I don't like him."

Jamie pointed to Erin. "He just called, and I think he might be a problem, so keep an eye out, okay?"

"You want me to shadow you for a while?" Becky asked Erin. "I can square the books first and then trail you if you need me. Extra security is always a good idea."

Especially when it looks like Becky.

"I'm good, Becky. I'll let you know if I need anything."

Jamie ignored Erin's directive to her employee. "Yes, keep a closer eye out, Becky," Jamie said. "I don't trust the guy."

Becky nodded, turned, and walked away, leaving the three friends to finish their conversation. Erin slid into her chair, her body limp, seemingly drained from the conversation with Reggie. "You don't think Boxer's going to be a huge problem, do you?" Her expression clearly begged for some sort of comfort.

Jamie and Cookie exchanged a quick glance. "We'll figure out how to deal with him. Just let Becky be your shadow for a while until we come up with something solid."

"I hate having someone follow me," Erin said. "It reminds me of my dad's security detail."

"Better Becky than Boxer, right?" Jamie asked.

Erin brushed a long blond strand of hair away from her face, tucking it behind her ear. "Yes, Becky is the better choice. I just don't want this to be a permanent thing—me needing security."

Jamie understood her friend's concern. "Don't worry. We'll take care of it."

Jamie and Cookie walked over to Erin and hugged her while she remained sitting in her chair. Cookie gave Erin a pat on the head. "No leaving without Becky, okay?"

Erin begrudgingly agreed and waved them out of her office. "Go on, now."

Cookie and Jamie turned to leave. They closed the door behind them and were halfway down the hallway before Cookie stopped. He turned to Jamie, his face creased with worry. "You think Boxer's going to be a problem?"

Jamie nodded. "Absolutely."

CHAPTER SEVEN

JAMIE AND COOKIE RETURNED TO her Tahoe, but Cookie's cell phone rang as he opened the car door. He checked the screen then answered the call with the touch of his finger. "Hey, bro, what's going on?"

Cookie leaned against the outside of Jamie's Tahoe, his considerable weight resting against the passenger's door. Jamie stood opposite, on the driver's side, while Cookie bargained with his brother. She half listened to the one-sided conversation while she checked email on her phone.

"Is he okay?" Cookie asked.

Jamie deleted spam messages and scrolled through what remained, her attention to her phone serving as a cover for her eavesdropping.

"Why can't Bobo help you? What's he doing?" Cookie paused, listening. "Okay. I'll be right over, but you stay put until I get there." He rubbed his forehead in exasperation as he disconnected.

Jamie could see he was concerned. "Everything okay?"

"Nothing major, but my Uncle Cleo knows better than to do work up high outside his house, but he's stubborn. Broke his ankle. He knows not to be on a ladder by himself."

"Stubborn runs in both our families, yeah?"

Cookie rumbled a half laugh, and they both climbed in the car. "Can you take me back over to Hemingway's so I can get my car? My cousin is dropping Cleo off from the hospital, but then he's got to go to work. I need to stay with him until my aunt gets off work." Cookie tapped his hand on the car window, and his head turned away from Jamie as he stared out.

Jamie considered offering more comic relief but decided against it. She could tell Cookie, annoyed as he was about the change in plans, was also genuinely concerned about his uncle. "Sure, no problem. After I drop you off, I'm going to run by that house and see if Kristen's hiding out there."

Cookie turned his concern from his Uncle Cleo to Jamie. "Are you sure? If it gets too late, maybe you should wait for me to go with you."

Jamie waved off his offer. She knew his family needed him, and if Jamie did find Kristen, she preferred to keep their conversation between the two of them. "I've got this. She's probably freeloading in this house, and I'll tell Brian that the case is closed. I'll text you if I need anything."

Jamie pulled into Hemingway's parking lot and put her vehicle in park. Cookie's frown appeared permanent, the result of realizing he would be Uncle Cleo's caretaker for a bit.

"I'll let Deuce out again before I go. Okay for Marty to keep him here 'til one of us gets back?"

"Sure. I'll make it up to him later."

"You're like an absentee doggie parent. Pretty soon, you'll start spoiling him with dog toys because you never spend time with him."

Jamie stifled a laugh. He was right, but she wouldn't say it out loud. "I'll make sure to take him on some extra beach trips soon." She wiggled her hand in Cookie's direction, shooing him. "Get out of here. I'll let you know if I find Kristen."

Cookie leaned across the seat and hugged Jamie, his ample arms squeezing hard. "See you."

She waited for Cookie to go inside. The foreclosed home was in a neighborhood less than fifteen minutes away. It was getting late, but Jamie wanted to put this case to bed. Kristen was most likely camping out in an empty house or partying with her friends, completely unaware that her family was worried about her.

Just one more stop, Jamie thought. *Just one more stop…*

———————⋯⋯———————

Jamie drove down Seascapes Avenue, which led to a new housing development that catered to vacationers searching for a summer home. As she pulled into the main entrance, she winced at the homogenous beach-themed entry walls promising a never-ending island holiday. She saw little imagination in the South Texas real estate market these days. People just slapped some baby-blue paint on a starfish, stuck it to a wall, and demanded top dollar for the privilege of tracking sand in the house.

Though she didn't know the neighborhood well, she figured she could find her way by turning here and there. It wasn't a huge development—a few blocks of unimaginatively designed abodes with small yards and tacky statues posing as lawn art. The small homes were nestled close enough to allow neighbors to almost peer into one another's windows with little effort. The thought of living publicly held zero appeal for her.

Jamie followed one road to the end of a cul-de-sac and found the realty sign Beth had mentioned. Like many foreclosures that sat on the market for months, that one appeared shabby and unloved. Weeds had blossomed around the sides of the house, and the windows were dirty and smeared, the blinds down. Jamie could tell from tire tracks in the tall grass that someone had parked there. The tracks also indicated someone had lousy parking skills… or was in a hurry.

She pulled into the empty driveway and reached into her bag to verify that her gun was where it should be. She didn't like venturing into an unfamiliar setting unprepared.

She moved with caution up the driveway, noting the lack of cars anywhere in the area. Definitely a good place to crash for a little bit. No nosy neighbors, and not much street traffic. At the front door, she saw the realtor's lockbox hanging from the doorknob. She turned the knob and stopped short. *Still locked.*

Jamie glanced around then proceeded to the rear of the house. Not much of a back door overhang to speak of, save for a small concrete slab and a porch that must have been built by two drunken college students on break. There was no trash or party litter, nothing dumped around the back to draw attention. She tried the doorknob, and it gave way with a creak. Leaning into the door, Jamie moved slowly and adjusted her weight to minimize the noise announcing her entry.

She stepped inside with care and surveyed the bare room. She saw a breakfast nook, judging from the hanging light's position and the alcove's proximity to the kitchen. The stench of old food greeted her, made worse by the closed windows and lack of air conditioning. The atmosphere felt stale, still, and steamy. Jamie decided to leave the back door open to circulate some air because her gag reflex threatened to strike. She moved to the living room, noting the scattered magazines, pizza boxes, and several empty 7-Eleven Slurpee cups attracting ants.

Jamie continued with caution, observing the different brands of take-out food containers. There were no surprises—pizza boxes, yellow boxes from the local fried chicken drive-through. *By free crash pad standards, this place isn't bad.* She stopped for a moment, taking note of the stillness in the house. She wondered if Kristen was hiding somewhere in one of the back bedrooms. Maybe her niece worried an intruder had come inside.

"Kristen!" she called out. "Are you here? It's Jamie!"

No response.

Jamie ignored the knot in her stomach as she moved tentatively down the hall toward the first bedroom. She took a step inside and stopped cold. On the floor, Kristen lay atop a navy blanket, but clearly not at rest. Her body was twisted in an unnatural way. Her face was turned to the wall, but her right arm remained outstretched, palm open, her torso turned toward the open door.

Then Jamie noticed the needle on the floor. She rushed to look at her niece's face.

Kristen's eyes were open with a haunting vacancy, gray and glassy.

"No, Kristen, no…" was all she could whisper.

Jamie knelt over her lifeless niece, studying her chest, waiting for it to rise and fall with breath, but only haunting stillness remained. Kristen's eyes, once flickering with anticipation of things to come, revealed nothing but the end of a turbulent young life. Jamie silently talked back the sobs, grief seizing her heart. Kristen was supposed to be hanging out with friends, not lying cold and alone on the floor of a foreclosed house.

Jamie forced herself to focus on the details of the scene. Careful not to disturb anything, she observed Kristen's clothing. The girl wore a spring break T-shirt and cutoff jean shorts. Her feet were bare.

Jamie's instincts told her something was off. Had Kristen really overdosed? Neither Dylan nor Beth had said Kristen dabbled in any hardcore drugs, certainly nothing with needles. Jamie remembered Kristen once telling her how much getting a flu shot had scared her as a kid. Dylan had said she didn't use serious street drugs and had been clean for some time. Had he lied, or did he just not know what she'd been up to? Jamie's suspicious mind wondered if something else was at play, or was Kristen simply another body to add to the statistics?

She remained kneeling and began gingerly checking the girl's pockets, careful to avoid the surprise prick of a needle. As she slipped her hand in the back left pocket, she felt something. A piece of paper. She pulled it out gently and examined it. Jamie focused on the folded two-dollar bill she held between her fingers, a calling card she had seen only once before.

Jamie sat on the ground next to Kristen. The weight of seeing her niece helpless on the ground was a crushing weight. Jamie's hands came up to cover her face, which contorted in a soundless sob. Her shoulders shook with the regret she'd carried for so long, but no tears came.

Despite her grief, she could have no release, not when it ended this way.

Their relationship.

Kristen's life.

Jamie would use her pain the only way she knew how. She would discover the truth, regardless of the cost. Her hopes of conciliation with Kristen withered in her hands, and all that remained was grief.

Grief and the desperate need for answers.

CHAPTER EIGHT

JAMIE SAT ON THE CONCRETE front step of the abandoned house. She couldn't bear to be so close to Kristen's body, but she couldn't move too far away. She felt the pull in opposite directions, wanting to comfort her niece but understanding it would never be possible. She could feel tears threatening, but she used her anger to keep them at bay. She couldn't unravel again; that would have to wait until later.

A Port Alene sheriff's department car emerged at the end of the street, red and blue lights flashing, invading the darkness with their demanding, colorful chaos. The car pulled up in front of the abandoned house where Jamie kept watch. The car parked, but the lights remained flashing.

Detective David Herrera stepped out of his squad car, all six foot three of him, and walked toward Jamie, who remained sitting on the stoop. He kneeled down next to her. "You okay, Jamie?"

She shook her head. "No, David. No, I'm not."

Jamie and Cookie both considered David Herrera to be a stand-up professional, a good man with a good reputation. Her work required keeping a solid relationship with the Port Alene Police Department but doing so in such a way that she didn't divulge more than necessary in any case. It was akin to walking a tightrope of honesty and discretion.

"She's inside?" Detective Herrera stood up and extended a hand to Jamie to help her up from the step. She held his hand for only a moment and, once up, released his grip and dusted off her backside.

Jamie pointed over her shoulder at the front door. "She's in the back bedroom. I didn't touch anything other than the front and back door. And her. I touched her briefly."

"You came in through the back?"

"Front door was locked."

"I called the coroner. He'll be here as soon as he can."

Jamie nodded, keeping her hands in her pockets, her mind turning over the last hour's events. It didn't feel right—the house, the body, the needle, the two-dollar bill. She contemplated how much to reveal to Herrera. She knew the Port Alene Police Department had rarely been called upon to investigate crimes of any magnitude. Not because they didn't have the skills or smarts but simply because the environment gave them a daily diet of DUIs, speeding tickets, and bar fights.

And this was personal.

Jamie followed Herrera into the house, and he continued toward the bedroom. Jamie stopped at the hallway, watching while Herrera examined the room, walking carefully around Kristen's body, taking note of the sparse details of the room.

"I'm not so sure this is what it looks like." She felt compelled to advocate on Kristen's behalf and let him know that she wasn't a junkie. "She doesn't have a history of using hard drugs. And I know she was scared of needles."

Jamie relayed the information she'd gleaned from her conversations with Dylan and Beth—that Kristen sometimes dropped off the grid to be alone, that she seemed fine, and that she never dabbled further than prescription drugs and the occasional joint.

Herrera stood over Kristen's body and looked at her for a moment. He then knelt down, carefully studying her arms.

"See? No track marks," Jamie said.

Herrera nodded. "People shoot up in all kinds of places. Between the toes, other places hard to see at first glance. We'll make sure to do a thorough examination."

"I'd appreciate that. Thank you."

The numbness infiltrated her bones as she watched Herrera finish his analysis, taking notes as his eyes searched for any small detail that might provide insight.

Herrera emerged from the bedroom. "She doesn't have any personal belongings with her. If she carried a bag, it isn't here."

Jamie had no idea if she carried a bag or not. What she knew about Kristen's life could fit in a thimble with room to spare. "She's not wearing any shoes, either."

"Wel , this is Port Alene," Herrera said. "Shoes and shirts optional. It's a beach town."

"Not even flip-flops? Isn't that a little odd? Would she walk around in this heat without shoes?"

Kristen had no personal belongings with her. Even junkies—and Kristen wasn't a junkie according to Jamie's sources—had something they kept close, an item they cared about. They were often fiercely protective of their few possessions.

Jamie's thoughts returned to the two-dollar bill, her fingers manipulating the clue hidden in her pocket. She didn't want to hand over the bill, but she also knew that withholding evidence would hinder the investigation. She grasped the bill and held it up for Herrera to see. "I found this in her jeans pocket. You know what this means."

Herrera accepted the bill from her, his features tight as his eyes examined the bill. "Let's not jump to any conclusions here, Jamie," he cautioned. "It doesn't necessarily mean—"

"But it could."

"We'll look into every lead. I promise. But this, on its own, isn't proof of anything."

Jamie nodded, understanding that pushing the topic further would lead nowhere She stood next to the detective, hands in her pockets, which were empty without the bill that had taken space there moments ago.

"Jamie?" Herrera extended his arm, gesturing her to the front door.

She nodded and turned to glance over her shoulder one last time. She moved tentatively back to the bedroom, stopping short of stepping inside. It was painful to be so close.

Detective Herrera moved toward the front door, giving her a moment alone.

"I'm so sorry," was all Jamie could manage. She blinked against the burning in her eyes and walked to meet Detective Herrera, who followed Jamie outside.

"I'll call her father and let him know we found Kristen," Jamie said.

He nodded. "Have him call my office, and we'll let him know what we find out And give him my condolences."

Jamie headed to her car, drove a block, then pulled over. She leaned her crossed arms against the steering wheel and buried her head in them. She couldn't allow her grief to weaken her. She needed it. It would be the fuel propelling her forward in finding who was behind Kristen's death.

Kristen was gone.

And someone was going to pay.

CHAPTER NINE

JAMIE ARRIVED AT THE GOLDEN Star Racetrack just before the gates opened at ten thirty. The parking lot was beginning to fill up with the cars of early betters eager to start the day by placing their sure bets. Jamie knew the feeling.

The evening had been long, time stumbling in small steps through the dark hours, and she had spent the night alone with only the company of Deuce and a bit too much whiskey. While she'd wanted to call Cookie to tell him about Kristen, she couldn't bring herself to reach out, not to Cookie, not until she could find the right words to explain how her discovery would affect his life. And she couldn't call Erin. She needed to sit alone with her grief, maybe to suffer a bit, maybe to wallow in some self-pity. A small part of her also felt as though she owed it to Brian to tell him first before anyone else. She didn't know if he deserved it, but he was, after all, Kristen's father—a lousy one, yes, but still her father.

Jamie fumbled with her key ring as she leaned against the hood of her Tahoe. She told herself she need not hurry inside, but deep down, she knew the truth. She didn't want to have this conversation, and she certainly didn't want to be in this place. The knot in her stomach tightened. A flutter of nausea created tiny waves inside her, butterflies daring her to lose her breakfast. She pushed off the hood and made her way to the front steps.

Let's get this over with.

When Brian had called shortly after Jamie's discussion with Detective Herrera, she told him they needed to talk in person, motivated by equal parts compassion and strategy. She wanted to see Brian's face when she delivered the news to determine if he knew more than he was letting on. She knew he'd grown up as she had, with a master's degree in deception.

Jamie stood by the front steps of the track, breathing in the salty South

Texas air. She wanted to fully experience this moment of anticipatory rush, the tingling in her senses. Those with addictive personalities knew that itch—the internal pressure that built then desperately searched for release. Coming from a long line of addicts who indulged in legitimate vices as well as illegal ones, Jamie knew her own risk of having her toes dangling just over the line of compulsion. She knew the ways to keep the risk in check, but she wondered at times if she were too confident. The racetrack was where she went when she wanted respite. Gambling opened the floodgates for her, serving as her escape, if only for a few moments.

She remained standing still while other patrons maneuvered around her to open the large double glass doors to the lobby. She overheard speculation about the day's races and plans of strategies for bets. One man, whose sad excuse for a fedora clashed with his red plaid shirt, recited his bet list while studying the day's sheet. From the looks of him, his horse had not yet come in.

Jamie knew she was there on solemn business, but still, her itch to place a bet remained. It would be her undoing one day. She spotted Brian, leaning against the outer railway as people hurried around him to find seats. Jamie approached slowly, her steps deliberate and measured. She leaned on the rail next to him. His eyes, strategically shielded with sunglasses, remained fixed on the track.

He acknowledged her presence with a slight nod. "Wanting to see me in person... This can't be good news."

"Brian, take your glasses off and look at me."

He hesitated but then did as he was asked, and in taking off his glasses, he revealed one hell of a shiner. It was a fresh wound, neatly contained around the right eye socket. Two small cuts above the eyebrow were held together with a butterfly stitch, and the skin around the eye had a purplish hue.

Jamie winced at the sight of it.

"A small business disagreement," he explained.

Jamie studied his face. "Seems you came up short in the negotiations."

His glance moved between Jamie's intent stare and the horses lining up in their gates on the track. "So, tell me. Did you find her?"

Jamie nodded, realizing that she must deliver the news with compassion. Kristen was his daughter, and even though there was no strong bond between the two siblings, she knew that the news she brought would forever change him.

She moved closer and turned her body toward him, her eyes demanding to be met with his. "Brian…" She reached for him, but he pulled away. "I need to talk to you."

He shook his head. "Just tell me, Jamie." He remained staring straight ahead, either unable or unwilling to make eye contact with his sister. "Is she gone?"

Jamie could only nod. She resisted the urge to reach for him in any way, to comfort him, as they stood together with the news of Kristen's death taking space between them. A tear rolled down his cheek, but he quickly wiped away any evidence of heartbreak.

Jamie took him through finding the foreclosed crash pad, discovering Kristen with a needle nearby, and the police speculating on an overdose. She made sure to include her belief that Kristen's death, if it involved drugs, was done *to* her rather than *by* her. Kristen wasn't a drug user. That much she knew, and she wanted Brian to know too.

His expression remained stoic as she spoke, his jaw tight. His body was rigid, and his hands gripped the rail in front of him, knuckles whitening from his intense grasp.

"Did you know anything about her using?" Jamie asked.

He shook his head. "No, but I guess that doesn't mean anything. We've always been good at hiding bad behavior, right?"

Jamie was surprised by his willingness to consider that his daughter had died of a drug overdose, especially since Jamie believed there was more to her death. Maybe she was grasping for a better explanation. Maybe she was blind to what Kristen had been capable of before her death.

"Did they find anything on her?" Brian asked. "Anything that could explain if someone was with her? Or what happened?"

Jamie knew he was fishing for information. She was careful not to respond with even a hint of suspicion in her voice, hopeful that he would reveal more than he intended.

"What do you mean?"

His eyes were fixed on the track. "Nothing in particular. Just anything that points to someone being with her or…"

Jamie tilted toward him, a small gesture, but for her, a large gesture of openness. "She didn't have any jewelry on her, no purse, not even a pair of shoes. All I found was a two-dollar bill in her back pocket." She kept her eyes trained on his expression as she said those words.

His jaw clenched ever so slightly—a tell. "I always gave her a two-dollar bill for good luck."

That clinched it. With that one lie, Brian had confirmed he knew more than he was sharing. At this crucial moment of discovering that his only child was dead, he'd lied to Jamie's face.

"So, what happens now?" Jamie asked, careful to keep her arms uncrossed, not wanting to show any defensiveness. If she kept her guard down, he might slip and give her a glimpse of what he kept close.

Brian put on his sunglasses, shielding his eyes from Jamie's scrutiny. "I don't know what happens now. We pick up the pieces and go forward."

Jamie's experience warned her not to lose her temper, but she had now depleted all her reserves of patience. This wasn't a real-estate scam gone bad. His daughter, her niece, was gone. *Gone.* And it didn't seem to move him.

Jamie's voice now rose above polite conversation. "That's it? That's all you've got? Your kid is found with a needle in her arm in some abandoned house, and you're just going to move on? Was she that disposable?" Two older men standing twenty feet away turned at the sound of Jamie's voice, but she pretended not to notice. She didn't care who heard her. Part of her wanted the world to know what a coldhearted bastard her half brother had turned out to be.

Brian turned his back on his sibling, just as he had done with his daughter. He began to walk away but stopped, turned to her, and pointed his finger at her. "You have no idea how I feel. You don't know me."

Jamie said nothing more as she watched Brian walk across the betting lobby and out the door. She wondered what truths had left with him, what truths would be buried with Kristen, and what the chances were that she could uncover them.

Her brother, the client, could no longer be trusted, even in the investigation of his own daughter's death. In one short exchange, Brian had placed himself at the top of Jamie's list. She would have to search for answers, knowing Brian would likely stonewall her every step of the way.

CHAPTER TEN

J AMIE KNEW SHE NEEDED TO talk to Cookie alone, to have the one conversation she would have done almost anything to avoid. Still emotionally raw from her confrontation with Brian earlier that morning Jamie wished for an afternoon by herself with nothing more than a few beers and her research notes. Her instinct to retreat pulled strongly, but her loyalty to Cookie took priority. He deserved to know the truth because his life and Kristen's were intertwined. He just didn't know it yet. It was up to Jamie to connect the dots and make sense of the way her niece's life and his brother's life crossed in a most cruel manner.

She'd asked Cookie to meet her for an afternoon scuba dive, her strategy to cover difficult territory against the comforting backdrop of Gulf waters.

"You ready to go?" Jamie asked as she stood at the edge of the pier, watching Cookie steer his pride and joy, a fishing vessel he'd named *Sweet Mama* after his sweet mama. *Sweet Mama* was a bay boat that he used for fishing, diving, and impressing new girlfriends.

It wasn't a spectacular vehicle, but he'd bought a lot of boat for his buck thanks to the weak economy and a glut of fishing vessels on the market. The saying "The two best days in a man's life are when he buys a boat and when he sells it" worked in his favor. He understood the time and attention boating life required. Unlike many who found maintenance to be a hassle, he found comfort in the necessity of it. It also proved to be a place of respite. Cookie retreated to his floating haven whenever he needed to think things through.

Jamie had counseled Cookie that he would never find a wife as long as he was so attached to his mother and his boat, but Cookie believed the trio to be a package deal. Jamie had a private bet with Erin on how long Cookie would remain a male spinster. Of course, men could have children well into their sixties, so his biological clock wasn't a factor.

Jamie figured her own clock was broken. She had no maternal instincts, and although she actually liked kids, she never would have sought out their company or admitted her affection out loud. She thought it best that her lineage die out. Being an aunt, lousy as she was at the job, had been the closest she would get to such a role.

"Is my gear on board?" Jamie asked as she stepped over the side of the boat, the water shifting enough to keep her off balance.

"Got everything. Checked the tanks, and we're good to go." Cookie took note of Jamie's faded orange T-shirt and jean shorts. "You got your suit and mask in that bag?"

She nodded. "You're such a good dive wife, checking everything ahead of time." She studied her friend in his water gear. Cookie was built like a linebacker and, at the moment, testing the limits of his wet suit. In spite of his size, he could remain neutrally buoyant, and in terms of skill, Jamie wouldn't want to have anyone else as a partner. He was adept at moving underwater, being observant of the surroundings, and making sure they didn't descend too far too quickly.

He pushed the gas handle forward and left the dock for the Gulf Coast. He nodded to a cooler tucked underneath the bench seat on the boat. "There's beer in the cooler."

"We'll save that for after. No reason to dive stupid."

"That's what I meant," Cookie replied, winking at her. "I'm not a bonehead novice."

Too many accidents occurred when newbie scuba divers drank all afternoon then decided to spend a few hours in open waters. And drinking too much after surfacing was no smarter. Jamie and Cookie strictly adhered to one beer after a dive, and only after drinking water to combat the dehydration. They had heard enough horror stories from friends running diving charters that they knew not to take stupid risks.

They moved through the bay for a few minutes. *Sweet Mama*, under Cookie's steady guidance, traveled at a slow and steady pace. This vessel was their private place, and they rarely brought anyone else with them on the boat save for a lady friend needing Jamie's approval or other divers needing a lift out to open waters.

Cookie pushed his boat full speed ahead, and they braced themselves for a choppy ride. They counted four other boats on the water, likely hobby fishermen or winter Texans hoping to land a fish worthy of a good story. Cookie recognized most of the regulars by their boats and sometimes commented when something looked gossip-worthy. That day's topic was Barney Martin, a local businessman who looked as though he'd taken the day off for some play. Cookie waved to him, taking note of the woman on board, a blonde wearing a black-and-white-striped sundress.

"I see that Mrs. Martin is off visiting her mother again. I wonder who he's got covering at the store this time?"

Jamie couldn't help but laugh. The island was a tough place to keep a low profile. The population ranked less than ten thousand locals and maybe another few thousand visitors on any given weekend.

"I hope it's someone who can keep a secret, because it seems like Barney's got a bunch of them," Jamie replied.

"That man's shameless. I don't think he even tries to hide it anymore. I saw him liplocked at Studabakers with some touristy-looking chick. They were in the back corner booth behind the pool tables."

"If he isn't careful, maybe one day we'll find his body floating somewhere out here."

"I don't think his wife cares, really," Cookie replied. "I mean, she has to know, and he's still walking around. Of course, she spends his money like a drunken sailor on leave. Who needs two Porsches on the island?"

Once they'd traveled a few miles out into the bay, free from the close company of other vessels, Cookie eased off the gas and let the boat idle. He surveyed the surrounding scenery. "This is all I need, you know that? I could spend all day, every day, out here—fishing, diving, coasting."

"Well, it's all you need 'til you get hungry and go running to your mom."

Cookie nodded, hard-pressed to deny Jamie's observation. "That's true, but then I'd be right back out here." He pointed to a small red cooler off to the side of the bench seat. "By the way, Mom sent fish tacos. We can eat after we come back up." He reached with his right hand to put the boat in neutral. The roaring sound of the motor diminished to an idle. The clouds burned off, offering little shade against the intense sun. Jamie felt the weight of the pending conversation pressing down, the heat only upping the intensity. She could feel Cookie studying her face, trying to read her. They both knew the discussion of Kristen was necessary. She had told him little about what had happened, preferring to have the conversation in person.

"You want to tell me what happened?" he asked.

Jamie had planned on waiting until after the dive, wanting him to enjoy some time in the water before discussing what she had found. "It can wait, Cookie. Let's dive first, and we can talk about it after."

Jamie could tell Cookie's bullshit radar pinged as soon as the words left her mouth. His eyebrows rose a notch, and his lips tightened. "You sure you don't want to talk about it now? You don't even have your suit on."

She could feel his eyes studying her expression, and at that moment, she knew her poker face was nonexistent.

He pushed again. "I know this must be hard for you, Jamie, but you'll feel better if you just talk about it."

Cookie, like always, was looking out for her. She hated what would come next because she couldn't protect him from the truth, nor should she. He would never forgive her if she kept something so important from him.

"It's just that I found something, and you need to know because it involves you."

The boat now drifted in waters twenty feet deep, according to the navigation system. There were no other boats nearby, although a stray vessel could be seen out in the distance.

Cookie extended his arm toward the water. "Just us out here in one of my favorite coves. No ears out here but the fish. And they don't have ears, so we're all good. Plus, if I betray your trust, you can hit me over the head and make me swim with the fishes."

Godfather jokes were a staple in their relationship.

Jamie was tired of avoiding the topic. She had to come clean and prepare herself for Cookie's reaction. He deserved to know.

She sat down on the small vinyl bench next to the boat's wheel. "So, you know that we found Kristen with a syringe nearby, and we're waiting to hear confirmation that she died of a drug overdose."

Cookie remained standing but leaned back against the boat's center panel, his arms crossed. "That's what you said. I'm so sorry." Cookie rubbed his eyes with his right hand, his thumb almost digging into the socket.

"Do you think she overdosed? Or do you think it was a setup to cover something else?"

Jamie traced her finger along the ridges of the boat's cushion, noticing its frayed edges and yellowing hue. She focused her attention on the stitching as she answered, not yet ready to meet his eyes.

"I don't think she was on drugs. I think her death was a signal to someone, maybe even to Brian. He's not telling me everything. Pretty sure I caught him in a lie."

She sighed, clasping her hands together, her forearms resting on her knees, her eyes studying the boat's floor. "I think she was murdered, but I don't know that the police will rule any different from accidental overdose. On the surface, she looks good for it."

Cookie reached over from his post, his arm outstretched to touch hers. "Must have been hard being the one to find her. I should have been there with you. You shouldn't have had to do that alone."

"I wanted to go alone, Cookie. That's not on you. It was my decision. I had no idea I'd find her that way." Her voice rippled with the beginnings of tears. "I was just going over there to yell at her for worrying everyone and wasting my time, and..."

Cookie leaned forward and hugged her tightly. Jamie allowed herself only a moment before she gently pushed away from his embrace, not wanting to completely fall apart.

She sniffed, wiping the tears from her eyes with the heel of her palm. "So, there were a few things that didn't add up for me when I found her. She didn't have a bag or anything personal with her, which I thought was strange since she was supposed to be using this foreclosed house as a crash pad."

Cookie nodded in agreement. "Never met a woman who doesn't have something she carries all her stuff in. And men know better than to venture in there."

Jamie appreciated her friend's humor in the moment, short-lived as it would be. "I know, right? Here's the thing, Cookie. She wasn't wearing shoes, either."

Cookie thought about it for a moment. "No shoes? You didn't find them anywhere?"

"Nope."

"You thinking what I'm thinking?"

"Taking someone's shoes makes it harder to run."

"Exactly."

"We know someone that does this."

"Yes, we do. And it gets worse."

"Like how much worse?"

Jamie sighed. She really didn't want to say the words, but she pushed them out in a rush. "I found a two-dollar bill in her pocket."

Cookie remained still, but Jamie could feel the tension in the arm that comforted her. His grip tightened, and his easy manner, full of compassion for Jamie's loss, dissolved in the discovery that Kristen's case and his brother's were connected.

Cookie pushed himself from a leaning position and stood at attention. His words spilled out quickly as he realized what Jamie was trying to say. "How did Kristen get tied up with the likes of the Deltones? This is bad in a way that you don't want to know. After what they did to my brother..."

Jamie rose from the boat bench and moved closer to her friend. His body was still partially covered by his wet suit. The top half was folded down and felt hot from the Texas sun.

"This isn't your battle, Cookie. You didn't sign up for this, and to be honest, when I started looking for Kristen, I thought she was pulling one of her disappearing stunts. This wasn't anywhere on my radar. I had no reason to believe that she would be involved in something on this scale."

Cookie watched the water in the distance. Jamie resisted the urge to crack a joke or break the silence. They both often hid behind dark humor, a survival technique necessary to deal with the painful realities of the cases they worked, but at that moment, she held her tongue. This one hit too close to home, for both of them.

Jamie waited for him to speak, and after what felt like an hour but was no more than a minute, he reached for his dive gear. He moved to sit on the end bench and kept his eyes trained on his tank. He was fidgeting, really. She knew from experience that Cookie had triple-checked his gear before getting on the boat. He was meticulous that way.

"That tank's fine."

He sighed. "I know it's fine." He kept his hand on the tank's valve.

"Cookie, this isn't your fight. You've finally put Manny's death behind you…"

"I never put it behind me," he corrected her. "The Deltones gunned down Manny, and now it looks like they've taken one of your family, too. This fight is mine, Jamie, whether you want my help or not. You know there's no way I'm standing on the sidelines with this one."

Cookie's soft features hardened, a deep determination claiming his compassionate smile. He was a gentle soul until pushed too far, and having his little brother left on the beach to die had closed off a section of his soul. From what Jamie had heard, Manny's demise was meant to serve as a warning to anyone who dared consider opposing the Deltone family and their rules, although Cookie's family had never discovered why he had been targeted. Someone had placed a two-dollar bill in Manny's pocket, a way of claiming responsibility for his death. The intimidation worked. It worked because the Deltones understood that killing a rival wasn't nearly as powerful as killing a rival's family member.

Jamie wished nothing more than to ease Cookie's pain, but she understood that gift was not within her power. She sat next to him, placing her hand atop his, which was still holding the top of his dive tank.

"Cookie, Manny's death took you down a dark path for a long time. I hated watching you walk away from some things that you really cared about, you know? That rage, that anger, it swallowed you whole."

"I appreciate your being there for me, Jamie. I know that was hard on you, too."

She dismissed the comment. "It wasn't hard on me. It was hard on you, and I don't want to drag you back into that again. I don't want you to feel that you have to go there again, out of loyalty or anything else. I can handle it."

"First of all, you aren't as tough as you think you are," Cookie said. "I mean, you've got a mouth that can talk your way out of anything, but your fight skills suck."

"I have a gun, Cookie. And I'm a damn good shot."

"Yes, but the Deltones are all about surprise. You won't have your gun when you need it. Trust me. You need me if you're going to find out what happened to Kristen and what she was mixed up in, where she fit in his world."

"I know I need you, Cookie. I just don't want to need you."

"Well, if it makes you feel better, you don't have a choice. You aren't dragging me into anything. You know I still want my shot at bringing down their operation. I just needed a reason, and now I have one."

The pair sat silently together, watching the waves ripple and reflect the sun's rays.

Jamie's mind was lost in thoughts of revenge or justice; she hardly cared which.

CHAPTER ELEVEN

J AMIE AWOKE TO THE SOUNDS of glasses clanking against dishes and muffled conversations below. Living in the loft above Hemingway's had many benefits—cheap rent, food, beer on demand, and free emergency dog sitting. But the downside? Sleeping late was almost impossible.

But not for Deuce.

Jamie gave a low whistle in the hopes of waking up her furry roommate.

Deuce ignored her, apparently upset with her for pawning him off on Marty, although she knew that her pudgy companion received more attention and fried food than he could handle when serving as Hemingway's mascot. Still, the portly bulldog could hold a grudge far better than a socialite snubbed at a cocktail party. He slept on the floor, seemingly unaware of her presence, even when she intentionally made noise by scraping her dining-room chair on the floor.

The term "dining-room chair" was a bit of a stretch. It was more like a padded chair that Jamie "borrowed" from Erin's Senior Seaside Adventures. In fact, most of her modest abode's décor came from Erin's castoffs. Jamie found no joy or purpose in most domestic duties. One time, Cookie had accused her of frat-house living but without tacky girlie posters plastered on the wall.

She would never admit it out loud, but she refused to settle in and get comfortable even though she called Port Alene her home. She still kept her ditch bag stocked and underneath her bed, ready for the moment she would need to disappear and begin somewhere else.

Old habits died hard.

After leaving Cookie's company, she'd called Brian's cell phone three times and had yet to get a call back. His callousness surprised her, although she scolded herself for being surprised. It was par for the family course.

"Jamie! You up?"

She heard a key turn in the front door lock, and the door opened, revealing Cookie in all his bright-Hawaiian-shirt splendor. This morning's selection combined bright yellow hibiscus in a pattern against a navy background. Jamie actually liked this choice, but she never would have told him for fear of encouraging him to further blow his earnings on clothing that only seemed appropriate in bars, luaus, and casinos, which, once considered, were really Cookie's favorite places, anyway.

Cookie balanced two disposable coffee cups with lids along with a brown paper bag emitting the enticing aroma of breakfast tacos. Food and coffee would always garner Jamie's attention. Cookie's backpack hung off one shoulder, the strap wrinkling a hibiscus flower into a dot.

"I thought we could get a jump on the investigation this morning." Cookie pulled a chair out from her dining table and placed the breakfast bribes on its surface.

Jamie brushed her hair away from her face but was sure she was suffering from severe bedhead. Deuce had immediately relocated from a sleeping position to full attention at Cookie's feet.

"Taqueria San Juan's is the best," Jamie said. "Did you bring him a taco? Please tell me it isn't bean and cheese."

Cookie shook his head. "No, I decided to be nice to you today. Bacon and egg today, his favorite."

Jamie looked at Deuce, who ignored her for Cookie. "You need to go outside first before breakfast. Just give me a minute. Cookie, don't feed him yet. Seriously."

Cookie held his hands up to Deuce. "Sorry, buddy. Have to wait."

Jamie tucked into her tiny bathroom to handle her morning routine and brush her teeth and hair. She made a clicking sound to Deuce and pointed to the front door. "Let's go handle your business." Deuce ignored her until she opened the door. He then waddled his way to the front door, where Jamie knelt down and hoisted him in her arms. His stocky body could handle the stairs, but it was hard on his joints, so sometimes she carried him. She was sure Deuce felt that was how all transportation should be handled.

Jamie had become adept at balancing Deuce in her arms while walking down the flight of wooden stairs. Thankfully, they weren't too steep, and it was a snap as long as she wasn't in a hurry or tipsy. Once down the stairs, Jamie turned right and slipped out the private back door into the restaurant's grassy yard. Jamie appreciated the private door, which allowed her to bring clients in and maintain discretion rather than walk through the bar.

Deuce stepped onto the grass, gingerly at first, sniffing his way through the stubby blades to find his favorite potty spot. He handled his business without dillydallying. The sound of traffic passing the restaurant buzzed in Jamie's ears, and she shook off the sleep that had followed her outside. Deuce stomped his paws then made his way back to the door.

Once inside, Deuce stood at the base of the stairs, waiting for Jamie's response.

"You can do it. I don't need to carry you both ways."

A standoff ensued for only a few seconds until Deuce decided he would rather get to his tacos than hold out for a lift up the steps. He hoisted his stocky body up the stairs, with Jamie trailing him. Once at the top, he scratched at the door, and Jamie reached over to let him inside.

Cookie had started without them.

"Really? You couldn't wait five minutes?"

Her friend had no shame. "Hey, I brought everything, and I had to smell it on the drive over. I'm hungry."

Cookie reached inside the bag and pulled out a taco wrapped in aluminum foil. As he unwrapped it, Deuce stomped his paws in excitement and barked. Jamie handed Cookie Deuce's dog dish and a knife. "Make sure you cut it up really well."

He scoffed at her instruction. "Uncle Cookie is the breakfast master. I got it. You go handle yourself." He winked. "Don't you want to put something on that you didn't roll out of bed in?"

Jamie nodded, unable to argue with his comment. She walked the few feet it took to reach her dresser, yet another hand-me-down from Erin. She pulled open the top drawer, quickly selected a T-shirt and shorts, then excused herself to the bathroom to change. She could hear Cookie talking to Deuce the entire time, and she smiled, grateful to have him around, especially now.

Jamie emerged from the bathroom a bit more pulled together. She'd fastened her hair in a ponytail and had even opted to add a hint of mascara and lip gloss. She walked to the table and sat across from Cookie. Deuce's breakfast taco was long gone, his face now staring at an empty bowl. She could see the expectation on his furry face.

"That's it, buddy," Jamie said as she waved him away. "You don't need another one."

Deuce ignored her, his attention still on the bowl. Jamie glanced at Cookie, noting there were three aluminum balls on the table. Cookie was on his second one. She reached inside the bag and pulled out a selection, placing it on a napkin. She then took a sip of coffee and immediately felt better.

"I needed that," she said.

Cookie nodded. "Eat your tacos."

Jamie obliged, and the two sat silently for a few minutes, absorbed in their own thoughts while finishing their breakfast. Deuce had finally given up, retreating to sleep by the edge of the couch.

Cookie crammed the last corner of tortilla in his mouth then reached for the napkins and other remnants to return to the paper bag. "Okay, let's get set up to work." He reached into his backpack and retrieved his laptop. He booted it up, staring at the screen as the operating system loaded. Jamie, still lingering over her coffee and the last bits of her breakfast, felt him looking at her.

"What?" she asked. "Don't give me those judgy eyes. Unlike you two"— she waved in Deuce's direction—"I like to taste my food."

Cookie said nothing but smiled, his attention on his laptop screen. Jamie retrieved her own laptop plus a notebook and pen from her satchel then returned to her seat next to her partner. She opened the notebook, a Dollar Store special composition book with a faint coffee stain on its surface, and selected a fresh page.

"Okay, we're going to need to map out all the connections we understand at this point." In the middle of the page, Jamie drew Kristen's name and circled it. She then drew lines to the names of those in her niece's social circle. Brian went to the center above her; Dylan and Beth went beneath her. Jamie then drew a line off to the side and started listing other names: Boxer, Manny, the Deltones.

Cookie glanced at her list. "We need to understand how the Deltone family is structured: who is in charge, liaisons, foot forces, anything we can figure out. Kristen has to be tied to them somehow if they're claiming responsibility for…" His words fell off before he could finish the sentence.

Jamie let his hesitancy hang between them. She didn't want to say the words, either.

"Let's split up the background work. Do you want to take the Deltone org chart, or do you want me to handle it?" Jamie felt that giving Cookie that task would help him channel his anger into something tangible, useful—but only if he was ready.

He nodded. "I've got it."

"Okay. I'll handle Kristen's circle. We'll see how they might overlap."

Cookie nodded and picked up his cell phone. "Let me see who might be able to help me. I can also check out some social-media sites. Always amazed at what people post."

When it came to tech skills, Cookie's far exceeded Jamie's—in part because he was a social being and loved being online. Jamie would have rather had a root canal than an active online presence. One on one, her investigative skills were strong. She excelled in more intimate connections, whereas Cookie would walk into a chat room or ballroom and be the center of attention. Together, they covered each other's shortcomings, and their investigation efforts benefited from their differences in style.

Jamie's skip-trace training taught her that she needed to track Kristen's last movements, to discover how and with whom she had spent her last days. A girl with her upbringing might be hard to track because she had likely grown up learning how to stay off the grid. Still, she was young and, from what Jamie had learned so far, at times careless. So Kristen's case started where every case started—the Internet.

Jamie began with simple searches of Kristen's name in FriendConnect, one of the most popular social-media sites, but her first attempts turned up nothing of any value. That wasn't unexpected. While Jamie found social-media sites useful in some cases, her experience proved that pounding the pavement and speaking directly with people turned up the most useful leads. She could study their responses and had learned when to push for information and when to fall back and use surveillance. Technology had its place, but nothing trumped looking others in the eye and asking pointed questions.

Still, Kristen was a millennial, a generation born with a USB cable for an umbilical cord. She had left her digital footprints somewhere. It was simply a matter of uncovering them.

Jamie mulled over what she could remember from past interactions with her niece and half brother. She could picture Kristen's face, her confidence—it was an effusive trait. But the truth was that she knew little else.

Jamie could feel Cookie studying her face. "You need to talk it out, Jamie, to make the connections."

"I know, but I don't want to bother you while you're working."

Cookie grinned. "I'm a master multitasker. So go ahead. Bounce some stuff off of me."

"Okay." She still stared at the screen, her FriendConnect search bar coming up with nothing of value. "When I think about Kristen, I think about when she was younger and I taught her how to create a basic secret code. You know, with a book and a written decryption key."

Cookie grinned at her. "That sounds perfectly appropriate for some weird reason. I mean, knowing your family."

She smiled at the memory. "She wanted to know how I handled taking surveillance notes and other stuff."

"Keep going."

Jamie leaned back in her chair. "Well, we both loved to talk about traveling. Maybe it was our upbringing and all the moving, but we used to make a list of places we wanted to visit one day. I even bought her a travel book years ago just to, you know…"

"Remind her of you?"

Jamie nodded. "Yes, and to remind her that she could choose her own life, although I'm not sure she was ready for those decisions."

"We're all invincible at that age," Cookie said in a way that felt more like fact than opinion, although Kristen had proved the exception to Cookie's rule.

Searching the deep corners of her memory, Jamie struggled to bring more to the forefront. She tapped her finger on the table, the pace quickening to the point of near frenzy. "There wasn't that much between us, Cookie. We didn't have deep conversations as a general rule, or explore our darkest souls."

Cookie leaned back in his chair and sighed, placing his hands behind his head, his neck supported by the latticework of his fingers. "Remember what we tell clients. It's often the little things that give us the next lead."

He was right, of course. Jamie had to put herself in both chairs—client and investigator. She had to turn the script on herself to be a better witness for the case.

She sat quietly, staring past her computer screen, and let herself remember Kristen. For so long, she had pushed her niece—and her brother—to the corner recesses of her mind, never allowing them to claim any emotional space. Now she needed to let her guard down. It was difficult, allowing in that bit of longing for a relationship she had denied for so long.

Deuce had retreated back to his dog bed, likely dreaming of more breakfast tacos. Cookie hummed the melody of some popular pop song sung by whatever flavor of the month graced the radio with her auto-tuned voice. It did have a catchy beat, though. Cookie made it work.

Jamie thought back to one of her earlier conversations with Kristen when they were sharing tricks of the trade. They both loved getting creative with aliases, drawing names from favorite characters from books, movies, and television shows. She recalled Kristen talking about a time when she hid out in a local motel under a false name.

What was it again?

It was a comic book character, but not as popular...

What was her name? Irons... something. Jeremy Irons? Definitely not the actor...

Natasha Irons.

That's the one.

The memory brought a smile to her lips. Cookie pretended not to notice, his humming uninterrupted by his not noticing.

She takes over superhero work for an injured uncle and battles Lex Luthor. Kristen had loved comic books, especially the lesser-known cult favorites. Jamie's "random facts memory" was broad and bountiful. She was certain it was why she could never remember birthdays or passwords. Too much miscellaneous data already claimed her brain space.

Living under an alias—or six—was a common technique, making her wonder if Kristen might have used the Natasha Irons name elsewhere.

Jamie typed the name into her online search engine, and within seconds, relevant results filled the page.

She clicked on a link. It led to the name Natasha Irons but with Kristen's photo attached—a FriendConnect account.

"Aha. I've got something."

"Your trip down memory lane shook something loose?" Cookie leaned over and surveyed the results on the screen. "Natasha Irons?"

"Comic book popular, not of Wonder Woman fame, sometimes a cult favorite, sometimes not. Kristen liked her."

Jamie skimmed over Kristen's main page. Natasha had some friends, many also using superhero names, some more recognizable than others. Variations on Superman and Batman made their appearance, and at first glance, the conversations seemed fairly trivial. There was small talk about the latest movies, characters, and events around town. Jamie scrolled through a couple of selfie photos, one of Kristen grinning in front of a boat, the word "Freedom" peeking out from the corner. Another photo showed her in what seemed to be a nightclub, the lighting dark with colored strobes and nothing telling in the background. Discussion topics on her page consisted of comic conventions and famous actor sightings. Still, there had to be some deeper meaning somewhere in one of those online conversations, one of those relationships. Jamie continued reading, searching for something, anything, which might prove useful. She clicked on each profile photo. Each one was another twenty-something she didn't recognize. Then, finally, she saw a face she knew.

Her screen name identified her as Connie Coy, but Jamie recognized her simply as a waitress from Tricky Dick's, a local sports bar on the island, known for its nonstop broadcast of sporting events and cheap happy-hour specials. Marty called the place a pimple on the face of Port Alene—ugly, touristy, and lacking all the subtlety required of a local watering hole. The dive offered mediocre food and kitschy décor. Every time Jamie ate there, she suffered guilt, as though she were cheating on Marty. He once claimed he could smell their fries on her. He had taken it personally and hadn't talked to her for the rest of the day.

Jamie read a conversation thread between Connie and Kristen—as Natasha—discussing plans to meet for drinks at Tricky Dick's the week before she'd disappeared. It was the last conversation thread between the two. There were no follow-up or "great to see you" comments. Jamie wondered if Connie had indeed met with Kristen or if her niece had gone missing before their date.

"There's no comments on being a no-show or changing the meeting, so maybe she and Connie talked before..." She didn't want to finish the sentence. Cookie had the decency to leave it be. With his confused expression, Jamie tilted the computer so he could read Connie's comments on Kristen's page.

"So you think you need to meet with her?"

Jamie nodded, her expression rife with apology. "She's a waitress at Tricky Dick's."

Cookie raised an eyebrow. "Ooh, you know how Marty feels about that place."

Jamie knew all too well. "No take out, no evidence. Dine-in only. And besides, I'm working a case. You follow the evidence wherever it leads."

"You need to work on that guilty look. Marty smells betrayal like Deuce smells tacos."

She pointed to Cookie's computer. "You need to focus on your investigation of the Deltones. I expect to see a flowchart with details once I get back. We need to see where Kristen might have fit, if anywhere. I'm guessing she may be connected somehow with one of the Deltones' lower-level people."

Jamie stood up, stretched, collected her bag and keys, and dropped her cell phone into her bag. Deuce opened his eyes, looked at her, glanced at Cookie, then returned to his nap. She wondered if she should be offended that her pup wasn't concerned about her departure. As long as Uncle Cookie was close food and belly rubs were guaranteed.

"I'm going to run by you-know-where to see if Connie's on shift. I'll let you know what I find when it's over."

Cookie stood up and waved to Jamie to come close. She obliged, giving him a quick hug. "I'll text you and let you know if I find anything."

She left Cookie and Deuce to tend to her loft and closed the door behind her, hoping another would soon open.

CHAPTER TWELVE

J AMIE ARRIVED AT TRICKY DICK'S just as the lunch crowd arrived. Dressed in a navy T-shirt, khaki shorts, and running shoes, she served as a poster child for island couture. Jamie felt fairly sure she owned a pair of heels, but she had no idea where they were. She only wore them if a role required it or if she was going on a date. Neither opportunity had presented itself in some time.

Jamie entered the restaurant and nodded at the hostess. The bar always staffed several attractive women to work the front of the house. Good Business 101. She also suspected that Dick personally hired every hot blonde, at least that was her professional hunch. She spotted Dick speaking with one hostess, but he stopped the conversation to greet Jamie as she stood taking in the décor Marty found offensive—for good reason. Wall space was violated by plastic kingfish, battered fishing poles, and enough pirate kitsch to offend Robert Louis Stevenson, even in death.

Dick lumbered toward her, his beer belly leading the way, affecting his gait, and arriving slightly ahead of the rest of his body. Dick Dobbs took his sweet time getting to Jamie. With his size, he had no choice.

He wrapped his burly arms around her in a full bear hug. Jamie wondered if that was how she had obtained her traitor's whiff. Maybe it had been transferred from foe to friend, then she'd carried home evidence of their illicit food tryst with the scent of fried betrayal.

"Jamie, sweetie. It's been so long since I've seen you!" He stepped back and looked her up and down for a moment, but not in a sleazy way. He seemed more like a father who was appraising a child's appearance. "You're getting too skinny, you know. It's because they don't feed you right at Hemingway's. Marty always shorts on the serving size. Cheap bastard."

Jamie had to laugh. "Don't tell him I was here. You know how jealous he gets." She glanced at the busy back of the house, crowded with wall-to-wall customers. "So, how're you doing?"

Dick gestured toward the full seating room. "Business is good, can't complain. We got all the snowbirds coming back for the season, so we're ramping up our senior specials. So damn competitive now, you know? Did you hear that Arnold's Cafe is offering an all-you-can-eat buffet for four bucks? That's just crazy. It doesn't matter, though. We've got all the atmosphere."

Jamie had to agree with him. The place was a tourist's dream with TVs broadcasting football, baseball, and other games on sets mounted throughout the restaurant.

"So, what brings you to my fine establishment? Need a burger to fatten up those bones?"

"I'm looking for one of your waitresses. Connie? Is she working tonight?"

He nodded. "Yeah, she's working. I'll go get her for you." Dick turned and walked past the hostess stand toward the back bar, waving down a waitress who was standing in the wait well. Jamie noted Dick pointing in her direction, and Connie nodded, soon making her way to the front.

She was heavyset and short by most standards at barely five feet tall. Her long black hair was secured with a hairband glittery enough to have been plucked right out of the seventies. She wore a denim skirt, flip-flops, and a shirt that read, "I'm not short. I'm fun-sized." She had full-sleeve tats down both arms and was pretty in a most unconventional way. Her smile was sincere, and she had a hint of dimples surfacing. The girl would have been easy to pick out in a lineup.

"Connie?"

She nodded. "That's me."

"Can you set us up with a table that's out of the way? I need to talk with you for a minute."

Connie's expression morphed from casual to cautious. "What's this about?"

"I'm Kristen's aunt."

Connie's confusion turned to empathy. She reached for Jamie's hand and squeezed briefly before releasing it, a sort of momentary commiseration of shared grief. "I'm so sorry about what happened to her."

Connie's knowledge of Kristen's death caught Jamie off guard. She then scolded herself for showing any surprise. *Rookie mistake.* "How did you hear about it?"

"You know, it's the island. Bad news travels fast." She stepped in closer to Jamie and whispered, "I'm glad you're here. I was worried who might show up."

Maybe Kristen confided in Connie after all. Jamie glanced around the restaurant. "Can we talk someplace a little more private?"

Connie led Jamie to the back of the main dining hall, to a place better suited for a clandestine discussion. Slightly secluded from other tables, the table they chose was tucked in the corner with no one on either side of them and a sixty-inch television above them broadcasting horse races.

I might have to hang out here more often. Jamie could almost feel Marty on her shoulder like a foul-mouthed conscience, spewing obscenities at her.

Dick personally came to check on their table, took their drink orders, and advised Connie not to spend too long off the clock. He then went off to tend to his flock.

Connie had an honest, sweet face, an odd contrast to her outrageous clothing. Of course, Jamie had been fooled by such contradictions before.

"So, you're Kristen's aunt?" Connie smiled. "You know, it's funny because I see you now and then, but I never made the connection between you and Kristen."

Jamie tapped her forefinger on the table. "Yes, but I'm her aunt in name mostly. We weren't as close as we were when she was younger, and I didn't know she had been in the area until recently." Jamie leaned forward. "How did you and Kristen meet?"

Connie's eyes lit up. "We met at a Comic-Con in Austin, if you can believe that. We met at one of the panels and just hit it off. We got together for drinks or dinner now and then."

Just as Connie finished her sentence, another waitress placed two water glasses on the table, plastic tumblers with the Tricky Dick's logo. She smiled briefly at both ladies before leaving to tend to her other tables.

Jamie took her notepad and pen from her bag. "Can you tell me about the last time you saw Kristen?"

Connie nodded. "Yeah, I saw her over a week ago."

"Did she say anything unusual?"

Connie hedged, her eyes looking past Jamie and into the crowd. "Not really. Why?"

Jamie felt that she could be open with Connie about her suspicions. "I'm sure you've heard some speculation about how Kristen died."

Connie nodded. "You know how talk travels on the island."

"I absolutely do." Jamie tapped her finger on the table, considering how to best explain the situation to Kristen's friend. "I'm not sure her death is what it seems—whether drugs were involved—but I need to know if you remember anything she said, any fights she had with friends, anything that might help me prove her death wasn't accidental."

Connie leaned in closer. "I think you're right." She quickly surveyed her surroundings before continuing. "Look, Kristen had a lot going on in her life, sure, but she was also pretty ambitious. She might have gotten drunk partying sometimes, but she made it clear that she wasn't interested in hard drugs, especially anything with needles. She's seen firsthand what that looks like."

"Did she know someone who got hooked?"

"Her mom. She didn't talk about it much. She just said that she didn't have any intention of ending up like her."

"Her mom is still alive, though, isn't she?" Jamie wondered how dysfunctional that question sounded, considering the inquiry was technically about her sister-in-law. In truth, Jamie had only met the woman once, and that had been enough. Pamela Thorn was a thorn in every sense of the word—prickly, rude, and painful. And that was when she was sober.

"Yeah, she's alive, if that's what you want to call it. Kristen didn't like to talk about her, but she said once that she is just always high out of her mind, and Kristen didn't want to know what her mom had to do to earn money to stay that way."

"I saw that you and Kristen had a conversation on FriendConnect, but I couldn't tell if you two ever met up. It seemed to just drop off."

Connie shook her head. "No, we never did. I had something of hers, and I was supposed to give it back to her. I never had the chance." Connie reached for the plain silver chain around her neck and began fiddling with it.

Jamie prodded her. "What did she give you?"

She pulled on the chain slightly to reveal a single small key that had been tucked underneath her shirt. "Kristen gave this to me last time we spoke. She said she needed me to keep it safe and she'd get it back from me when things cooled down. Gave it to me when we met last week. Ever since I heard what happened, I haven't known what to do." She touched the key dangling at the end. "I was afraid to hide it and afraid to take it off."

Jamie stared at the necklace, wondering what the key opened, imagining how hard it must have been for Connie to keep it after hearing of Kristen's death. "You must have been pretty scared."

Connie nodded but said nothing.

"Did she say what she was waiting for to cool down?" Jamie asked.

Connie shook her head, her hand still protectively covering the key. "No idea. She wouldn't talk about it. She said that it was better if I didn't know anything."

"May I?" Jamie held her hand out to receive the key, although she wasn't yet sure Connie was ready for it to leave her possession. When the girl hesitated, Jamie consoled her. "I'm the best person to keep this key, trust me. In addition to being Kristen's aunt, I'm also a private investigator."

"You're a PI, and you didn't know that Kristen was back in the area?" Connie pursed her lips together and leaned back in her seat. "I didn't mean that how it sounded. I just meant—"

Jamie held her hand up. "It's okay. Kristen and I are both very well-trained at staying out of each other's circle, and it seems that she was spending more time in Corpus. You know how easy it is to hide in the big city."

"She did always want to meet in Corpus," Connie noted. Seeming satisfied, Connie slipped the key and chain over her head. Her dark hair momentarily tangled itself in the chain, so she reached behind her neck and unhooked the fastening. She placed the key on the table and slid it across to Jamie, her hand concealing the key.

"I actually feel better now that this isn't around my neck. I thought about taking it to the cops, but I had no idea what I'd even tell them."

Jamie wanted to comfort her, to tell Connie everything would be okay, but she knew better than to offer such things. Instead, she said, "I promise I'll let you know if anything comes of it." She then continued her questioning. "So, what was the deal with her FriendConnect account? Calling herself Natasha Irons? Was that just part of the Comic-Con thing?"

Connie smiled. "It was just a funny thing for her. She loved comic books—the alternate identities and walking between two worlds. She didn't want to use her real name—said it wasn't smart." Her smile dissolved as she spoke of Kristen. "She said someday she would just start over and I'd never hear from her again and that I should be happy for her because it meant she was free."

"Free from what?"

"She didn't say. She'd ramble on sometimes. I know she was working some with her dad, but she never discussed the work. I just assumed it wasn't really... legal."

And your assumption would be right on. Jamie wondered if the Natasha Irons identity had more clues to share since it was how she had found Connie. She reached over and touched Connie's hand. "I'm going to figure this out, okay? But you need to be honest with me and not hold anything back, even the bad stuff. Trust me, with my family history, I'm in no position to judge."

"I can't really think of anything. We didn't have big, important conversations."

"What about Dylan? Did you know him or anything about him?"

Connie continued to origami the hell out of her napkin. "He was okay most of the time, but he had a wandering eye. She didn't like it, but she didn't like him enough to get jealous. She was ready to move on."

"Was he dangerous? Angry ever?"

"I never saw him out of control. He keeps his head on straight. Those other losers do whatever he tells them to do."

Connie's description of Dylan matched Jamie's gut reaction to their meeting. *No big surprises there so far.* She then asked, "Did she have any other men in her life?"

Connie hesitated, and Jamie picked up on it immediately, in the same way Deuce instantly knew if she had jalapeno poppers in her bag.

Connie sat silently for another few moments. "I don't know if there was actually another guy in her life, but I do know that there was someone she had her eye on. She'd usually tell me everything, but with this guy, she was real secretive. I tried to get her drunk once, and she still didn't cave. It could have just been a crush, or it could have been something more. Don't know for sure."

Jamie continued making notes. "Anything else? I mean, I know a girl like that may not have traditional hobbies, but did she do anything else?"

"She loved to draw and loved photography. She was always drawing, doodling. She was spending some time at the Youth Art Center. You know the owner? Marcus Holliday?"

Jamie nodded. "Of course. His father owns half the coast."

"Well, I think he was taking an interest in her work. She had me drive her to the gallery sometimes, and she'd stay there for hours. I know she was working on a portfolio, and he was helping her with it."

The silence sat between them for a moment, then Connie added, "But Kristen was a pretty talented artist. I know she hoped her art would be shown there one day. She never took it seriously before, but she seemed to be into it lately. He paid attention to her, and I think she liked it."

Jamie considered the possibility of a relationship between Kristen and Marcus, but it didn't seem likely. Someone with his money and recognition could have anyone he wanted. Why would he be interested in Kristen? What did she have to offer that Corpus Christi's socialites lacked?

Connie's eyes followed Jamie's hand as she made notes. "A lefty, eh?"

Jamie nodded. "Yep. I've got handwriting that would put a doctor to shame."

Connie checked her penmanship. "That's pretty scrappy."

Jamie wanted to keep Connie talking. "So did you ever see the two of them *together* together?" Jamie put added emphasis on the first "together."

"Maybe Kristen was a little starstruck. He's in the papers, he's got money, knows everyone. She loved celebrities. Easily impressed. She thought being close to them made her more special, too."

Jamie decided to move to the family. She had only heard Brian's side of things and wondered if he had any skeletons that needed to be freed from the closet. "So, tell me about Kristen's home life."

"What home life?" Connie deadpanned.

"What about her dad?"

Connie shrugged. "He seems like he's good at getting Kristen to do what he wants."

Jamie felt as though she knew Kristen better through Connie's descriptions. The girl certainly divulged more than Brian had, which sadly, wasn't unexpected.

"She had a locker at the Youth Art Center," Connie replied. "Maybe she left some stuff there." She thought for a moment. "Maybe that's what the key is for."

"It's possible."

Jamie reached into her back pocket and pulled out a business card. She slid it across the table. "Give me a call if you think of anything else."

The two women parted ways. Connie returned to her waitressing duties, while Jamie found herself stepping more deeply into Kristen's life, unsure of where the road would lead next.

Jamie returned to Hemingway's, opting for the back door in an effort to sneak up the stairs to her loft without Marty getting wind of where she had just spent her time. She opened the door to find Cookie gone and Deuce sleeping atop a pile of Jamie's dirty laundry. She opted for a long, hot shower and a change of clothes. After that, she felt she had appropriately covered her tracks and could get back to work.

Several hours passed as she searched through Kristen's FriendConnect account as well as other online sites her niece might have used. Not having Kristen's cell phone or laptop made the task far more difficult, but Jamie patiently sifted through one digital dead-end after the next. It was soon dark, and Jamie had little to show for her efforts other than a headache from staring at her computer screen.

Jamie's cell phone chimed, diverting her attention away from her investigation. She picked up the phone and saw a text from Erin.

Get to my warehouse now.

Erin was by far the most diplomatic member of her small circle of friends, so Jamie knew something was wrong. Erin never issued orders or missives to her friends. The girl would use smiley-face emojis at least once in almost any text conversation. Jamie responded, letting her friend know she was on the way. Then she sent Cookie a text.

Meet me at Erin's warehouse.

And bring Arnold.

Just in case.

CHAPTER THIRTEEN

J AMIE CIRCLED ERIN'S BUILDING ONE final time before pulling her Tahoe into a space a block away. The building, a three-story brick warehouse, seemed like an ideal candidate for restoration. With a few financial resources and attention, the place could easily convert into a revived downtown monument. Erin had once mentioned turning it into something more than a drain on her account, but for the moment, it remained just that.

Jamie searched for signs of Cookie's car, but she had clearly arrived first. She sent him a text asking for an ETA, and he answered not by return text but by pulling his car in behind hers. He exited and remained in a crouched position as he walked toward Jamie's front passenger's door. After struggling to get inside, he slammed the door too loudly for Jamie's liking.

"Your ninja skills are slipping, Cookie," she whispered.

"Like you've got room to talk," he said in hushed tones. "I'm not the one that dropped a glass bottle on the Gipson stakeout."

She fixed her eyes on the steering wheel, not daring to make eye contact after that comment. "I thought I had it, okay?" She glanced his way, unable to keep a straight face. "Boy, you jumped like a scared cat when that happened." Her voice changed to a more serious tone. "You bring Arnold?"

Cookie patted his jacket pocket. "Loaded and ready for trouble."

Unlike Jamie, Cookie didn't carry his piece all the time, even though he should have, considering the company they sometimes tailed. Most jobs didn't require firepower—Cookie's size and considerable intimidation skills proved plenty effective. Jamie, on the other hand, felt exposed without her messenger bag complete with firearm and random tools of the trade, including a lock-picking kit and a deck of cards.

"What the hell is going on? Did Erin explain anything?"

Jamie shook her head. "No idea. I sent her a text letting her know I was out here but I haven't heard back yet. Something's definitely not right. You know how she is."

"She's not much for ordering people around. It's like having a sorority girl for a bookie."

"She's all smiles until you stiff her. Then she sends Becky after you."

They continued their banter about Erin and what might have been wrong, but it was soon interrupted when Jamie's phone pinged. She checked the screen. "It's from Erin. She's telling us to move quietly toward the back door of the building. Walk, no cars."

Jamie and Cookie left her car and walked casually as though they belonged on the back street at night. Successful surveillance was all about confidence, and Cookie had that role down. Jamie looped her arm through Cookie's as if they were a couple. They'd done that routine on countless jobs before and had even joked about how it always felt a bit weird since their relationship was closer to that of siblings. They'd been friends and worked together long enough that they could anticipate each other's moves, ideas, and on-the-fly ridiculous schemes. Jamie could begin making up a story, and Cookie could finish it and make it believable. They completed each other's sentences like an old married couple.

As they neared the building, they stayed on the opposite side of the street until the last possible moment. A small flashlight flicker caught Jamie's eye. She tapped Cookie's arm and pulled him with her across the street. They increased their stride, hoping to make it inside before walking into unexpected trouble.

Entry to the building was through a large metal door that had hinges spattered with rust layers and deterioration. The door was a foreboding thing, and Jamie felt as though its purpose was solely to keep people out. She forced the full weight of her body into prying it open enough to slip through. Once she succeeded, Cookie braced himself against the door in an attempt to gain enough access to squeeze through the opening. After making his way inside, he left it open a crack, probably concerned the door wouldn't yield a second time if it were to latch shut.

The room they entered felt vast, empty, and humid—clearly a warehouse—with some metal stairs and walkways dotting the perimeter.

The concrete floors and open space resembled every other warehouse Jamie had ever visited save for the one item in the middle of the room.

A young woman sat handcuffed to a metal chair, a slice of ratty duct tape covering her mouth, her ankles bound in a similar manner. Her eyes were wide but calm, darting from Jamie to Cookie and back. Jamie's first instinct was to comfort the woman, to tell her it was okay, but she knew better than to reach out before she understood what they had walked into.

Who was this woman, and how had she ended up in Erin's building? Jamie had never thought of Erin as the kidnapping type. She knew there had to be another explanation because there was no way Erin would have been willingly involved in something so sordid.

Erin came out from behind a concrete pillar in the corner of the room, her slim figure breaking the darkness. "Boxer told me he had a delivery and needed the building tomorrow, so I came here to give everything a look and check the security system, and I walked in to find this... uh, her." She glanced at the woman. "Sorry."

Jamie gestured to the woman then looked at her friend. "Erin, what the hell are you doing working with Boxer?" Jamie couldn't believe Erin would make a deal with the devil's mini-me.

"I didn't have much choice," Erin said, clearly rattled by Boxer's threats. "He said he'd leave my clients alone if I let him use my building for a couple of deliveries. I didn't completely trust him"—she signaled toward the captive woman—"and with good reason."

Jamie moved slowly toward the woman, who didn't flinch or move as Jamie neared. She seemed calm, almost unnervingly so. Slim frame but tall, long black hair messy from restraint, her eyes meeting Jamie's without hesitation. Jamie placed her hand over the duct tape and prepared to pull, prefacing her action with, "This might sting." She ripped off the tape, revealing a red ring of flushed skin similar to a clown's mouth. Not a good look, but if it hurt, the woman didn't show it. What on earth had Boxer done?

"Can you get these handcuffs off me?" she asked. "They said they were going out for supplies, but they're coming back, and I know that's not good for anybody here."

Jamie reached into her bag and fished around until her hands came upon her lock-pick case. She pulled it out, unzipped it, and removed a slim metal tool. "Who are you, and why does Boxer have you here?"

The woman tried to wiggle her wrists free from the handcuffs binding her hands. "You don't really want to know that, do you? Maybe it's better if you keep out of this."

"In my world, ignorance isn't bliss. It just gets people in trouble. Keep your hands still." Jamie fiddled with the handcuff lock for a few moments before she heard a click and felt a release. She pulled the cuffs apart, freeing the captive woman. "So, talk. We should at least know why Boxer held you hostage in Erin's warehouse."

Erin stood with her arms crossed, studying the woman. "For a woman who was shackled to a chair, you don't seem too rattled. This a regular thing for you?"

She shrugged. "Where I come from, these are standard negotiating tactics. Now, getting some chains and going out on the Gulf—that makes me nervous."

Erin continued to push. "So, what's the deal with you and Boxer?"

Boxer's prisoner ran her hand through the dark strands of her tangled hair. She then pulled on her black hoodie, straightening it as though it were wrinkled. "He's trying to make a deal with my father, and it wasn't going his way, so he hoped to make his point by making me disappear for a bit. I don't think he'd seriously hurt me. He's not that stupid, and I know he doesn't want the wrath of Daddy Deltone to rain down on him."

Cookie and Jamie looked at each other. The mystery woman just dropped the bomb of a big name as though it were an afterthought. Cookie straightened his stance, his eyes remaining on her. "You're Deltone's daughter?"

She nodded. "I'm the youngest, the least important by family standards, which is why Boxer was even able to get to me in the first place. My sister Eve—she's untouchable. And smart people know better than to try."

"So, she's the next in line?" Jamie asked, working to get as much information about the Deltone family as possible. Boxer's captive seemed to think that Deltone lore was common knowledge.

She nodded. "My father was never blessed with sons, but he doesn't discriminate. He understands that women are as capable as men, sometimes more so. We have certain… advantages… that men don't."

"So Boxer is using you as leverage?" Erin asked. "For what?"

"I don't think I should get too deep into the details of the family business."

Cookie remained focused on her, his expression stern. "Anyone who follows your family's turf wars on the island knows your reputation."

Jamie watched Cookie's rage slowly smolder and build. She could see it in the stiffness of his stance and the hardness in his face. He stepped closer to the woman, his eyes narrow and angry. "My brother was killed by a Deltone feud last year. I know something about how your family does business."

Her eyes remained locked on his, her demeanor still calm. If she felt threatened or intimidated, she hid it well. "What was his name?" she asked simply, as though they were talking about the weather.

Cookie stood uncomfortably close to her, claiming her space. "Manny Hinojosa."

She nodded in acknowledgement and looked right into Cookie's angry eyes. "I liked Manny. Good kid. He didn't belong in that group. He didn't have the heart for this life."

"You mean, because he had a heart at all?" Cookie's tone was something Jamie rarely heard.

She nodded. "He wasn't built for this work, and I'm very sorry for your loss. Like I said, I liked him." She then said, "To clarify, he wasn't hit by our family. Someone wanted to pin it on us to start something bigger."

Cookie remained unconvinced. "He had a two-dollar bill in his pocket—your family's calling card."

She nodded. "True, but people who know that sometimes try to use it against us, get us mixed up in business that isn't ours. Manny's death? That wasn't us."

Jamie bit her lip as she listened to their exchange. Cookie rarely spoke about Manny's death, but she knew he carried it with him every day, and Jamie had picked the scab by sharing the details of Kristen's death. Cookie's face strained, stern and tight. His stance was rigid, and his eyes were dark.

Jamie knew she needed to shift the conversation before the woman's captors returned. "You owe me a favor now that we've released you."

"Maybe," she replied. "I'm not safe yet. We're still here."

Erin nodded. "Let's go. We can't let Boxer know we were here. He needs to think her family rescued her. There's no telling when his goons will be back."

Erin signaled the others to follow her to a side exit door. She crouched down, peering out the window. "Okay, let's go." They made their way out the door, single file. Erin left it open slightly as a way of leading Boxer to believe someone might have broken in to rescue the Deltone daughter.

They strode across the street toward Jamie's car. The woman extended her hand. "I'm Marissa, by the way."

Jamie shook her hand. "Jamie."

"So, about this favor?" Marissa asked.

"I'm trying to find out if a girl named Kristen was involved with your business at all. We found one of your calling cards." She held two fingers up to represent what she'd found in Kristen's pocket.

"Dad likes the two-dollar bill. Very effective. But like I said, some people use it to throw blame our way."

Jamie kept her attention on Marissa, working on a read. She knew something. "Maybe you should get a new calling card. Or better yet, maybe quit killing people."

"I can ask around. There was a girl that became an issue—not sure if it was yours or not. I'll call you when things calm down."

"I guess you don't need my number?" Jamie asked.

Marissa shook her head as she walked away from them. "I'll find you, don't you worry."

Girl stole my line.

Marissa disappeared into the darkness, soon slipping from view as she crossed the sidewalk and ducked between some bushes. Her movements were agile, suggesting such confrontations and evasions were truly all part of a day's work.

Erin took a deep breath. "We need to get the hell out of here now."

"Where's your car?" Jamie asked.

"I had a friend drop me off, just in case I got stuck and had to run. Besides, I have you."

"Lucky girl, you are," Jamie replied.

Cookie's demeanor remained icy and rigid, guarded. They piled into Jamie's car with Erin slipping into the back seat. Cookie sat silently while Jamie started the engine. As she pulled away from the curb, she reached over to him. "Are you good?"

Cookie nodded. "Someday." He then looked over his shoulder at Erin. "You think Boxer is going to retaliate for this?"

"He's got no proof that I was here, but there's no telling what he'll do when he finds his bargaining chip gone."

"He's not known for rational behavior, you know, so I'd step up your security for a while. I hope you're good at playing dumb when he comes calling."

Erin's voice trembled, and Jamie could tell she was rattled from how quickly her business entanglements had escalated. "All I want to do is run my little booking business. I don't want drug territory wars and kidnapping. I'm a simple girl with small-town dreams."

Jamie sped up once she turned out of the neighborhood. She couldn't leave fast enough but reminded herself that getting pulled over for speeding would only add to her problems. She'd just sprung free a drug lord's daughter, one whose family might lay claim to both Manny and Kristen's deaths. She hated it, but she had no choice. If Marissa could provide a tip on what had happened to Kristen, the risk would be worth it. But if Jamie came up empty, all she would have left to console her would be Boxer's wrath and Erin in his crosshairs. She wasn't sure her conscience could bear that, but given the circumstances, it was all she could do.

You play the hand you're dealt.

CHAPTER FOURTEEN

ORNING ARRIVED AS AN UNWELCOME guest, although the sounds of the morning crew prepping for lunch meant that she had slept later than she'd intended. The clank of dishes and glasses carried up the stairs, sounding almost as if Marty himself were leaning over her bed while she slumbered. She had no business sleeping in anyway, not with what had happened the night before.

She turned her face into her pillow and groaned quietly. She knew it was time to get her butt out of bed. Her nighttime meeting with Marissa crept to the forefront of her brain from the recesses of her memory. Her concern for Erin's safety was also in her thoughts. Erin had promised to send her a text verifying she wasn't in the trunk of Boxer's mob mobile once he'd discovered his prize had escaped. Jamie reached over, her hand fumbling on the nightstand for her phone. Erin had sent a group message to both her and Cookie, saying she was okay for the time being and that Becky was by her side. The wrath of Boxer had not yet descended upon them. That knowledge buried itself in Jamie's stomach, causing a brief moment of nausea to wash over her.

Jamie's roommate snorted, momentarily interrupting her panicked thoughts. "Hey, Deuce." She reached her hand over the edge of her bed to give him a rub behind the ears. He waddled over to the opposite side of her bed, and with agility that was unexpected from a stocky, slobbering dog, he hoisted himself up on her mattress with all the grace of a pig on roller skates. He landed in belly-flop position and stayed there. Jamie eyed her furry friend, surprised her portly companion didn't snap his stubby legs in the process of making his way up on the bed. Deuce shoved his face into hers, snorting and nuzzling her tangled hair. He was a loving, albeit loud and grubby, roommate.

She rubbed her hand over Deuce's head and scratched him behind his left ear. He growled a low bulldog purr, like a cat but with slobber.

Deuce had landed in her life by a combination of poker skill and a little luck during a Texas Hold 'Em tournament. One man had been so committed to the tournament that he'd actually put Deuce up as a bet. *What a dumbass.* Deuce was a full-bred English bulldog with papers; his monetary worth was estimated at about twelve hundred dollars. Wayne had lost that hand to Jamie, and she'd gladly taken the dog as partial payment, figuring any moron who was willing to bet a prized companion in a card game deserved to lose him.

She pulled herself up from bed. She needed clothes... clean clothes. When was the last time she'd done laundry? She reached over to a chair she used as a general clothes-dumping area and chose a pair of yoga pants—although she'd never done yoga in her life—and a tank top. She collected them to wear after her shower. While she would never admit it, Jamie often worked cases while standing in the shower. Something about the water falling over her face, the steam, and the absence of other distractions helped shake insights loose, ones she feared she would otherwise miss. She'd lost count of how many times she had taken showers explicitly for that purpose.

Jamie headed for the shower and took her time enjoying being pelted with hot water. Her mind turned over the events of the previous day, trying to make sense of all of it. She stood under the hot water until it turned cool. When she got out, she wrapped her hair in one towel and covered her body with a second one. With her hair still wet from the shower, she finished getting dressed just as her cell phone rang. She checked the number, took a deep breath, and decided to let it go to voice mail.

She tried to keep her kid sister, Grace, at a distance. The girl was trouble in a tight dress and manipulative beyond shame. She reminded Jamie of their mother. Her sister had, after all, learned at the high heels of a master.

Grace had a way of getting people to do things for her without directly asking. She would come to her target, lamenting her life's difficulties, even using another person's misery and twisting it to demonstrate how it affected her. Grace didn't want to appear helpless, but close, as if she had just done so much for so many for so long that she couldn't possibly take on *one more thing*.

But now the rules were different. Kristen was dead, and Jamie's little sister shared some traits with her departed niece, such as the kind of behavior and decision-making skills that led her straight to trouble. As much as Jamie wanted to write off Grace's phone call, she couldn't do it. Kristen's death had changed things. What if Grace really needed help this time, too?

Jamie's phone rang again.

"Hello," Jamie said, not acknowledging Grace's identity.

"Hey, Jamie. It's me."

"Hi, Me. How are you doing?" She tried to keep the conversation light.

"Oh, I'm all right, I guess. How are you?"

Jamie never knew how to answer that question. She wanted to get her sister off the phone as quickly as possible. She had things to do. "I'm tied up with some cases right now and a little worn down, but other than that, I'm doing okay."

"You sound different," Grace said.

Jamie tried to pass it off. "I'm okay, just tired. Surveillance means not getting enough sleep sometimes. You know how it is."

Grace giggled into the phone. "Yeah, my current job has me working nights. It's like I sleep half the day now, and I'm all turned around. The world is so different at night, so much more alive, you know? I like it."

Jamie wasn't the least bit surprised by Grace's revelation. "So, what are you doing now?"

She considered tossing a joke about her sister dabbling in the escort business but thought better of it... just in case it was true. If it was, she didn't want to know about it. Plausible deniability and all that.

"Oh, I'm working at Firefly Rouge on the Strip," Grace said. "It's this fantastic upscale restaurant and night club."

Jamie resisted making a quip about table dances and tips. She knew it was a sore spot with Grace, who viewed herself as far more upper-end than the rest of her relations.

"Oh, really? What do you do there?"

"I'm the hostess on the ten-to-five shift. It took me a good week to get used to it, but I'm on the reverse schedule now. It's a really nice place. You should fly up here and visit."

"I'm not planning on coming to Vegas anytime soon. It's really not my scene."

"It used to be," Grace teased.

Jamie clenched her jaw, reminding herself to parse her words with caution. "I know. Used to be. Past tense."

"Well, it's probably for the best. It's not like you want to lose ten grand again like last time. Probably better that you don't have so many gambling opportunities there. Vegas is no place for addicts."

Grace knew exactly which buttons to push, and Jamie couldn't help but take the bait. "I know you aren't calling me an addict since you're the one who's been through rehab three times."

Grace quickly backpedaled. No doubt she had temporarily forgotten she was talking to her sister and not a mark. Jamie knew her secrets and was more than willing to call her on every one of them.

"I didn't mean it like that. I just know that you didn't like being that out of control, that's all."

Jamie silently conceded that point. It had definitely been one of the lowest times in her young life. She still wished she could mentally erase that six-month period, not that she could remember all of it. And that was the worst part—the days that remained a mystery.

"No problem," Jamie said. "I know you can't help that things sometimes come out of your mouth like that."

Her sister responded to her comment with silence.

Jamie continued. "So, to what do I owe this phone call? It's been like a year or more since we talked."

Grace's voice became upbeat. "You know me. Never been good at keeping in touch with people. I was moving around. I was working up in Atlantic City for a while, and that was going pretty well until I realized that I didn't like Jersey that much."

Jamie translated her sister's true meaning. Grace had moved because she'd scammed someone she shouldn't have and they were out looking for her. That meant it was time to relocate.

"So, did you go back to Vegas to be with Mom and Dad?"

"They're actually why I'm calling."

Jamie sighed. She knew it. Grace was the only sibling who kept in contact with their parents. "I haven't talked to them in a long time, Grace. I don't even know where they are."

Grace sighed then waited a beat. "That's the problem. Dad doesn't know where Mom is."

"This is not the first time that's happened." Jamie's scoff was unmistakable. "When she wants a break, she takes off. She turns up when she's ready to work again."

Grace sighed with force into the phone, as if she was trying to blow Jamie's protest away.

Jamie did not want to get involved. She did not want to know. Well, possibly a small part of her did, and that small part was what always caused her crushing heartbreak. She hated to admit it, but even as a grown woman, she longed to have a mother she could depend on.

Finally, she relented. "What's the problem?"

"Well, she said she was going to spend some time in Colorado visiting friends. She and Dad were going to meet up here for a job they were supposed to start last week, but she never showed. He can't get ahold of her. She hasn't called. Nothing."

What is it with the women in my family just dropping off the grid on a regular basis? Always running from everything, even one another.

Jamie knew better than to be alarmed at this early stage. Their mother was notorious for her disappearing acts and dramatic reentries. It was how she convinced herself that she could still influence people. She would get them to worry, get them to search for her, then show up after she felt sufficient time had passed in which people would have missed her. It pissed Jamie off every time she did it, and each time, Jamie vowed not to get caught up in her games. But every time, she would falter and start to care—and regret it afterward.

Jamie rubbed at her temple to ward off a looming headache. "Look, I don't know what kind of game she's playing, but we both know that's what she's doing. Maybe she's angry at Dad, and she's making him pay for something."

Yeah, like fathering another child through an affair.

"Grace, don't trick yourself into believing that you actually understand anything about their marriage, because you don't. None of us do."

Grace took offense to this. "I know them better than you do. I still see them and spend time with them."

"And work with them?"

Grace hesitated for a moment. "Yes, I work with them. And they still have it, just in case you're wondering."

Jamie reached for her temple and gave it a small press. "I'm not."

"You've always been a skeptic, Jamie, but I know you. You use your con skills in your PI work. I know you do."

"Yeah, but I'm not screwing people. I'm trying to help them, not steal money and leave town."

"Jamie, I'm serious. You need to help us find Mom."

She put the brakes on that idea immediately. "Did Dad do anything wrong?"

Grace paused. "Well, there might have been a cocktail waitress…"

"That's it. She's pissed, and she'll show up when she needs more cash. She's going to make him squirm a bit, like always."

"Okay, I see your point." Grace sighed into the phone. "I'll give her a few days to see if she calls. Will you help me then if she doesn't turn up?"

Jamie thought of Kristen. "Yes," she replied with a sigh. "I'll help you." She then changed the conversation. "Have you heard from Brian lately?"

After a moment of silence, Grace said, "No, why? I really don't have any reason to talk to him. Mom would kill me."

Jamie decided to throw her baby sister a line to see if she would take the bait. "He asked me to help him find Kristen. Seems like lots of our family members are just dropping out of sight."

"Oh." More silence passed before Grace asked, "So did you find her?"

Jamie softened her response. "Yeah, we did."

"What was she doing?"

Jamie waited for a moment before responding. She hated saying the words aloud. "She's dead, Grace."

Her sister gasped into the phone. Jamie couldn't tell what Grace knew since the phone masked most of her tells, but Jamie hoped that if her misguided sibling did have any information, she would walk through the door Jamie had opened.

"That's awful. I'm really sorry, Jamie. The last time I talked to her…" Grace's voice trailed off, a silence more telling than she'd likely intended.

"The last time you talked to her... what?" Jamie asked.

"It was nothing, Jamie. She was excited about this guy. And she knew I would appreciate it."

"What did she tell you?"

"Not much. Just that he was going to help her with something big and she couldn't tell Brian about it because..."

"He would end it?"

Grace hesitated. "Yes. He never wanted her in a serious relationship."

"Because he couldn't control her anymore?"

"He needed her for his own work."

Jamie understood the desire of a daughter needing her father's approval all too well. "Let me know when Mom makes contact, okay? A text is fine. And don't tell her I care because I don't."

"Yes, you do."

"Stay out of trouble, Grace."

"Where's the fun in that?"

Jamie hit End on her phone, her little sister's words still hanging in her thoughts.

She worried about Grace and her dependent nature, her need to be noticed by their parents even if it meant being used by them. Jamie could live without her family. Unfortunately, Grace couldn't, which meant her future, like Kristen's, would likely be paved with poor choices. And like Kristen, Jamie wouldn't be able to save her, either.

CHAPTER FIFTEEN

J AMIE'S DECISION TO RETURN TO the Youth Activity Center by herself didn't sit well with Cookie. He felt that it was his responsibility to be her shadow, her comic relief, and her heavy. She loved him for it, but she also felt it best to return to the YAC on her own, to see how Marcus Holliday would respond to her. Besides, he had his hands full researching the Deltone family's architecture. Jamie would need to know the names of the key players to see who Kristen might have hitched her wagon to.

Jamie had spent time researching Marcus Holliday and his endeavors, a task made easy due to his family's high media profile. The YAC was completely funded through donations by the wealthy Holliday family as well as other private donors, and its purpose was to inspire at-risk youth— kids with crappy home lives, absent parents, and kids who were awkward, bullied, or easily coerced by a negative influence. That seemed to accurately describe most teenagers in general. The YAC had received praise and media coverage upon its opening and on and off ever since, particularly during the holidays. The center was positioned as a safe haven for kids without families.

Jamie knew she had to tread carefully in her dealings with the Holliday family. They wielded extraordinary influence in a good part of the state, and their political connections would likely shield them from most external threats. They had already proven they could dodge jail time. The eldest son, Edward III, had allegedly killed a woman while he was legally drunk, yet he'd gotten off with a tearful apology in front of scads of reporters and a promise to someday serve community service, which according to the newspapers, still hadn't been fulfilled. A wild child in his youth, Edward's every misstep had been well-documented in local tabloids and magazines: his underage partying at local clubs, his antics that had gotten him unceremoniously relocated out of not one but two private schools, and the long list of broken hearts that increased whenever his current love interest was supplanted by the next "it" girl.

Marcus Holliday, however, appeared the opposite of his elder brother, at least based on the lack of media coverage. Marcus was rarely mentioned in print, yet when he was, it was related to some sort of award or community project. He either behaved better or he had a more effective public relations manager. Jamie was curious to understand how this man had become an infatuation for her niece and if he had been anything more.

She parked her Tahoe in the front row of the parking lot at the Youth Art Center. She had to admit it was a beautiful addition to the island. She realized that, for someone who prided herself on her observation skills, she had completely overlooked these details of the décor when she had come to interview Beth the first time. Jamie approached the front door of the building, peeking inside the glass-paneled doors. As she stepped inside, she surveyed the interior. She noted a reception desk toward the back of the room, where a young woman sat and talked on the phone. The girl seemed far less concerned than the kid who'd been manning the front desk during her last visit with Cookie.

Jamie took the opportunity to scope out the sitting area. The main entryway was designed to be a gallery, so visitors walked directly into an area showcasing sculptures, paintings, and professionally framed photography. Below each work of art rested a photograph and corresponding paragraph about its young artist. Jamie evaluated the one closest to her, a pencil sketch of two teens on skateboards, their path appearing to travel up to the sky. Jamie was taken by the sketch then looked at the photo below it. A picture of a teenage girl with chestnut-brown hair pulled to one side was displayed below the print. Jamie read the accompanying paragraph, which described the artist's love for charcoal pencil, her dreams of going to Paris, and her favorite model skateboard.

Jamie continued viewing each piece. All artwork was accompanied by the artist's biography and photo. Jamie didn't notice anything in their statements hinting at their troubles, their station in life, or even where they went to school—if they went to school at all. The short paragraphs highlighted only the artists' passions, what they hoped to be, and what they dreamed of accomplishing in the future.

Jamie had almost completed her viewing when she came across the last photograph.

It was Kristen's.

So, this is what she really looked like. She had a beautiful face, but not the kind celebrated in magazines. Her hair was windswept and messy rather than coiffed, her bright-green eyes were almost electric, and a faint cascade of freckles was strewn across her nose and cheeks. What struck Jamie the most was that her eyes were bright, even hopeful. She wondered if Brian had ever had an opportunity to see her in such a way. Had anyone?

Kristen's featured artwork was a black-and-white photograph. Jamie recognized the location—the far pier off the Boardwalk, a place where kids hung out to skip school, smoke pot, and squander their potential one day at a time.

Kristen had named the photograph, *The Pier to Nowhere*. The image felt dark and somber. The stretch of wooden walkway seemed to disappear into the ocean, and figures of people along the boardwalk disintegrated into the background. Was that what Kristen feared would one day happen to her—that she would disintegrate into the background?

Jamie stood for a long time, gazing at the image. Sadness welled up inside her—sorrow for never getting to know this young woman and for never taking the opportunity to be a guiding force. Whether or not Jamie's influence had been a positive one would remain an open topic for discussion. She may have become one of the straighter arrows of her family's bloodline, but then, the bar was frighteningly low. She was lost in thoughts of her niece when she realized someone stood behind her. She turned and recognized him immediately.

Marcus Holliday.

His face was tan and young, but something about him felt older. Maybe he'd spent too much time in the unforgiving island sun or living in the shadow of his nefarious older brother? An old soul seemed to live in that thirty-something body. It was evident in his eyes and his expression.

"Ah, that's one of our newest artists."

"Yes, I can see that. What can you tell me about her?"

He seemed to examine Jamie, possibly deciding how to proceed. "Forgive my manners. My name is Marcus Holliday. I'm the director of the YAC. And you are?"

She extended her hand. "Jamie. Nice to meet you."

"Do you live in the area, Jamie?"

"Yes, I do. On the island, actually."

"It's a wonderful place to live. Unfortunately, more and more people are figuring that out. Seems like we're getting lots of new people moving in permanently."

Jamie agreed. "We love the snowbirds and the tourist money, but I wish they didn't stay so long."

"Agree a thousand percent. I've lived here most of my life, and I'm still kind of skeptical about newcomers."

"I've only been here a few years, so I guess I still count as a newcomer."

"Where were you before that?"

Jamie skirted the question. "Oh, here and there. We moved around a lot when I was a kid, and I kept up the habit until recently. I'd never found a place where I wanted to stay for any length of time until coming here."

"We have a good thing going here. We can go into Corpus, but we don't need to. We're big enough on our own; everything we need is here. It's big and small, if that makes sense."

Jamie thought for a second. "It does."

"So, what can I do for you?"

"I actually came to speak to you." She pointed to Kristen's photograph. "About Kristen. I'm her aunt, and I need some help."

Marcus nodded. "Of course, of course." He gestured toward the hallway. "My office is back here."

Jamie followed him through the main gallery and down a wide hallway, which broke off into several other rooms. Jamie glanced through each doorway as she walked past. One area contained an open lounge, where several kids hung out, playing card games, video games, sketching, or reading. Jamie noticed a group of four kids collaborating over a sketchbook.

Marcus noticed Jamie's interest. "We have several spaces here where the kids can create, draw, sculpt, or paint. We even have a darkroom for those kids who want to go 'old school' with film. There's a certain beauty to the film process that I think gets lost in the digital world."

He continued. "We wanted them to have a place to hang out with other kids who showed artistic inclinations. We worried that if they weren't here creating, they'd be back on the streets, getting into trouble. So we provide a hangout, and we also have vending machines with drinks and snacks. We even order pizza and Chinese for dinner for kids who don't seem to have anywhere to go or who would prefer to be here rather than home. You wouldn't believe the environment some of these kids live in."

Oh, yes I would. Was this where Kristen spent her time, away from the chaos of her father's schemes?

They continued past the living room and several other doors. The building was much larger than it appeared from the outside, and the walk to Marcus's office took longer than she had expected. At the very end of the hall, they came upon a bright-red closed door with several hand-painted designs on it. The images seemed random to Jamie. Collectively, they made no sense to her.

Marcus pointed at his door and laughed. "Some of the kids got together to repaint my door for me. I told them to create whatever they wanted, and it looks like they each wanted something different. I like it, though. I can tell from looking at the art who painted which design."

Marcus opened the door, and they entered his humble office, a decent-sized space but not ostentatious, certainly nothing Jamie would expect from a man with a Holliday family pedigree. The walls held several framed images of Marcus and his kids, artwork from past and present students, and a few clippings from newspaper coverage. His desktop held four bowls of different kinds of candy, a large Tiffany reading lamp, and a planner. Jamie fought the urge to read it, certain that if her nosiness were detected, Marcus would be less willing to share anything he knew. Plus, she sucked at reading things upside down.

"Here, have a seat." He gestured to a pair of leather-backed chairs, weathered either from time or by design. They each held a hint of ranch-country décor.

Jamie sat down, making an effort to loosen her posture and seem relaxed, although she felt precisely the opposite. "I appreciate you making time to talk to me."

"Of course. So, how can I help you?"

Jamie straightened up in her chair, her posture more alert. "Kristen's father, Brian, came to me a few days ago, asking for help. Have you ever met him?"

Marcus shook his head. "No, I never did, but most kids prefer not to talk about family."

"I understand that completely. I loved her, but we hadn't been close in some time, so I wouldn't be surprised if she never mentioned me."

Marcus leaned forward, his forearms resting on the desk. "A lot of these kids have pretty bad family situations, so my expectations about who is in their lives are usually pretty low."

"You must deal with this issue a lot," Jamie said.

Marcus nodded. "Common theme around here. Absent fathers, absent mothers, living with friends, grandparents, under the bridge, not finishing school, being bullied when they do try to go back." He leaned back in his chair. "I find drinking helps. Me, not them."

Jamie considered whether or not to reveal what she knew about her niece's fate. It was still too early to tell if Marcus had anything to hide. Did Marcus know Kristen was dead?

"It seems Kristen's been out of contact for several days, and her friends haven't heard from her," Jamie finally said.

"Well, I wish I could help you, but I haven't seen Kristen in almost a week. She'd go off for a bit and then come back, sometimes angry and out of sorts. She'd work through it with her art and get back on balance. Then the cycle would repeat."

"Do you know if she was mixed up in anything? Drugs, theft, anything like that?"

Marcus shook his head. "No, but that doesn't mean she wasn't doing something she shouldn't. It's kind of standard operating procedure for these kids. Sometimes they take the new path over time, sometimes not."

Jamie was a bit surprised by his matter-of-fact nature about helping kids in crisis. "You're very pragmatic about this whole thing. Some kids make it, some don't, just another day at the office?"

Marcus sat quietly for a moment before responding. "I don't mean to sound cold, but being sentimental can get you in trouble. You can't pin your hopes on these kids finding their way to something better. All I can do is make a space for them to come, and the rest is up to them. I've lost several kids, and it hurts every time. If I don't distance myself some, it will eat me alive, and I won't be able to help them at all."

"I can only imagine," Jamie replied. She inhaled deeply and pushed a stray hair from her face. Leaning forward, she clasped her hands in front of her lap. "So, here's the difficult part." She paused for a moment before revealing what she knew. "Kristen's dead."

Jamie kept her eyes locked on his and watched his expression now that the truth hung between them. The natural instinct is to avert the eyes when bad news is received, but Jamie always knew the power of the tell on someone's face in those first micro instants of a revelation.

Marcus's expression remained the same—solemn and a bit detached. He ran his hand through his thick dark hair and sighed. "I know."

It was Jamie's turn to be surprised. "And you know how?"

He replied quite simply. "A young woman found dead in a foreclosed house on this island is coffee shop talk. Bad news travels fast, unfortunately. And Kristen had been spending time here, so..." He then turned the question on her. "Why didn't you tell me this right away?"

"Don't take it personally. I don't trust anybody. Job hazard."

He leaned forward a bit in his chair as if he were preparing to share a confidence. "Kristen was a good kid, but she was ambitious, and she wasn't afraid to work people, if you know what I mean. If she could get something from someone, she'd do it. She had a good heart, I could tell, but she also looked out for number one."

Jamie grimaced at his characterization, hating to admit that it sounded accurate.

He continued. "I didn't take offense when she treated me that way. She's not the first. I mean, these kids do what they need to so they can get by."

She felt a momentary need to make excuses for Kristen, to explain away her behavior as a result of her upbringing, but realized it didn't matter. She was who she was, and it had landed her in an early grave. No amount of rationalizing would mitigate that fact.

Jamie decided it was best to be open with Marcus. "Look, I barely knew her, and she was my niece, so anything you can tell me would help. Anything you can think of would be useful."

He seemed to consider her request. He held his hands up as if he had nothing to offer. "I don't know what I can tell you other than she loved drawing and photography and being away from her family. She didn't talk about her friends, and she didn't share much about herself. She was someone who could talk a lot but not tell you much."

A valued skill of a con—talking without sharing. Jamie knew a bit about that tool of the trade. She found herself intrigued that Marcus had picked up on that particular characteristic. He certainly seemed more self-aware than his party-for-the-paparazzi older brother.

"Did Kristen leave anything here?" Jamie asked. "One of her friends mentioned that she might have kept some of her things here."

"I think she did. We can go check if you'd like." A cell phone buzzed, and Marcus pulled his from his pants pocket. "Excuse me for just a second." He stepped aside to the corner of his office while he took the call. His side of the conversation sounded as though he were just answering questions about some sort of fundraiser.

While Marcus took his phone call, Jamie surveyed his office once more, her eyes taking in the framed photography on the wall behind him, most likely works of kids from the center. Her eyes drifted to a stack of comic books resting atop a small table next to her chair. Something on the cover rang familiar: *John Constantine, Hellblazer*. She remembered seeing that comic book character's name before somewhere on FriendConnect. Jamie felt that more than coincidence was at play, although having comic books in a facility that catered to kids in trouble didn't necessarily mean foul play. It was possible Marcus had just used the comic books as a tool to relate to the teens in his care.

Jamie noticed a photo of several kids standing by a fishing boat. The name *Chelsea's Freedom* was painted in blue script across the back, the color matching the sizeable awning that covered the top deck.

Marcus disconnected and slipped his phone back in his pocket.

"That's a nice boat," Jamie noted, pointing to the photo.

Marcus nodded. "Would like to spend more time taking her fishing."

"So you take the kids out on it sometimes?"

"Now and then." He turned his chair around to look at the framed picture. "It's good for the kids to get away from things sometimes, and being out on the water clears your head like nothing else."

"Did Kristen ever get a chance to go?"

He pursed his lips and shook his head. "No, although I wish we would have. I think she would have loved it."

"I'm sure that's true," Jamie said. "Not that I knew her so well. I'm just suspicious of anyone who doesn't like being by the water." She straightened her posture in her chair. "So, back to Kristen and her behavior. Have you heard anything? Even a rumor might give me something to follow."

He shook his head. "I do have a question for you, though."

Jamie leaned back in her chair, her fingers laced together in her lap. "What is it?"

"How close are you with Kristen's dad?"

Jamie rolled her eyes. "Not at all. It's a long story, but… We're related, but we aren't family. Why do you ask?"

"I got the feeling that her relationship with him was difficult."

"What makes you say that? Did she say something specific?"

He shook his head. "No, she was always real careful about what she shared. I know he called her a few times and texted, and she'd make some offhanded comment about ignoring him. Nothing specific, but it didn't seem like she wanted him to know where she was."

"He and I don't have a good relationship, either," Jamie said. "I'm only here because I want to find out what happened to Kristen. If he had asked me for anything else, I never would have picked up the phone." Jamie then asked, "Is it okay for us to check her locker now?"

Marcus nodded. "Of course. Let's go take a look. Before you leave, do you want to give me your number in case something comes up?"

Jamie reached into the front pocket of her bag and pulled out a card. It simply had her name and cell number, no silly logo and no fancy artwork. Cookie said it resembled a calling card for a hit man. She held it between her fingers and reached across Marcus's desk. "Yes, that would be helpful. Even if it's something small and seems unimportant, please call or text me."

Marcus accepted the card, placed it on a stack of papers, then stood up. "Let's go check Kristen's locker to see if she left anything you might want to take with you."

Jamie trailed Marcus out of his office and down the hall. Two doors down, they turned left. Marcus stopped at a door with a placard that announced "Storage" in black and white letters. When they walked in, Jamie thought it definitely looked like a large storage room. Off to the left was a stand of cleaning supplies on a plastic table, and a mop, broom, and bucket were propped in the corner. On the wall to the right were three banks of lockers, silver and battered. They looked as though they had been rescued from a high school hallway.

"Here we go," Marcus said.

Jamie began to reach in her bag for the key Connie had given her to see if it would open the lock, but Marcus pulled a key ring from his pants pocket. He flipped through the numerous keys until he found the one for the lockers. It didn't look like the one Connie had given her.

"She was adamant about a top row locker on the corner, so it's easy to remember." Marcus turned the key in the lock and opened the door. He then stepped back and made room for Jamie. "Please"—he pointed toward the locker—"take a look."

Jamie turned to face the locker. A small black sports sack, the kind with rope-style handles to wear as a backpack, rested in the center. The logo on the front read, "Island Art Symposium." The words were rounded in a stylized circle.

Marcus pointed to the bag. "We had a lot of those bags printed for an event last year. We have extras to give out if the kids want them. They seem to like the style."

Jamie retrieved the sack from the locker. She pulled open the top, and the elastic loosened to show the contents. She noticed a few items of clothing and a small cosmetic bag. She quickly closed the sack back up. "I'll take a closer look when I get home."

Marcus nodded. "No problem. Let me know if you need anything else." He gestured toward his office. "I need to get ready for a meeting."

They shook hands, and Jamie watched Marcus return to his office. She took Kristen's bag, slung it over her shoulder, and left the storage room in the opposite direction, heading for the front lobby.

As she walked out to her car, Jamie felt the weight of Kristen's bag on her shoulder. She realized it was far heavier than she'd expected because it carried the expectation of finding the truth behind her niece's death. Even though she had come away with one clue, she still had no explanation. Marcus had lied to her about Kristen being on that boat, and she needed to know why.

CHAPTER SIXTEEN

"How did it go?" Cookie asked as he continued typing on his laptop, his meaty fingers quickly punching at the keyboard.

"Interesting." Jamie stood close to Cookie, not quite staring over his shoulder at the table, clutching Kristen's nylon backpack to her chest.

"Looks like you found something." Cookie's eyes glanced at the bag then up to meet hers. "You didn't look inside yet, did you?" He said it in such a way that it was more an affirmation than a question.

Jamie pulled out a chair and sat down next to her friend. "I wanted to wait until I got back. I didn't want to look inside it alone, and I sure didn't want to look inside with Marcus Holliday standing there. It feels like it's mostly clothes, anyway."

"How did you feel about Holliday? What's your take on him?" Cookie now gave Jamie his full attention, leaning back in his chair and turning his body toward her. "Did he play you straight?"

"Not completely." Jamie pointed to Cookie's laptop. "Pull up her FriendConnect account."

Cookie tapped away at the keyboard, opening a new tab in his browser and typing in Kristen's information. "Okay, now what?"

"Go through her photos until you find one of her taking a selfie by a boat."

Cookie did as instructed and pulled up the image on the screen. Jamie pointed at the name in the corner. "You see that word 'freedom'? Marcus has a fishing boat named *Chelsea's Freedom*."

"Okay, so she was on his boat?" Cookie asked.

"Marcus said Kristen had never been on his boat."

Cookie stared at the photo on his screen. "It's possible that she just took a photo in front of it, you know, the way teenagers often do to create their perfect online lives."

"Do you really believe that?"

"Not really," he said. "But it's possible. We have to look at everything, right? Maybe he lied because he was worried about how it would look if he had her on his boat, especially if it were just the two of them."

Jamie rubbed her eyes with her forefinger, digging her thumb into her temple to soothe the headache now surfacing. "Here's the thing. I just don't see any kind of personal relationship going on there. He seems pretty grounded, he talks about these kids with compassion, and he seemed to get that there are specific boundaries to being at his facility."

"But he lied."

She nodded. "But he lied."

Jamie patted Kristen's bag, which she had kept on her lap, then placed it atop the table and pulled open the elastic band. "Let's get this over with." She reached inside with her hand and felt the rough texture of a pair of jeans. She pulled them out and placed them on the table. Next came a nondescript navy T-shirt with the tiny embroidered logo of a polo player on the breast pocket; the soft fabric was creased from being bundled inside. Two more shirts, a pair of shorts, a cosmetic bag, and a brush were all that remained at the bottom of the bag. The cosmetic bag had clearly done hard time in the backpack, its once light-pink floral pattern now faded. Jamie unzipped it to inspect the contents. An eyeliner, lipstick, and several tampons in colorful wrappers composed the top layer of items.

"So, are the tampons here to keep people from looking any further, or are they just there to be there?" Jamie pulled the items out of the bag. More cosmetics followed—a black powder compact, a tube of mascara, and some makeup brushes. At the bottom, she found one curious thing—a cell phone.

"Ah, the old hide-a-burner-phone-under-your-tampons trick," Jamie said. "Basic black, cheap design, probably bought at a superstore somewhere."

Her discovery had Cookie's full attention. "That hiding stuff inside girlie necessities is pretty smart. Most guys won't bother venturing any further once they see that." He held his hand out. "Can I check it?"

Cookie inspected the phone. His finger pressed buttons on the phone as he pulled up the recent calls list. Only one phone number was listed in the call history. "I can try some reverse-lookup directories and see if we get lucky."

"Do your magic," Jamie instructed him. She patted down each item of clothing and turned out the pockets to see if she had missed anything before bundling them back into the bag. "That's it. The standard grifter's legacy—a few everyday items and a lot of unanswered questions."

Cookie took a break from inspecting the phone and turned his attention to Jamie. "It must be hard living like that, bouncing from one place to the next, not really owning anything of your own, living out of a backpack."

Jamie stood up from her chair, stretching her arms overhead and letting out a sigh. "It's all she knew, I suppose." She walked a few steps to a nearby window, the view of the ocean providing brief comfort. Having the freedom to be anywhere at any time could be its own prison, a lesson Jamie had learned all too well from her time on the take with her family. Having a few roots, no matter how shallow, in Port Alene had helped Jamie more than she would admit to anyone. Being part of a family, even one cobbled together with friends and bar mates, had changed her, softened her some. She knew it was good for her personally, but the jury was still out on how it had affected her professionally.

"So, the key that Connie gave me didn't fit her locker," Jamie said, still looking out the window.

"Did you try it?"

She turned around to face Cookie, who was still staring at his computer screen, typing commands she couldn't see. "No, I was going to, but then Marcus pulled out his set, and the key looks completely different. I didn't want to show it to him in case he knows something we don't."

She returned to her chair and peeked over Cookie's shoulder as he continued typing. "You working on the reverse directory already?"

He nodded. "My guy has his people adding all kinds of data from social media and other places where numbers are published. If this guy is super careful, we're out of luck, but if he's got it registered somewhere, we'll find it."

"So your guy has people now?"

Cookie nodded. "Yep. Business is good."

"Maybe we should go work for your guy instead. We can sit behind a desk and eat chips and M&M's all day. It's got to be more fun than handling divorce cases."

"No way," he replied. "I need to be around people. I'd go nuts being trapped in a room full of computer geeks all day."

"I hear they have good snacks, though," Jamie said.

As Cookie continued working on his laptop, Jamie reached for her notebook, which was covered by a stack of napkins from Hemingway's and some plastic utensils. Marty knew she hated doing dishes, so he allowed her to pilfer his food-to-go supplies. She opened the notebook to the next clean page and wrote Kristen's name at the top. She just needed to brain-dump her thoughts. She wrote about the key, about Marcus lying to her about Kristen being on the boat, about Dylan, and about the FriendConnect account with the Natasha Irons comic book identity. None of the information was new, but somehow, having all the moving parts down on paper for her to consider helped her process everything differently.

"Ha! I've got something." Cookie clapped his hands together and rubbed them as if he were warming them over a fire. "The name on the account is Elena Mendoza." Cookie continued typing, searching for more details about Elena Mendoza, cross-referencing her name with search filters for Port Alene and the surrounding areas.

"Should we call the number and ask for her?" Jamie asked. "It's a risk. If the number is in a burner phone, there has to be a reason."

Cookie nodded. "Okay, I'll do some searching and see what I can come up with. Check FriendConnect for any Elena Mendoza accounts and see if she shows up."

Jamie retrieved her own laptop from the kitchen counter and returned to Cookie's side. "You know, this would be so much easier if we had found her phone."

"I'm guessing that's gone for good," Cookie replied. "All we have is what she left online, which isn't much."

Cookie ran through the list of possible Elena Mendozas, happy to find there were only two that seemed likely. One of the two was twenty-eight years old and a kindergarten teacher in nearby Rockport. The other was in her sixties with a very active social-media presence that seemed to center around her grandchildren and all the brilliant things they had done in their short lives.

"I'm thinking it's the teacher. Older than Kristen but closer in age, although she would be way too well-grounded to be friends with Kristen."

Cookie pointed at the screen. "There are two numbers listed on Elena's account. Maybe we should call the other one? We can use the billing storyline to ask about this number?"

Jamie nodded. "Okay, just let me spoof my number so it looks like it's coming from her cell phone carrier."

He continued typing. "I love these databases, by the way. So useful."

Jamie cringed, knowing that most people had little knowledge of how easy it was to spoof a phone number and make it look as though the caller was calling from somewhere else, like a legitimate business. Databases that looked up cell carriers, reverse lookups, and other tools online made finding someone with only a ten-digit phone number pretty easy. The right software, which was available to most anyone on the Internet, could mask a caller's identity, pulling information from the unsuspecting party with ease.

"You want me to handle the call, right?" Cookie asked. "I'm way better at social engineering than you are." He held his hand up. "No offense."

He was right. Social engineering was an important skill, and it was the secret behind most hacks, ranging from garnering basic information to stealing someone's identity, and even locking them out of their own accounts. The key behind social engineering was making sure the hacker had enough basic information to fool someone else into giving him important, sometimes confidential, information. Bounty hunters were some of the best at using these tools of psychological manipulation, understanding that most people wanted to be helpful, especially if you position yourself as a victim or someone trying to save a loved one from a crisis. Humans were almost always the weak link, the failed gatekeepers opening the doors to their own secrets. Even the best hackers understood that tech alone wouldn't get a job done; the con artist needed the right information first, which meant getting someone somewhere to tell him what he wanted to know.

Cookie shared his attention between his phone and his laptop, preparing for his call to Elena Mendoza. "If she doesn't answer, I'll just hang up. Not like she can call me back on this imaginary number." Cookie dialed the number he had found using his reverse search database and placed the phone to his ear. His eyes looked up toward the ceiling as he waited for a human voice on the other end of the line. He nodded at Jamie then began his phishing expedition.

"Hello, Ms. Mendoza?" He paused. "Hello, this is David Willis with PrimeTime Mobile. How are you?"

He paused again. It was too risky to put the phone on speaker, so Jamie simply sat and listened to Cookie's end of the conversation.

"Good, thank you. Listen, I'm sorry to bother you, but I'm calling about a second number that's attached to your account? It's 361-522-3432. Is that yours also?"

He paused.

"Oh, I see. Yes, ma'am. We just noticed some international calls being billed to that number, and we believe they're fraudulent so we're going to have them removed. You don't need to do anything, and we will contact him also on that line to let him know."

Another pause as he listened.

"Oh, I see. Well, lots of people are lousy about answering their phones, so we can just leave a message. No problem."

Jamie could hear the faint voice on the other end as Cookie listened.

"No, nothing you need to do on your end. We have your account protected, so everything is fine. Thanks so much. Have a good day."

Cookie ended the call and placed the phone on the table. "So, that phone is for her brother. His name is Ritchie. She said he was supposed to remove it off her account, but he hasn't done it yet because he doesn't like having things in his own name. And he's lazy."

Jamie laughed at the comment. "Sounds like a freeloader… or someone that wants to keep his name off of records."

"Maybe he's both."

"If this guy's a criminal, you know most of them are actually pretty sloppy. They cover one area and then slip up somewhere else."

Cookie laughed. "That's so true. Criminals on TV are so much smarter than the ones on the streets." He typed Ritchie Mendoza's name along with Elena's into his online search. "This might take some time and some asking around. We can't just dial the number and ask Ritchie what Kristen was doing with a cell phone that had his number in it."

Jamie stood up from her chair and crossed the loft space in a few steps then returned to where Cookie sat at the table with his attention still focused on his laptop.

"I keep thinking about how Marcus lied about Kristen being on that boat," she said. "I think we should try and find *Chelsea's Freedom*."

That got Cookie's attention. "You mean, just go drive up and stare at it or…"

"We could probably get on and take a look around, just see if there's anything worth seeing."

"You think there's something more to it than Marcus just taking her out on it?"

She held her hands up, palms open. "Why hide it otherwise? He was open about helping her, about her spending time at the YAC, so why not be open about the boat? It's clear from his photos that he's taken other kids on it, so what makes Kristen different?"

Cookie closed his laptop, giving Jamie his full attention. "Something tells me we're going on a field trip."

Jamie nodded. "You like boats, right?"

CHAPTER SEVENTEEN

"T HIS IS ONE OF MY favorite places," Cookie said as Jamie pulled into the parking lot for Coastal Adventures Marina. Its location was close to the ferry line, where boats transported cars from Port Alene across the Corpus Christi ship channel to nearby Rockwall Landing, another popular small-town destination. "Maybe if we take on a few more divorce cases, I could get one of these." He waved his hand toward the impressive lineup of fishing boats and cabin cruisers.

It was a nice dream. The marina touted some beautiful vacation vessels, ranging in size from modest to monstrous. Jamie's car was parked perpendicular to the first row of boats, and she could see a gate with a keypad on the left side of the walkway. "We need a gate code," she said, her forefinger glancing to the left.

Cookie smiled and pulled out his phone. "No problem." She could see him searching for something on his phone's browser, then he pulled up the phone number for the marina. "Here we go," he said, dialing the number.

"Hi, this is Bill over at J and R. I'm supposed to do some maintenance and review for *Chelsea's Freedom*, Mr. Holliday's boat, but I don't have the access code. I think I left it at the office."

Cookie grinned as the other person spoke.

"Okay, and the slip number?"

He paused again.

"Okay, great, thanks." Cookie ended the call, clearly pleased with his performance. "Slip forty-six. Gate code is 1230."

"You should have looked up a real maintenance company name first. You got lucky."

He scowled. "Hmm. Good point, but the kid on the other end of the phone could care less. I think I was interrupting some reality TV watching. Didn't seem too on the ball."

"Still, you got lucky."

"Lucky is my middle name."

"No, your middle name is Francis."

Cookie wagged his finger at his friend. "Okay, that's a closely guarded secret. Besides, Saint Francis of Assisi was one of my mom's favorite saints."

"You ain't no saint," Jamie joked.

"He wasn't either... at first, anyway." Cookie reached over the middle seat console and swatted his friend. "Can we get off this topic and focus on the task at hand?"

Jamie dropped the teasing and studied the line of boats in front of them. "Doesn't look too busy today. Not many people out and about."

"We've got some storm clouds coming in, so that could be helpful. Not as many people wanting to take their boats out."

Jamie tilted her head and took note of the changing weather. Texas weather changed quicker than a teenager changed her mind, and it was every bit as unpredictable. Jamie reached behind her seat to grab her prop, a nondescript black tool bag. It looked official enough and had some weight to it.

"What do you have in here?" Cookie asked.

"It's just my random crap bag from my car. A few tools, some jumper cables."

"That should come in handy on the boat."

"Smartass. You ready to do this?"

He nodded.

Jamie reached into her bag and fumbled around until she found her baseball cap. She retrieved a hair band from the cup holder and deftly contained her long auburn mane—abused by humidity into a wavy mess—and tamed it into a simple ponytail. Placing the cap on her head, she figured she was now bland enough to fit into the scene without attracting attention. Cookie, too, donned a baseball cap and was wearing a plain black shirt with khaki board shorts, but his size left him less likely to blend in with a crowd.

They waited a few moments, just long enough to let the people who were walking on the pier move away from where they had parked. Then

Jamie and Cookie stepped out of her car and casually walked toward the pier to the gate. Cookie punched in the key code with authority, and a clicking sound signaled they were in. He reached for the gate, swung it open, then held it for Jamie as she passed through while carrying the tool bag, which Cookie then took from her once they were through the gate.

She looked at the numbers on the slips and noted they were standing near the fifties. "Must mean we need to go a couple of rows over."

They walked with purpose, as if they belonged. The goal in this situation was to remain in the background as much as possible and, if having to engage people, to make sure that those people forgot them quickly.

Jamie continued walking next to Cookie, glancing from one boat to the next, reading the names of each vessel, and chuckling at a few of the choices. So far, *Here Fishy Fishy* and *Money Pit* were her two favorite choices, but *Wetted Bliss* was also a contender. The weather turned a bit cooler, and the coastal breeze grew stronger. Her pace quickened as she glanced up and noticed a new roiling band of rumbling gray clouds. While rain was certainly a welcome guest that rarely visited South Texas, she hoped it would wait a little longer to arrive.

Jamie and Cookie continued walking along the pier of docked boats, when her eyes fell upon *Chelsea's Freedom*. She was a beautiful and respectable vessel, not a grand braggart of a boat that would be expected from someone of Marcus Holliday's means. Maybe Marcus preferred a bit of privacy himself, not wanting to attract too much attention while on the water. Most men with money preferred to announce that fact loudly with an expensive party boat, complete with bikini-clad bimbos arranged on the forward deck, but Marcus seemed not to fit that mold. Still, Jamie cautioned herself not to think favorably of this man, who obviously played some meaningful role in Kristen's life. The lie he told still stuck in her mind.

Jamie glanced around briefly and saw only two people even remotely close by. They were about five boat slips down and appeared involved in hosing down their deck. Cookie stepped closer to *Chelsea's Freedom* then stepped over the toe line and onto the stern of the boat. Jamie followed him. She moved quickly out of sight, down the stairs to the lower deck. Only then did she take in her surroundings.

The interior whispered elegance, with its warm wood tables and caramel-colored leather furniture, accented by strategically placed turquoise throw pillows. The galley kitchen had stainless-steel appliances and granite countertops. The bench seating area could easily double as a home office with its table layout and large porthole, perfect for peering at the majestic ocean.

Cookie took in the cabin view. "Wow, this is much nicer on the inside than it looks on the outside." He ran his hands along the kitchen counter. "Can you imagine what it would be like to take this boat out?"

Jamie agreed, her eyes still taking in the space. It wasn't a large cabin, but it was well-appointed. The galley kitchen was modest in size but not in finishes. The main living room area seemed comfortable and compact, and the kitchen led from it, narrow but fully equipped. The cabinets were a warm oak color with brushed silver handle pulls, and the surfaces were clear of clutter. Jamie walked to the bench seating, which had teal-colored pillows decorating it and pull-out drawers. Jamie noticed the cabinets underneath had small circular locks.

Interesting.

Cookie signaled to the back. "I'm going to check out the sleeping quarters."

Jamie followed him. Like everything else, the rest of the boat was compact but attractive. A queen-size bed and some small drawers lined both opposing walls, and a small television was mounted on a wall stand in the corner. Jamie reached to open the drawers and found surprisingly little inside—a few T-shirts, some underwear, socks, and a pair of tennis shoes. Most of the space remained unclaimed.

Jamie looked around the room. "I don't see anything with a lock in here, which is odd since it's the bedroom. You'd think this is the place to hide something."

"True," Cookie noted. "But maybe he lets other people stay here and so he doesn't keep anything important on the boat."

Maybe. Maybe not.

"I saw something back by the kitchen I want to check out."

Cookie nodded as he continued going through the drawers, making sure to leave no detection of his snooping.

One beauty of boat design existed in the careful use of space, making sure every square inch served a purpose. Jamie crouched down and placed her bag underneath the galley table. When she did, she raised her head just enough to bang it on the underside. "Dammit," she muttered. She rubbed the top of her head in hopes of taking the edge off the pain. It was like hitting a funny bone—enough force in just the right place could make even someone's grandma curse like a sailor.

Jamie returned to the trio of drawers underneath the seated bench. She reached into her pocket, retrieved the key, and inserted it into the first lock. The drawer opened.

"Cockie, the key works." Jamie's pulse quickened. "Maybe we'll finally get some answers."

Searching the drawer, she found a few maps, pencils, a pair of wayfarer sunglasses, and some rubber bands, but nothing worth locking up. She opened the next drawer and was greeted with equally uninteresting items—extra paper plates, utensils, napkins, and some fishing line.

Frustration began to take over, and Jamie wondered why Kristen would bother asking Connie to protect a key to some useless drawers. Maybe the key also opened something else on the boat.

Last drawer. Jamie turned the key in the lock and pulled the drawer open. She found a section of old newspaper, nothing worth noting unless one wanted to keep a souvenir of the latest fishing reports. When she picked up the newspaper, she saw something else—a plain black composition notebook.

"Find anything good?" Cookie asked as he leaned over Jamie, who was still squatting.

"Maybe." She pulled the notebook out, stretched her legs, then cradled the notebook over her forearm as she opened it to study its contents. It reminded Jamie of the books used in high school chemistry labs or writing classes—black-and-white-mottled cover and lined inside. Turning to the first page, she noted that it seemed to be a journal. She began reading.

Then she spotted her own name.

Whose journal is this?

She skimmed the page, reading.

I don't know what to do. I can't see a way out. I know I've made some mistakes, and I'm afraid I'm going to pay for those mistakes by finding myself in the trunk of a car. I sure as hell wouldn't be the first. Ritchie said he would make sure that I'm okay, but I don't know that I can trust him.

She continued reading.

I know that my dad doesn't want me talking to Jamie since the family thinks she abandoned them.

This was Kristen's journal.

Jamie's mother had disappeared more often than Houdini during her childhood, and *she* was the one that abandoned the family? Damned family revisionist history.

She continued reading.

I don't know what to do right now. Marcus says he can fix things, but I'm not so sure about that.

Cookie read over Jamie's shoulder. "It looks like your hunch paid off." He placed his hand on her shoulder. "Let's take this and go. We've been here long enough. Don't want to push our luck."

Jamie nodded, slipping the journal into her shoulder bag. She followed Cookie to the front of the boat, where he retrieved her tool bag before they ascended the steps to the deck. The sky had turned darker, and the rumbling clouds threatened to downpour. Jamie stepped off the boat and onto the walkway. Cookie hopped behind her, surprisingly nimble given his size and the weight of the bag he carried.

A man standing at the far end of the dock spotted the duo making their exit. His scruffy beard almost seemed cliché for a fisherman. "Hey, what are you doing on Mr. Holliday's boat?" he barked.

Jamie considered herself an expert on talking herself in and out of trouble. "I'm sorry. I told Susan that I was going to drop by the boat because I can't find my cell phone and I thought I left it here."

He studied her face. "I don't remember ever seeing you here." He then looked at Cookie, and his sternness softened, perhaps due to the fact that Cookie himself was a far more imposing figure.

"Well, I could say the same thing about you," he replied. "How do I know that you aren't here to steal Marcus's stuff off his boat?"

He wasn't amused. "Because anyone here can vouch for me. I don't think the same could be said for you."

He was smarter than he looked, which was going to be a problem. Jamie decided to get out while she could. "Look, it's about ready to rain, and Marcus knows we're here."

His attention turned to Cookie's bag. "What do you have there?"

Cookie shrugged, his expression unconcerned about the entire interrogation. "Just some tools and cables. Had to help someone jump-start her car earlier by the ferry. A real pain, but we got it going."

The man seemed confused. "Maybe I should just call Mr. Holliday to double-check."

"I think that's a great idea," Cookie said as he and Jamie exchanged a glance. Before the man could respond, Cookie took the bag and shoved it into him, knocking the guy backward and onto the ground.

Jamie and Cookie darted for the gate, and once outside, kept running to their car. Jamie fished for her keys in her bag while running and almost tripped over Cookie, who was keeping an impressive pace.

Cookie glanced behind him. "He's up and moving," he yelled, his breath quickening with the pace of his feet.

The two hustled to the car, and Jamie turned over the engine before the questioner made it to the gate. She peeled out of the parking space, leaving their pursuer by the gate, nothing more than a figure in her rearview mirror. A downpour of rain erupted, and water rushed onto her windshield. She slowed down, not wanting to hydroplane and ruin her escape.

Cookie's breathing was still heavy, as was hers.

Jamie wiped the sweat from her brow. "You owe me a new set of jumper cables."

"I haven't run that hard since Jenny Williams's dad caught me kissing her on the porch," Cookie said between huffs.

The two worked to catch their breath, their gasps as loud as the air conditioner, which was blowing cool comfort on their faces. Cookie's forehead still glimmered with rain droplets, his dark hair flat and mussed from the downpour.

Jamie's body began to chill from sitting in wet clothes. "You realize we're going to have another problem now, right?"

"Marcus knows we were on the boat?"

She nodded. "Marcus knows we were on the boat."

CHAPTER EIGHTEEN

"T HAT WAS EXCITING," COOKIE SAID as he sat in the passenger's seat of her car, peeling pistachios and dropping the salty shells into the cup holder.

Jamie stared at him, making note of the mess he was making in her front seat. "Are you going to clean that up?" She glanced down at the discarded halves with a smirk on her face. "And how can you eat right now after what just happened?"

Cookie shrugged. "You know me. I can always eat, and all that running made me hungry. I need real food now. How about tacos? Tacos are good."

"My car still smells like jalapeno poppers. Tacos are a no-go." The two had driven around for a while, making sure no one had followed them from the marina. Confident that they had left their trouble at the dock, Jamie pulled into her regular space behind Hemingway's. "We can have Marty make us something while we take a look at the journal and figure out what to do next."

Jamie and Cookie took the side door into Hemingway's and moved toward a corner booth they called the conference table. Marty tried to keep it open as much as possible since it doubled as a meeting area and makeshift office for the duo. Unfortunately, his way of keeping it open was to leave dirty beer glasses on the table. Jamie wrinkled her nose at the cloudy pilsner glasses housing small amounts of stale beer and God only knew what else. She pushed everything to one corner.

They slid into the booth, and Jamie put the bag next to her on the seat. Marty threw them a nod across the room, and Cookie gave him a signal for a round of drinks. He yelled to Marty, "And some food, por favor!" Cookie would be hungry at his own funeral.

Jamie pulled out the journal she'd taken from Marcus's boat. She scooted closer to Cookie so that he would be able to better read the journal alongside her. She tended to read more quickly than him, so she waited for his nod of approval to turn the page.

"A lot of this is just rambling," she said. "What happened each day, ideas for photography shoots…"

"It's a snapshot into her life, what was important to her, right?" Cookie asked. "You know that sometimes the little things lead us to the big things."

They continued reading together, and Jamie felt her heart rate quicken each time she saw her name written. "Listen to this. She wrote that Brian said I couldn't be trusted because I walked out on the family. Maybe she wanted to talk to me about her trouble, and they told her not to?"

"You can bring it up at the next family reunion," Cookie riffed. "But it won't make you popular."

Jamie wrinkled her nose. "I lost that popularity contest a long time ago. You know, Brian hasn't called once to ask how things are going. You think that's weird?"

"Honey, your entire family is weird. I don't think there's anything that's out of bounds where they're concerned."

"Good point."

They continued flipping the pages. Cookie pointed to a paragraph decorated by doodles of flowers and other scribbles. Jamie went back to the page she remembered reading on the boat. They had a second name.

"Here it is," she said. "See this name? Ritchie? Isn't that Elena's brother's name? The one in the cell phone? Clearly, she had something going on with him."

Cookie agreed. "Definitely need to do some work to figure out why Kristen had his number in a burner phone. It's not like we can just call the number and ask him."

Cookie reached over to flip a few pages forward. Jamie shot him the stink eye in jest, but he ignored her as he always did. "Check this out. It's like some random notes about where some people are eating dinner or walking their dogs, almost like—"

"A surveillance journal?"

He smiled, tapping his finger on the open page. "Yeah, like she was passing the time and just writing whatever she saw. Like she's bored to death."

Jamie nudged Cookie with her elbow. "Listen to this. One of the things she writes about is how she feels like she's being pushed to do things she doesn't want to do. You think she means Brian? Or could it be Marcus?"

Cookie shrugged, keeping his attention focused on the notes. "Brian might have been involved. Did she have any other family that she was close to?"

"Not that I know of."

Cookie returned to skimming the pages. "You know, she writes about different places and gives pretty sharp detail, but it's all kind of rambling. Also lots of abbreviations—no idea what it means. I'm thinking that maybe the places she was writing about involve jobs she was working. Maybe we can check a few places and see what turns up. She has some initials and numbers here. It means something, but I don't know what."

Jamie also found more guarded musings about whether to stay in the family business or leave for something else. It sounded as though someone was putting a great deal of pressure on Kristen to take on work that she really didn't want to do, although she never wrote exactly what the work entailed.

The next page contained several rows of numbers, each row with three sets of numbers. Jamie stared at the numbers for several moments, prompting Cookie to ask, "What is it?"

"You see these numbers?"

"Yep, lots of numbers. Looks like a code of some sort. You know what they mean?"

Jamie ran her finger over the page. "This is a book cypher. Pretty basic."

"And you know this because…"

"I know this because I taught it to her. Just for fun, really, because she wanted to know how to hide information in case she ever needed a reason."

Cookie leaned closer and studied the numbers. "So, this means that we need the key text, and we don't have it."

She nodded. "There's another book out there that unlocks this code." Jamie thought about her time on the boat. "I didn't see another book anywhere, not in the bedroom, in the drawers…"

"Maybe she gave it to someone else for safekeeping."

That made sense. She had trusted Connie with the key to the boat drawer, but who would she have trusted with the second half of this puzzle? It would have had to be someone she could trust, but Jamie had yet to find many people who fit in that category.

Cookie continued looking at the numbers on the page. "We'll figure this out, don't worry." He signaled to the journal. "Keep going, let's see what else is here."

She flipped to the end of the journal and noticed a small notation on the back cover in the same handwriting. It simply said *John Constantine.* She showed it to Cookie. "I saw this name in Marcus Holliday's office. It's a comic book character. What do you think it means? I can't believe that it's a coincidence. Not with the whole Natasha Irons identity on FriendConnect."

"Here we go, my hungry friends." Marty brought the pair two draft beers and a huge basket of fried cod and French fries, then bussed the table of the stale beer glasses. Following close behind him was Deuce, the scent of food too much for him to resist. He wobbled along, prancing as much as a bulldog could muster. Cookie's face lit up as soon as he laid eyes on dinner, while Jamie was happy to see her pooch.

She leaned down to pet him. "Are you having fun with Uncle Marty?" She scratched his jowls and petted his head. "Don't eat too much fried food. It's not good for you." That statement most likely went in one doggie ear and out the other. She looked up at Marty. "Thanks for keeping him today."

Marty winked at the dog. "I should be paying you. Deuce is great with the ladies and great for tips. And I promise he's been outside a lot today. The waitresses love taking him for walks."

Even being raised in a bar, her pooch had had a far better upbringing than Jamie had.

"You're my man, Marty," Cookie said as he quickly claimed a handful of fries and put them in his mouth. Jamie reached for the beer and took a sip then pulled a fry from Cookie's plate. She reached down and gave it to Deuce, who chomped at the food, barely missing her fingers.

Marty looked down at Deuce. "Don't let her buy your love so cheaply, Deuce."

Jamie shot Marty the stink eye and returned her affections to her dog, petting his head and feeding him more bar food.

Cookie chided her. "You just said not to eat too much fried food, and now you're giving him fries?"

"One fry," she corrected.

Cookie stuffed several more fries in his mouth. "I'm just sayin'."

Marty made a nod toward the journal. "Got another job, eh?"

She nodded. "Something like that."

Marty had a clear "don't ask, don't tell" policy at Hemingway's. While he heard everything, he pretended to be dumb as a box of rocks if a delicate subject came up. It was just good business.

Marty left them to their food and speculation. Cookie seemed more interested in the former at the moment.

Jamie nudged him. "Cookie, take a breath. And leave some for me." She took a long draw from her beer. "Damn, I hate sharing food with you."

"I don't share," he replied.

"Exactly."

They made short work of the meal and left nothing but crumbs and two empty beer glasses. Jamie was ready to get back on the trail. "Let's move. We need to figure out the John Constantine thing and why he's in Kristen's journal."

Cookie wiped his mouth with a napkin, crumpled it, and tossed it on the plate. "Are you going to call Brian with an update?"

She thought for a moment. "Yes, but I need to figure out my angle. He's obviously hiding some things, even after I told him he had to be completely straight with me if I helped him find Kristen. I want to make sure I leverage the information I have in the right way."

Cookie wiped the salt off his hands then reached around Jamie's shoulder to give her a squeeze. "Sorry your family is so screwed up. I can't imagine not being able to trust your own parents."

She felt a pang of sadness but quickly pushed it down. "Well, I've got my own family—I have you, Erin, Marty, and Deuce. I'm good."

He nodded. "And you can borrow my mom anytime. If you need some motherly advice, a good meal, whatever, she'll take care of you."

"I know she would. And hey, if you ever need a crazy woman to sell your car out from under you, you can borrow my mom."

"Seems like a fair trade," Cookie deadpanned. He pulled a five-dollar bill out of his wallet and left it on the table for the waitress. "Let's get out of here."

The two went upstairs to Jamie's loft to get back to work. They needed to find John Constantine, figure out what role Ritchie had played in Kristen's life, and deduce who had the missing text that would crack the numeric code in her journal. Kristen's life may have been a mystery, but Jamie was determined to make sure her death wouldn't be.

She owed her niece that much.

CHAPTER NINETEEN

A LONG DAY OF DETAILED INVESTIGATIVE work had been followed by a late night of drowning their sorrows. Kristen's death and her connection to the Deltone family had weighed mightily upon Jamie and Cookie, and they'd relieved the pressure the only way they knew how—at the helm of Marty's bar.

Marty had been a bit heavy-handed with the pours.

Jamie woke up the next morning facedown on her bed with Deuce snoring loudly on the floor next to her. Her hair was a tangled mess of random strands sticking out every which way. She pushed it out of her face and glanced around the room. The room spun, and a touch of nausea washed over her, so she retreated to her pillow, facedown once again. After a few seconds, she tried again, more slowly this time, and when she looked toward her small living room, she saw Cookie scrunched up on the couch, his ass hanging halfway off the cushions. He could hit the floor at any moment. What the...

Tequila shots. It was all coming back now.

She remained on all fours while she gently slid off her mattress. Then she stood still for a few moments so the floor would stop moving. "Jose Cuervo is not your friend," she muttered. Jamie took her sweet time in getting to the bathroom, where she brushed her teeth and cleaned up the hot mess that was her hair.

After pulling herself together, she walked over to Cookie, leaned over, and shook him firmly. "Cookie, wake up. I feel like crap, and it's all your fault."

Cookie's breathing stuttered, but he didn't move. She shook him with more force, her hands on his shoulders, rocking his entire upper body in an effort to jar him awake.

"Stop it, Jamie. I hate you right now." Cookie's voice was muffled by the couch cushion in which his face was buried.

"No, hate comes your way, Cookie. You're the one who pushed the tequila shots."

He tilted his head upward. "It seemed like a good idea at the time." His head plopped back down on the safety of the cushions. "And Marty wasn't helping, either. His pours were heavier than a barbell."

"Cookie." She pushed his legs aside and sat on a tiny corner of the couch. "We need to talk about what I asked you to do last night."

"Nothing happened last night," Cookie joked. "I mean, I'm sorry. I don't see you that way."

She reached over and pinched his arm hard. "You should be so lucky."

She then rested her arm on his leg, which took up most of the couch cushion. "Seriously, Cookie. You know what we need to do today."

That did it. Cookie groaned and turned his body, which prompted Jamie to move off the couch. He sat up, mostly, revealing his Hawaiian shirt, which was a wrinkled flurry of flowers. His hair fared far better than hers. "I know what you want me to do, and I'm telling you that I don't want to go."

"I know, but I think it would be good for you. It isn't his fault, you know."

Cookie looked her in the eye for the first time. "If he had been a better friend, maybe Manny would still be alive."

"There's only so much one person can do," Jamie replied. "You know that better than most people."

Cookie brushed his hair to the side and rubbed the alcohol-fueled sleep from his eyes. "I haven't seen him since the funeral."

"I know he's reached out to you, and you never responded."

Cookie remained silent.

"I think it's time," Jamie continued. "You have to admit that he's a solid lead. He can give us information on the Deltones and a read on what's going on right now when it comes to family territories."

Cookie remained on the couch, his gaze traveling past Jamie. After a few moments of silence, he said, "Let me get cleaned up, and then I'll come back."

"So you'll do it?"

He nodded. "Okay. Let's go see Albert."

It had been almost two years since Jamie had last visited this neighborhood. Her dashboard clock told her it was almost lunchtime, and the sunlight streaming through her car windows proved bright and fierce. This particular area housed an eerie mix of hope and despair, much like the halls of most high schools. She glanced over at Cookie, who had been unusually quiet on the drive over. The combination of a fading hangover coupled with apprehension kept his mood more subdued than usual.

They sat in her Tahoe for a good fifteen minutes, deciding when the time would be right to walk up the steps to the neatly kept house with its fresh butterscotch-colored paint and mended fence. A new row of violet flowers had been planted by the front porch. Care had been taken there.

The neighbors seemed a bit out of place for the area, but that was precisely the point. Stepford wife starter home on the outside, but on the inside... not so much.

Jamie kept her eyes on the front door, and it opened. A Hispanic man emerged. He was bald and had full-sleeve tats on both arms, so colorful that she could see them clearly from her car window. His stare would have melted snow in Denver upon first glance.

Jamie remained still, watching him come closer. She rolled down the car window, her eyes studying him as he walked to her car. He rested his forearm on the open space. "If you're doing surveillance, you suck at it." Then he cracked a smile and extended his hand to her. "It's good to see you, Jamie."

She squeezed Albert's hand then released it. "How's it going, Albert? I wish I could say I'm here just to chat."

"*Mija*, nobody ever comes here just to chat."

He glanced at the passenger's side. "Hey, Cookie."

Cookie cleared his throat. "Hey" was all he offered in return.

Albert signaled to the house. "So, you want to come in?"

Jamie shook her head. "No, too many ears in there, I bet. How many kids you got right now?"

He smiled. "Four. Just got two brothers trying to break from gang life. We may need to send them farther north, though. They got people lookin' for them. So here we are… hiding in the suburbs. At least our anonymous benefactor keeps us covered."

"Anonymous benefactor?"

"Yeah. He makes sure we have everything we need."

Jamie thought about a halfway house for gang members smack in the middle of this little neighborhood. "I don't think anyone will look for you here."

"The kids are good. They work hard—painting, fixing stuff, helping neighbors with projects." He held his hand up. "All closely supervised, of course. I'm working on some job training for them in San Antonio. We've got several kids out of the life and living straight now. Sometimes we lose a few, but what can you do?"

"Must be tough."

"Losing Manny was tough," Cookie said.

"Yes, it was," Albert replied. He seemed to consider saying more then looked at Jamie again. "So, you didn't come to talk about the old days. Why are you hanging out in front of my place?"

Jamie explained how Boxer had kidnapped Marissa and planned on handing her over to Acuna thugs in exchange for business. Then she told him about finding Kristen with a two-dollar bill in her pocket.

"Wow, when you jump in it, you're in it."

Jamie nodded. "You know how it is. Sometimes you don't go looking for trouble. It just finds you."

"Girl, it's got your address." He looked down at the street. "So, what do you want from me?"

Jamie tapped her finger on her steering wheel. "Look, I know you still keep your eye on what's going down in that world. You have to. I need you to tell me what you know about Marissa Deltone."

Albert let out a low whistle. "Wow. You jump right in there, don't you?"

Jamie nodded. "I helped her with something, and she owes me."

"She's the baby, but she's tough, you know? You piss her off, and it's lights out." He then added, "But she follows the family code, makes a big deal about it on the street. No kids, no wives. Only one for one direct. The Deltones run things old school, and they're not afraid to take out one of their own if they betray the family."

Jamie had heard the rumor that the Deltone family had put a hit on one of its own, an uncle that wasn't following the family creed. The guy hadn't been seen in person for a couple of years. The official Deltone line was that Big Mike Deltone was running some business in Mexico City, but others on the fringe of the business speculated the fishes in the Gulf of Mexico had digested him long ago.

Albert knew more than he was telling. She knew it, and he knew she knew it. Keeping his pulse on the families meant keeping his own kids off the street. Keep your enemies closer and all that...

"I think my niece, Kristen, was involved with a guy named Ritchie. Does that name mean anything to you? Maybe Ritchie Mendoza?"

Albert rubbed his chin. "Yeah, I know him. The guy has a reputation for being a loose cannon sometimes, you know? Gets hot fast, jumps too quick at small stuff, not much discipline."

"Who does he work for?"

"Right now, he works for the Deltones. Manages their street soldiers, the young kids coming up. I think he worked for a Jersey family a few years ago."

"Why would the Deltones keep him if he can be a problem?"

"He's a top enforcer. He gets results, keeps people in line. Plus, his grandfather was friends with Abuelo Deltone. Family courtesy."

"You ever hear the name John Constantine?"

He shook his head. "I don't think he runs with our group. Maybe his crew is north."

"Here's the thing," Jamie said. "I need to talk with Marissa."

Albert waved off her comment with both hands. "Oh, I don't know about that. Word gets out that I'm talking..."

"Lock," Jamie reasoned. "We saved her ass from Boxer. She owes me."

"And you owe me, Albert," Cookie added.

Albert's eyes locked with Cookie's. He glanced down at the street then looked directly at Cookie. "All right, look. Marissa's abuela is at St. Mark's Senior Care in Corpus. She visits her every Sunday afternoon after church."

Jamie wrinkled her brow. "Drug runners going to church?"

Albert shrugged. "Hey, we're all sinners. God doesn't grade on a curve, you know?"

A part of Jamie hoped Albert was wrong about that. Stealing from a grocery store and murdering a family shouldn't get the same consideration in Heaven. That was her position, anyway.

"You didn't hear it from me, right? I don't need Marissa coming up here and putting my head in a vice."

Jamie nodded. "You're a good guy, Albert."

He tapped the car door then stood up and pointed a finger at her. "Yeah, don't be spreading that around." He looked at Cookie. "You know, we named this place after Manny."

"Too bad he isn't around to see it," Cookie replied.

"That's why I'm doing what I do here. Manny was my best friend. You know that."

"You should have been a better friend to him before he died, Albert."

Jamie jumped in. "Cookie—"

Albert stopped her. "It's okay, Jamie. He's right. We were both in the life, and even though I thought about getting out, I didn't have the courage to do it, not until Manny was gone."

Cookie nodded, his face softening. "At least you admit it."

Albert hung his head for a moment. "Manny was my friend, and I'd do anything to have a second shot. I know I failed him. And you."

Jamie watched as Albert turned away from the car and walked up the steps back inside his suburban halfway house for wayward teenage gangbangers. She wondered what Manny might have become if there had been a place like that for him. Cookie looked out the window, and Jamie believed that he wondered the same thing. Manny's death was the catalyst that helped others like him, and while it was a cold comfort, it would have to do.

CHAPTER TWENTY

THE DRIVE AFTER MEETING ALBERT had been a quiet one. Jamie knew she had pushed Cookie to go with her, and judging from his silence, she couldn't tell if he was upset or contemplative. She had hoped seeing Albert and speaking to him directly would ease some of his pain, but Jamie now wondered if her strategy had been a sound one. The silence drove her crazy, but she knew how to navigate these uncomfortable moments. After several failed attempts to engage Cookie in conversation, she relented and turned on the radio. She turned on a country-western station for the sole reason that she knew it bugged the hell out of him. Forget waterboarding—if you wanted Cookie to talk, try K-Country 96.7 FM.

He lasted less than five minutes. "Seriously, J, turn that crap off."

"Are you done punishing me?"

"I'm not punishing you. I'm just... thinking."

"About?"

"About Albert and Manny and why Manny should still be here."

She couldn't argue with him. "You're right, you know. Manny should be here. Manny should be here, and Kristen should be alive. Lots of shoulds in our world." She looked over at her friend, who seemed a bit smaller than usual, hunched in the passenger's seat. "I'm sorry I made you go with me. I thought it was best."

The façade cracked, and a sliver of a smile emerged on Cookie's face. "You didn't make me, and you were right. I needed to go. It's just hard digging up these demons."

"Let's stop for Mexican food and eat our feelings. My treat."

Jamie pulled into the parking lot of Taqueria San Juan on Grand Avenue. The meeting with Albert had picked at the wound that was Manny's memory, and they needed time to process what they had learned before attempting to track down Marissa. Jumping from one fire directly into the next would certainly burn their investigation to the ground. They needed time to recover their balance, and that called for the best Tex-Mex on the island.

Once a local favorite, Taqueria San Juan had grown in popularity, and now the pair had to compete for seats with college students, snowbirds, and tourists. Jamie resented the hell out of it. She would have preferred for the place to stay off the tourist radar, but she understood the family who owned it needed all the tourists to make a living. So she stuffed her grudge in her pocket and elbowed a few hungover kids when she spotted a corner booth by a window. She signaled to Cookie to make way. The restaurant's atmosphere was bustling. Multiple conversations were happening at once, and the background noise of waitresses handling plates and glasses further amped up the decibel level. Cookie plowed ahead of her, making sure that everyone made room for him to pass. People couldn't ignore Cookie's presence even if they wanted to. He could have helped Moses part the Red Sea and would have done it in half the time.

The waitress smiled at them but didn't come to their table. She knew to bring two iced teas and two family specials—chicken enchiladas, tostadas, refried beans, and rice. A few moments later, their waitress placed two large Styrofoam cups of iced tea on the table, nodded, and left. Jamie reached for her cup and drank from the straw for several seconds. "Best tea in town. I don't know what they put in this stuff. I might like this even more than beer." She winked at him. "Don't tell Marty."

Jamie's attempt at comic relief had fallen flat. Cookie obliged with a half-hearted smile, but it was clear that the meeting with Albert still weighed heavily on him. She signaled to his glass. "Drink your tea. You'll feel better."

Cookie took a drink and returned the cup to the table. "I want to be mad at Albert, but I know Manny's death wasn't his fault. Manny never listened to me, either. They were both trapped in that life, but I see Albert, and it reminds me that he made it out and Manny didn't."

Jamie leaned in closer to the table. "Perfectly normal to want to make someone responsible."

"The Deltones are responsible." Cookie sipped his tea. "I know I need to place blame where it belongs."

"Do we really know that, though? Marissa said they weren't responsible. Why would she lie?"

Cookie gave her an incredulous look. "Because she was tied up in a warehouse and wanted us to let her go?"

Jamie wasn't sure responsibility for Manny's death should be placed at the Deltones' feet—at least, not completely. But she knew she had to tread this conversation with care. Cookie needed answers and needed someone to be held accountable for his little brother's death. She wanted to give him that. "Look, we cut her loose from Boxer's clutches. She knows she owes us a favor. And we're going to collect."

The twinkle in Cookie's eyes returned. "Okay, Miss Badass, we'll see how this goes."

Their waitress soon returned with two family specials. Steam was coming off the refried beans, and there was far more rice than either could finish. "Here you go. The usual." She turned to Cookie and winked at him. "You should try the chicken tortilla soup sometime. Best in Texas."

"Just might do that next time," he replied.

The waitress left to tend to her other tables, while Jamie and Cookie immediately picked up their forks. Jamie scooped up a healthy serving of enchilada, gooey cheese extending in a long string from her utensil to the plate. "I think that waitress likes you."

He smiled. "It's the power of the Hawaiian shirt."

Eating overcame conversation, and their table was quiet for several minutes while they enjoyed their meal. Cookie was always the first to finish because his bites were like his stride, covering more territory than his partner's.

Jamie had one particular concern about meeting Marissa, and while she hated bringing it up, she knew it had to be addressed. "If we actually catch Marissa at her grandmother's place, it's going to be difficult for you. Are you going to be able to keep your feelings in control? It's a big ask, I know."

Cookie reached for his tea and took a drink. "I can handle it." He looked directly into Jamie's eyes. "How about you? Are you ready for this? The anger, the rawness, it can catch you off guard. I know, speaking from experience…"

Jamie nodded, realizing she had been so worried about Cookie's response to Marissa that she had failed to give her own enough consideration. "You're right. I have no idea what it will feel like being face-to-face with her. This is the first case we've worked where we're both so personally involved."

"It sucks," Cookie observed. "Let's never do this again."

Jamie finished her enchiladas, leaving little except a spattering of rice. She tossed the napkin on her plate to signal she was finished, and their waitress appeared almost on cue to exchange the empty platters for the check.

Cookie stood up from the booth, and Jamie followed, taking the bill to the register to pay for their meal. Cookie left a five on the table as a tip and waited for Jamie to finish squaring the bill. He opened the door and held it while she walked through then waited while a family with three small children came through into the restaurant.

"Nice manners," Jamie said. "Your mama taught you well." She pushed the unlock button on her key ring and pulled the driver's side door open.

They both settled into their seats. Jamie tossed her bag in the back seat, while Cookie cranked the air conditioner on full blast. Warm air assaulted them, blowing Jamie's stray strands from her ponytail in random directions.

"It's going to be okay." Jamie forced a small smile. "Whatever happens, we're going to be okay."

Cookie nodded and reached over to give her hand a quick squeeze. Jamie wasn't sure the words she uttered were entirely true, and she was pretty sure he knew it. But whatever happened next, they would face it together.

CHAPTER TWENTY-ONE

"SO, THIS IS IT, EH? I expected it to have more security or reinforcements or something." Cookie craned his head to peer through the car window and surveyed the mediocre medical facility that was St. Mark's Senior Care. The five-floor facility's façade was composed of putty-colored stucco and redbrick accents. The front door was flanked by a long front porch with a row of rocking chairs, mostly unoccupied, except for two elderly ladies sitting next to each other, engaged in more talking than rocking.

Jamie and Cookie pulled into the parking lot, sat for a moment, and discussed how to approach Marissa. "Should we wait for her in the lobby, or does she have some super-secret back door reserved for coastal kingpins?" Jamie asked.

That did it. Cookie finally cracked a smile. "It could be hidden behind a bookshelf and lead out to an armored car."

Jamie inhaled and let out a long breath. In the background of her mind, she understood the painful importance of this meeting, but now, sitting in the parking lot, the gravity of walking through those doors flooded her senses. "So I think the best strategy is just to go in and see if we can get in during normal visitation hours."

"What if they only let family in? If you lie and they find out, we'll be dragging the river, looking for your body."

"Thanks for the reminder."

"That's what I'm here for."

Jamie cautioned her friend. "We need to keep it in check. She doesn't get under our skin. Right?"

Cookie stopped and looked Jamie in the eye. "We discussed this in the restaurant. I understand what's at stake here, okay? I'm not going to blow it by being emotional."

Jamie nodded, reached over and touched his forearm briefly, then pulled away. "I know, I know. I'm not questioning your professionalism, okay? But this is the first case where we both have personal ties, and there's a reason why we don't usually work personal cases—because they're messy and complicated. I'm not doubting your ability, just recognizing what we're taking on here."

The two sat together, no words between them, for several moments, until the weight of the silence proved too stifling.

"Okay, let's do this," Cookie said.

The pair walked through the front door, working to look as friendly and nonthreatening as possible. Cookie prepared to turn on the charm, which would give them every possible advantage. Jamie figured it best to let him take the lead in sweet-talking the receptionist.

It would take some effort. The woman had a stern teacher thing going on, with narrow black-rimmed glasses. And her gray-streaked hair was pulled so tightly into a bun that Jamie figured the woman must have been receiving a mini face-lift from the strain.

Cookie leaned on the counter, smiling at the receptionist. "Hi, I'm wondering if you can tell me which room Mrs. Deltone is in? We're friends of Marissa's."

Jamie almost choked on the lie.

"Do they know you're coming?"

He shook his head. "No, we weren't sure if we were going to be able to make it." He leaned in even further, his elbows holding his weight, his smile becoming more personal, connected. "We wanted to surprise her."

The receptionist studied Cookie's face, her frown easing, not to a pleasant expression but one that was a solid distance from angry. "She really doesn't like surprises, you know. Hold on a second."

Ms. Stern Face made a call then said, "She's in room one-twelve." She leaned toward Cookie and whispered, "Don't stay too long. She tires very easily these days."

Cookie nodded, while Jamie kept her expression straight, surprised that they had gained access to an important family member so easily. Then again, how dangerous could the senior Mrs. Deltone be if she had to live in a nursing home?

They walked down the hallway and came upon Room 112 at the end. They knocked, and an elderly voice said, "Come in."

Jamie and Cookie pushed open the door to find a sweet elderly lady, with smiling eyes and short gray hair, resting comfortably in a reclining bed. She was propped up by pink pillows, and her legs were covered by a crocheted blanket. She wore a navy floral nightgown, and the only thing out of the ordinary was the gun she pointed at the door.

"Forgive the hardware, kids. You know how it is."

Jamie liked the woman already. She held her hands up. "Hello, Mrs. Deltone. We're very sorry to disturb you. We're here looking for Marissa. We need to speak with her."

Marissa appeared from the bathroom, where the door had been cracked but the lights remained off. She walked toward her grandmother and sat on the bed next to her. "You can put the piece down now. They'll take it from you if they find it again. You know that."

Marissa stared at Cookie. "Manny's older brother, right? Nice to see you again."

He nodded but said nothing. Jamie could see his jaw clench, the tightness creating a small dimple in his cheek.

Jamie pushed to keep the conversation from turning to Manny's death. She didn't need Cookie unraveling before they got the information they needed. "Marissa, we need a favor. Can we talk about this outside? I'm not sure if your abuela needs to hear this."

Marissa waved off the comment. "She knows where all the bodies are buried." Marissa exchanged glances with her grandmother. "She's like a vault. Knows everything and guards it carefully."

Now she'd heard everything. The women in this family ran a tough crew. Even Grandma had a homicide history. She had such a sweet face, to the point that Jamie could almost forget the woman had greeted her by pointing a firearm at her.

Jamie resisted asking further questions about Abuela's rap sheet. Instead, she asked, "You know that favor we did for you earlier?"

Abuela Deltone gave her granddaughter a puzzled glance.

"These two are the ones who found me after the Boxer thing," she said. "They got me out of there."

The senior Deltone shuddered. "He's a toad. No code with that one. Someone needs to take him out."

"Maybe someday," Marissa replied. Then she looked at Jamie. "It depends on what you're asking for."

Until this moment, Cookie had remained quiet in the corner, taking up no space in the conversation. He took a single step from the back corner of the room, making his presence known. His tone was even and calm. "You might be rotting in the ocean somewhere if we didn't rescue you. We all know that." He took one step closer, and though he closed the space, Marissa didn't move one inch. "It's time for you to return the favor. You owe far more than what we're asking for."

Marissa wouldn't be so easily convinced. "I suppose it depends on what you want me to do for you."

Jamie placed her hand on Cookie's arm, signaling she would take over. "We need to make sure Boxer isn't an issue anymore for Erin. I'm not saying he should disappear. We don't need heat, and we don't want that on our conscience. He should know in very clear terms that she's off-limits. After all, this battle is between Boxer and your family. He just used Erin's building as a safe house. She had no idea anything was going down."

"Boxer was happy to hand you over to the Acunas to do God-knows-what, so this is good for you, too," Cookie added. "You need to let people know they can't take a Deltone hostage and walk away from that." He appealed to her pride and connected.

Marissa seemed amused by his comment. "I'm quite aware of how I need to respond. And what it means to my family's credibility."

"We have a bit of experience here, you know," Abuela Deltone said.

Jamie could feel her stoic expression crack a small smile. She couldn't help herself. Abuela was a handful. Jamie then took the lead. "I also want you to tell me what you know about my niece, Kristen. I know she was working for you at the time she died."

Marissa nodded, her expression more serious. No smile, no bravado on her features. "I'm sorry to hear of your loss. I will tell you that no head of this family ordered that she be... handled... in such a way."

Cookie scoffed. "Handled? She's dead, Marissa, but I suppose you're pretty used to that. People just die in your service, but that's part of the deal."

"You're talking about Manny, right?" Marissa asked.

Jamie studied Cookie's face, wondering if he would be able to keep his composure now that Marissa had poked at his wound. He didn't move or flinch. He said, "I deserve to know the truth about what happened to my brother. You claim you didn't kill him. Why should I believe you?"

"He was a good kid, that one," Grandma Deltone added. "Loyal. Didn't have the heart or the stomach for any of the tough stuff."

Cookie looked at Marissa's grandmother, his body becoming less rigid, his shoulders releasing their guarded position. "Thank you, Mrs. Deltone. He should still be here."

Marissa moved closer to her grandmother's bed. "I'm going to tell you something. You may believe me; you may not. I have no control over that."

Cookie stood with his arms crossed. "I'm listening."

"We knew Manny was being recruited by the Acuna family to run some logistics."

Cookie couldn't cover the surprise on his face. "I've never heard this before. That's not true."

"Again, you can believe me or not. That's up to you. We knew he was talking to them. The Acunas were trying to get information about our work. This kind of stuff travels fast back to us, you know?"

Jamie had been quiet, letting Cookie lead the search for answers, but she felt the need to keep Marissa talking. "You didn't retaliate and kill him because he was talking to them?"

She shook her head. "Manny came to us, told us the truth. He wasn't going to switch loyalties. He even told us some of what he learned about their operation." Marissa sat down next to her grandmother on her bed, her body barely balancing on a small space so as not to crush the fragile woman. "Manny's death is on the Acunas, not us. They killed him because he refused their offer, and they gave us credit to make it look like we were in the business of killing our own too easily. It makes them look like a better alternative."

"So the two-dollar bill signal?" Jamie asked. "That was the Acuna family making sure they put it on you?"

She nodded. "It keeps the cops looking our way and makes us look ruthless." She looked at Cookie. "We do… difficult work. But we aren't careless. And we don't throw our own people away unless they put our family in jeopardy. Manny didn't do that. And we aren't responsible for what happened to him."

Jamie knew Cookie well enough to see that Marissa's words had affected him, made him consider that the truth he thought he knew might actually not have been the truth at all. She had to admit that she believed Marissa. The woman seemed sincere, as though she wanted Cookie to know that her family didn't own Manny's death. Jamie wanted to give Cookie his answers, but she was also still waiting for hers.

"What can you tell me about Kristen?"

Marissa stood up from her grandmother's side. "Well, that one was more difficult because she got involved with one of our… lead coordinators."

"Ritchie?" Jamie asked.

Marissa's face registered recognition. She tried to hide it, but they both knew Jamie had confirmed the identity of Kristen's relationship within the Deltone family. "He has difficulty with restraint at times, but he is very good at what he does."

"What could Kristen have done that was so terrible that she deserved to die?"

Marissa held her hand up. "We never ordered that anything happen to her. Ritchie came to us after she had been found and said that she was alive when he left her at the house. He's done some stupid things, but I believe him."

"Someone left her in a foreclosed house alone to die," Jamie said. "Who would do such a horrific thing?"

Marissa stood stoically, her arms by her sides, her posture straight and strong. Jamie could see how this woman could lead a small army of men. Her calm confidence was impossible to ignore. "Kristen had been taking notes about our business, about our territories—specific dates and times of certain operations. Our intelligence told us that her father was trying to get cozy with the Acuna family and she was his way in. Maybe she betrayed the Acunas too."

A tightness filled Jamie's chest as she processed what Marissa had just shared. Brian had put his own daughter up to this work, and her loyalty to him was rewarded with her death? Cookie moved from the corner and stood next to Jamie. He didn't touch her, but his presence let her know he was there for her.

"This is Brian's fault?" Jamie still struggled to wrap her mind around the possibility that Brian would jeopardize his daughter's life for his personal gain so he could be in a position of true power.

"He's the reason she was in this situation," Marissa replied. "I think she liked Ritchie or at least saw some reason to be with him, and he was careless with how he talked. He took her into things where she had no business being. And we still have a problem, so if you need my help, I'm going to ask for yours in return."

Cookie scoffed at the comment. "You already owe us to be even. Now you want something else?"

"Wherever Kristen was making notes about... things... Ritchie didn't find it. That information is still out there somewhere. We need to get it back."

The missing journal. Jamie knew she had one of them, but Marissa's request meant that the second book, the one needed to decipher Kristen's code, was still out there. Where could Kristen have hidden it? She had been smart not to store both books together, but finding the journal was critical to everyone in that room. Or did someone else already have it? In the wrong hands, the journal could prove devastating for the Deltone family. Jamie and Marissa had a common goal. They needed to get the journal back before it fell into the wrong hands.

Jamie crossed her arms in front of her and considered Marissa's words. "Do you believe Ritchie? Really? That he left her at that house alive?"

Abuela Deltone, who had been quietly dozing on and off during their exchange, suddenly became more attentive to the conversation. "If Ritchie did anything, it wasn't under our direction. Bodies are bad for business. There are far more effective ways to keep associates in line. That's how I lead and how I taught Marissa to lead. I'm sorry you lost your niece, but she put herself in that situation. It was her decision to use Ritchie for information." So her sleeping was all a ploy of eavesdropping. The older woman turned her grandmotherly gaze to Cookie. "And Marissa gave you the truth about Manny freely. No strings attached. Because she knows what it is to lose someone and live without answers."

Jamie wondered when Kristen had realized that she had finally gone too far with a scam, the moment she realized that her current job was far more dangerous, the people far more nefarious, than anyone she had ever conned. Did she see her own end coming? Or did she just slip away, not realizing she would never wake up? Jamie's stomach still hurt, the pain of the truth about Kristen still finding its way into her bones.

"If I help you find Kristen's notes, I expect you to take care of Boxer. He is to make sure that Erin and her business, her customers, are all off-limits. He's not to even so much as sneeze in their direction."

Marissa nodded. "Oh, don't you worry. We are going to make sure Boxer is out of our business for good. And we'll make sure Erin is part of the deal. She seems like good people."

"One of the best," Jamie said.

"You have my word, as my abuela is my witness."

Marissa's grandmother said nothing but simply raised her hand in agreement. She then crossed her arms and closed her eyes. Old people could apparently sleep though anything, including a gang negotiation.

"It really is the men who make the messes, isn't it?" Marissa asked. "I suppose that makes us both the daughters of bad men. Your friend Erin too, yes? And Kristen. The men that have been lauded in fairy tales to care for us and protect us fall short. So we protect ourselves instead. They don't really control the battlefield—we only let them think they do. They believe they can do whatever they want to the women around them, but they don't understand how much power we wield because we don't flaunt it. We don't need the credit. The power is enough." She turned and smiled at her grandmother. "That's how we handle ours, anyway."

Jamie offered a small nod in acknowledgment of Marissa's truth. She was right. Jamie wouldn't admit it aloud, but she was right.

Marissa stepped back two steps, offering more space between her and Jamie. Cookie had since moved back against the wall, his shoulder next to the closed blinds covering the room's window. It seemed they had come to an agreement; they were all searching for the same thing but for different reasons. Jamie's chest was still tight with the knowledge that Marissa had shared with them. She needed to get out of there and make sense of what had transpired in the old woman's room.

"We'll be in touch," Jamie said.

"I know how to find you," Marissa replied.

Cookie nodded to Grandma Deltone then looked at Marissa. He said nothing but gave her a slight nod, a small concession, but huge by Cookie's standards.

Cookie opened the door, and Jamie followed him, neither looking back as it closed behind them. The woman they had once thought responsible for their loved ones' deaths was now an uneasy ally. That reality hung between them, an unspoken presence far more complicated than they ever could have imagined.

CHAPTER TWENTY-TWO

J AMIE AND COOKIE PARTED WAYS after their meeting with Marissa, each understanding that the other needed time alone to process what they had learned, to sit in solitary with the truth. They agreed to meet at Jamie's place the next morning to regroup and view Kristen's case with fresh eyes and the new knowledge of what she had been doing before she died.

Jamie had just finished running a brush through her hair when she heard a quick rap on the door and a key turning in the lock.

Cookie emerged a moment later, his hair still wet, probably fresh from a shower. He was dressed in the print of the day—a black shirt with white-etched flowers in rows down the front.

"New shirt?" Jamie didn't recognize the specific pattern. "I like it. It's subtle." She modified her comment. "Well, subtle for you, anyway."

"Thanks for the backhanded compliment," Cookie quipped as he walked over to her fridge. Deuce immediately perked up from his slumber once Cookie's hand grasped the refrigerator door handle. He opened it, reached for two water bottles, and handed one to Jamie. "You realize you have no food in your fridge."

"I have pickles. And blueberry jelly."

"That's disgusting."

"Who needs food with Marty downstairs?"

He shrugged. "Maybe some bagels or snacky things would be nice."

They sat together at her small table, drinking water and staring at nothing in particular. Deuce had decided to stay put since no food had been offered for his consideration. He snorted then closed his eyes, his nose creating a small whistling sound when he exhaled.

"You okay?" Jamie asked. "After the meeting yesterday?"

"I should ask the same thing," Cookie replied.

"I didn't like what she told me, but I believe what she told me. And I'm angry and sad for Kristen all at the same time."

Cookie tapped his fingers on the table. "I'm in the same place. I don't want to believe her, but I do. Manny's still not here, though."

Jamie leaned toward him and put her arm around his shoulders, resting her head on one. "Getting answers is a good thing. You know we don't always get them in our line of work."

He tilted his head and let it lean against hers for a moment. He then sat upright. "Okay, enough of that. Get off me."

"So salty this morning," she joked as she reached for her laptop. While waiting for it to boot up, she grabbed the water bottle and drank half its contents before placing it back down.

Cookie watched her, the humor plain on his face. "Little dehydrated, *mija*?"

"Shut up." She typed her password into her laptop. "I had one beer last night when I got back. One," she said with emphasis. "You can ask Marty. I was a total bore." Jamie directed the conversation back to Marissa and what the woman had shared with them the previous day. "So, what do we know now, assuming Marissa is telling the truth? Let's go through it all again."

Cookie rubbed his eyes and exhaled an exhausted breath. "*If* she's telling the truth, someone else saw Kristen after Ritchie left. And there's one more journal out there that completes the codebook she was creating about the Deltone business."

Jamie considered Cookie's summary of the previous day's events. "Kristen chose to hide one journal on Marcus Holliday's boat, right? Why?"

Cookie considered this. "She trusted him. It was convenient—an opportunity."

She ran her fingers through her hair and readjusted her ponytail. "Or both."

"Or both. Do you think he knew about it being there?"

Jamie typed his name into her online search engine, reading about Marcus's background again, hoping to find something she had missed during her preliminary investigation of him. "I'm not sure. The guy chasing us at the dock could have just been doing his job without Marcus knowing we might show up there. And he did let me search Kristen's locker without any problem. He opened it for me and let me take everything."

"True, but maybe whatever important was in there, he already took first."

"But the burner phone was in there, which leads us to Ritchie and his claim that Kristen was alive the last time he saw her."

Cookie made a clicking noise with his tongue. "Yeah, that doesn't make sense."

Jamie turned her laptop to show Cookie her online search results. "Look at this guy, Cookie. Comes from big family money, and no personal scandals here. Nothing. Is that even possible? Doesn't that kind of bank end up corrupting people? You can buy anything you want."

Cookie considered this point. "Maybe he's that one in a million? Super-rare moral guy who happens to be loaded."

"Well, if that's true, he's not just rare. He's a damn unicorn."

Cookie patted Jamie on the hand. "Well, maybe we should go see if that unicorn can give us the magic clue we need."

And with that, Jamie knew the next item on her schedule. She wondered if Marcus Holliday hated surprises as much as she did, not that she cared. He was now the most important thing on her list today.

Lucky him.

CHAPTER TWENTY-THREE

"H
I. WE'RE HERE TO SEE Marcus," Jamie said, leaning on the receptionist counter in a casual manner.

Cookie stood next to her, a winning grin on his face, full wattage, pointed at the young woman behind the front desk. If the girl were old enough to drink, it would have likely happened this year because her fleshy cheeks, straight blond hair, and young features all pointed to college age, sophomore at best. Jamie could see she wore a royal-blue T-shirt with the Texas A&M Corpus Christi logo on the front.

"Mr. Holliday is helping a student at the moment..."

Jamie waved her hand as if to dismiss any concern. "No worries, really. We'll just wait in his office like last time. We know where to go."

Cookie tapped the counter and gave the receptionist a wink. "Thanks for your help." He followed Jamie back down the hall toward Marcus's office. The door was closed, and Jamie tentatively reached for the knob and turned it. It was unlocked.

She stepped inside, with Cookie following close behind her, as if she would shield him from any danger that might leap from behind the door. Cookie closed it behind him, and the two stood, face-to-face, with one of Marcus's most private spaces—his office.

Jamie's steps came slowly, as though she were sneaking up on a friend. She moved timidly, carefully, until she came to the photos on the wall behind his desk. She glanced at his desk space but saw nothing of any interest—no papers, no planner, no scribbled notes or important phone number hastily written on a napkin. A Tiffany lamp made of stained glass, a pattern of beach waves decorating each panel, sat on the corner of the desk next to a glass jar half full of wrapped chocolate confections. A plain yellow notepad served as the centerpiece, but not a word or thought had been added to its surface.

This guy was good. Careful.

Cookie studied the photographs on a nearby wall. The three images, all related, showcased local themes. In the first one, a sandpiper, small in stature, stood alone on the beach, seemingly scanning the water for its next meal. The second image was of a seagull in flight, its body parallel to the ocean's waves. The third was of a local fishing boat known for bringing shrimp to the docks early in the morning for eager locals who stood in line to pick up a few pounds of the freshest seafood. Its name, *The Optimist's Club,* was painted in bright-blue script across its hull.

Cookie pointed to the photo. "Do you ever go get shrimp there?"

Jamie looked at him, and she was sure the stupidity of his question was evident in her expression. "Sure," she joked. "You know how I love to cook."

"My mom has me going there at least once a week to pick up shrimp. She swears they must have the best bait because the shrimp they catch are huge."

"I do like a good shrimp taco."

"I'll hook you up; don't worry."

Jamie studied the books, while Cookie took a cursory look around the office. He evaluated a set of golf clubs propped in the corner, some shrouded with black fuzzy covers.

"Why are some golf clubs covered and others aren't?" he asked. "I mean, do your favorite ones get to stay warm and the other ones know they aren't loved? How cruel."

"Who knows? Maybe the clubs double as dusters? I never understood how someone could waste an entire day playing golf." Jamie turned in Cookie's direction. "What's the point, really?"

Her attention turned back to Marcus's bookshelf, which lined the entire back wall of his office. A few bays were decorated with photos of Marcus standing next to people Jamie didn't recognize. Small wooden sculptures of island birds lined one shelf, while another shelf served as a display for seashells in every shape imaginable. A sand dollar had been placed in the middle of the arrangement.

Jamie read the names of the books lined up on Marcus's office shelves and noted an array of business books, memoirs, and local-interest books. *The Secret Life of Port Alene* bumped up against *A History of Fly Fishing*, with *Historic Corpus Christi* on the other side. He also seemed to have an affinity for thrillers, as Brad Meltzer, Lee Child, and Karin Slaughter took up considerable space with several titles per author. She turned her gaze upward to the row of books one step higher than eye level. Her eyes skimmed the row, and that was when she found it.

The Vagabond's Guide to Europe.

She knew that book.

She knew that book because she had given it to Kristen when the girl had started high school, before Jamie had made the list of family enemies. She signaled to Cookie. "Can you give me a boost?" she asked, pointing to the bookshelf.

Cookie took the few steps necessary to circumvent Marcus's desk and pushed his chair away to make room for his substantial presence. He placed his hands around Jamie's waist. "Ready?"

When she nodded, he hoisted her up a row with little effort, holding her suspended, allowing her to retrieve the book. Her forefinger slid across the top of it before she hooked it and pulled it toward her. Once the book was firmly in her hand, Cookie lowered her to the ground.

At that moment, Marcus Holliday walked through his office door, and his eyes immediately went to the book. "What are you doing with that?"

Jamie's stare threatened to burn through him. "I was going to ask you the same question."

CHAPTER TWENTY-FOUR

JAMIE CLUTCHED THE BOOK CLOSE to her chest as she stared at Marcus. Cookie kept his position close to his friend. The three stood frozen, each taking turns staring at one another. Marcus closed the door behind him and gestured to the two guest chairs opposite his desk. "Why don't you sit down?"

Cookie and Jamie exchanged a glance, and Jamie's nod was so small that it was barely detectable. Jamie walked over to claim a chair, and Cookie followed, sitting next to her. Marcus watched them as he moved to his seat.

The three of them all sat quietly, distrust in the air.

Jamie was the first to break the silence. "Why do you have this book?"

He tilted his head, looking more curious than angry about the fact that they had been in his office unattended. "What do you know about it?" Marcus's eyes moved between hers and the item she kept in her lap.

"I know that I gave it to Kristen a few years ago, so I would like to know why you now have it."

"How do you know I didn't just happen to have another copy of it?"

Jamie scoffed at the idea. "This isn't a very mainstream book. I mean, it was old when I bought it for her at a used bookstore. I doubt it's even still in print. Kristen was drawn to the title. She just had to have it." She turned the book over to reveal the small pink bookstore price tag, with a whopping two dollars and forty-nine cents printed on it. "I remember this sticker. I remember when I bought it. Too much of a coincidence."

Marcus leaned back in his chair, and his hand moved to his face, his fingers covering his lips. Jamie wondered if he was trying to decide whether or not to tell her the truth.

"Kristen gave it to me," he said simply.

"Why would she do that?" Jamie asked. "You seem like the kind of man who can travel wherever he would like at any time." She tapped the tome in her lap. "Without a poor girl's guidebook."

Cookie leaned forward in his chair, propping his palm on his knee. His posture was casual, his tone anything but. "We're not here to play games, Mr. Holliday."

Marcus held his hands in the air, his attention on Jamie. "Kristen didn't trust many people, and I'm sorry to say, she wasn't sure she could trust you, which is why she gave it to me." He pointed at Cookie. "And don't think I don't know that you have the other journal. You fit the description security gave me of two suspicious people boarding *Chelsea's Freedom*. I know her other journal is gone, and she trusted me to keep that safe too."

"You aren't very good at it," Jamie jabbed. "No offense, but maybe this skill isn't in your wheelhouse."

"Well, maybe your trustworthiness isn't a fair trade for being good at theft."

Cookie leapt to her defense, his stance moving from sitting to near standing. "You'd damn well better watch your tone here."

Marcus dug his thumb into his eye socket as if working away the underpinnings of a headache. "I'm not saying these things to hurt you. I'm only relaying what Kristen told me. She was unsure about being able to come to you for help, especially since her father had told her you couldn't be trusted."

Jamie inhaled deeply, holding her breath for several seconds before releasing it. A blow to the stomach would have been far kinder than Marcus's words. It had hurt to read it in Kristen's own handwriting, and hearing confirmation from Marcus's lips was akin to rubbing salt in a raw wound.

"Brian told her that?" she asked, already knowing the answer.

Marcus nodded. "Yes, and she told me about him, too. What a piece of work. So when you came here looking for information, and you said you were helping him, it just reinforced the idea that you were…"

"Untrustworthy." Knowing her niece didn't trust her when she died tightened the knot in her stomach and made it feel as if she were losing Kristen for a second time. It wasn't often that Jamie had no idea what to do next, but at that moment, she sat, taking in Kristen's perception of her through Marcus's account.

Cookie seemed to sense this and took the lead while she worked to get herself back in an investigative state of mind.

"Listen," Cookie said, "I can tell you that Jamie is one of the most trustworthy and loyal people out there." Jamie tried to interject, but he continued. "And Brian made sure that Kristen chose him over Jamie because he told her she had to. Jamie tried for years to help Kristen get away from his influence, and Brian knew it. So he made sure to cut her out of Kristen's life. Parents are good at manipulating their kids, especially in a family battle."

Marcus leaned back in his chair and ran his hand through his hair. He glanced between Cookie, who held his gaze, and Jamie, whose eyes continued studying the bookcase behind him. She hated to hear Cookie advocate on her behalf, even though she knew Marcus needed to hear it.

Marcus then nodded, his eyes on Jamie. "That makes sense. Like I said, her father seemed to have quite a hold on her."

Jamie nodded, saying nothing further but directing the conversation back to the pressing matter of the travel guide. "What did she tell you about that book? About the importance of it? Why did she trust you with it?"

Marcus swiveled briefly in his chair, moving it slightly from one side to the other. "Kristen got herself in some trouble, and I was trying to help her get out of it."

"Trouble with the Deltones?" Jamie asked.

He nodded. "She got mixed up with this guy, and then she started using him for information, which she wrote down."

"Using a basic code technique I taught her the last time I was still in her good graces."

He nodded. "She told me that her father had promised a rival family the information and said that she would turn it over to them."

"The Acuna family?" Jamie asked, not really needing confirmation. No one else came close to claiming significant territory. It was a two-family turf war.

"Bad people, as you well know, I'm sure," he said. "She was pretty scared, and now she had her father making promises she didn't want to keep. She knew that she was now compromised with both families, and there would be no way she could prove her loyalty either way. Her father put her in that position, all because some other guy promised him a position within the Acuna family."

"So, the two books together hold the code to all the notes Kristen had recorded about Deltone daily business?"

"Yes." He nodded at the book in her lap. "So, now what do we do?"

"I'm going to ask you to trust me with this book," Jamie replied. "Let me take t and keep both of them somewhere safe."

"You have no relationship with Brian?" he asked.

She shook her head. "He's a lying thief and a rotten excuse for a human being. The only reason I agreed to help him was because he was afraid that Kristen was in danger." She sighed. "He just failed to mention that he was the reason she was in the crosshairs in the first place."

Marcus considered Jamie's explanation, sitting quietly with his eyes moving from hers to the book and back again.

Cookie said nothing. He knew when it served the situation best to have Jamie be lead negotiator, and this case in particular called for Jamie to stay in charge.

"I gave Kristen this book, and it's the only thing I have left of her. Let me take it. Let me figure out how to make some of this right."

"You won't hand it over to Brian?"

She shook her head. "I'd run over him with a stampede of Longhorns first."

He smiled at her comment. "Can I ask where you're going to keep the books?"

She turned to Cookie and smiled at him; the two shared a knowing look. "Don't you worry. We have the perfect place."

CHAPTER TWENTY-FIVE

COOKIE AND JAMIE STOOD OUTSIDE Jamie's Tahoe, observing the chaos that was double-points bingo day. The entrance to the Senior Center & Snowbird Funhouse, a name bestowed upon Erin's business by Jamie, bustled with winter Texans descending from all over the island.

"Ever since she started offering free margaritas with every entry, Erin has been just raking in the green," Cookie said to Jamie, who was still trying to gather her things from her car. Cookie spotted two women, both using walkers, moving more slowly than the rest of the group, so he took the opportunity to walk over to the front door and open it for them.

"Thank you, honey," a gray-haired woman said. She was sporting blue polyester from head to toe, her shoes resembling the white numbers nurses often wore for long shifts. "Not many good-looking men with manners around here these days."

"No problem at all. You go in there and make some money," he said, offering the high-wattage smile he usually reserved for hot waitresses. Cookie then returned down the steps and back to Jamie.

"What the hell are you doing in there?" he asked, leaning over to peer at her through the driver's side window.

"I couldn't find my phone," Jamie said. "It slipped down between the seats, and you weren't here to call it because you were flirting with the seniors." She peeked into her shoulder bag, double-checking that she had both journals in her possession. She had checked them at least ten times—they weren't small or easy to lose—but she still felt the need to physically see both of them in her possession. She stepped out of the car, bag over her shoulder, and slammed the door shut then locked it with a double-tap of her key fob.

She and Cookie walked in the front lobby and were greeted by a packed house. Clusters of seniors were gathered, most holding frozen green drinks in small clear cups. More women than men filled the space, all chatting about topics ranging from the latest politics to gossip about Mrs. Sandoval and her much younger boyfriend. It was like a meeting group for people who had aged out of all the conventional online dating sites.

The woman decked out in blue spotted Cookie and hustled her walker over to stand by his side. Barely five feet tall but with solid posture, she looked up at Cookie's smiling face. "You going to stay here for a while and play? Free drinks and everything."

"Afraid I can't today." He pointed to Jamie. "My boss is making me work overtime. Got a lot to do."

The woman went from smiling at Cookie to grimacing at Jamie. "You really shouldn't be such a hard-ass, young lady. Take it from me. Don't work your whole life away. Not worth it. My husband, Bernie, rest his soul, worked nonstop until he turned sixty-seven—no days off, didn't take vacations, so dedicated. You know what happened?"

Jamie took the bait. "No, what happened?"

"Finally got him to agree to take a vacation. Hawaii. First-class tickets, the whole thing. Payment for my waiting patiently all those years. He dropped dead, just like that. Heart attack, no warning. Just on the ground, gone. Couldn't even get the money back from the airline."

Jamie listened to the woman's cautionary tale, both amused and enamored with her plain-speaking presence. "I'm so sorry that happened. I will definitely work harder at"—she searched for the right words—"work harder at working less." She glanced at Cookie. "I promise to give you time off so you can come back here for the next double-points bingo event."

The woman smiled so large, one would have thought she had won the lottery. "I'll be looking for you next time, okay?" she said with a twinkle in her eye for the large man sporting Hawaiian floral.

"I'll see you here," he said before gesturing to Jamie to get a move on.

Jamie stifled her laughter, almost choking on it. "You might have finally found someone who's too much woman for you."

"Thanks for that."

Jamie carefully navigated through the sea of silver to the hallway that led to Erin's office. Becky was standing outside the doorway as though she were Erin's personal bouncer... which she was.

"How you doing, Becky?" Jamie asked as she walked by her into Erin's office.

"Good." She offered a fist bump to Cookie as he passed her.

Erin sat at her desk, typing something that had her focused attention. Her straight blond hair was tucked behind her ear, revealing a large, dangling lapis earring. During moments such as this, Jamie wondered what it would feel like to be so polished, so well put together.

It seemed like a lot of work.

Jamie tapped on the desk. "Hey, Erin."

Her friend hurried through whatever she was typing on her computer then exited the screen with a tap of her finger. "Nice to see you," she said, "although the seriousness in your voice worries me a bit." She signaled to Cookie. "C'mere, you."

Cookie walked around the desk and gave her a hug.

Her hair fell in his face as she leaned in to give him a squeeze. "How's my hot boyfriend doing?"

"Quit calling him that, Erin. You're going to give him a big head."

"Too late," he joked.

"So, tell me what this is all about."

Jamie reached into her bag and pulled out the journal and the travel book. "I need you to put these in your super-secret vault, the one that you use for your most important papers... and stuff." She touched them. "These belonged to Kristen, and both the Deltones and the Acunas want them."

Erin stared at the journals. "Kristen's death was about what's in those two books?" She shook her head. "I'm so sorry, Jamie."

"It's okay," she replied. "I mean, it's not okay, but at least we can do something about it."

"You want them here long-term, or will you need them again soon?"

Jamie shook her head. "No, no, I just need you to hold them for a few days. I'm looking into a few things still, and there's no way these would be safe at Hemingway's or at Cookie's place. I don't have time to get a bank deposit box, so can you just take them for now? I want to take some time to go through the journals but not until I set up something more secure long-term. They need to be safe for now until I decide how to move forward."

Erin smiled at her friend and reached over for the books. "Of course. This is the perfect place. After all, who's going to think something so important would be hidden in a seniors' hangout?" She gestured toward her office door. "Why don't you two follow me to the room, and we'll get these locked up so you can see they're safe and sound."

Becky remained standing outside the door, her eyes on her charge. "You need me to follow you somewhere?" she asked Erin.

Erin shook her head. "No, I've got these two. I'm fine. Just stay here, maybe check on the crowd outside to make sure none of the patrons get too rowdy. Those free drinks sometimes backfire. Always get a wild one or two in the middle, wanting to do something stupid like start a mosh pit or stay awake past ten o'clock."

Becky grinned at the comment, and Erin led Jamie and Cookie to what she'd simply called "the room." The room looked like a basic office supply storage area. Reams of paper were stacked high next to other office supplies, cleaning supplies, and the like. Erin signaled to Cookie. "Can you move that table with all the paper on it?" When Cookie shot her a look, she said, "I know, I know. It's not that heavy."

He leaned forward and lifted the table, complete with all its contents. One ream of paper slid off, then two, then a third, each hitting the floor with a thud, which dented the corners of the paper packages. "Sorry about that."

Erin shrugged it off. "No worries." She then walked over to a beige area rug with a pattern of palm trees across its length. She leaned down, resting on her knees, then lifted the rug, revealing a safe built into the floor. The surface was stainless steel with a digital screen at the top and a second small screen toward the bottom. Erin typed in a code, letters and numbers. The safe clicked twice, then after a third click, the door opened slightly.

Erin opened the safe and placed the journals in quickly, not leaving time for eyes to fall on any other contents inside. Jamie knew it wasn't because Erin didn't trust her and Cookie, but rather because she wanted to get the safe secured quickly. Erin then closed and locked the safe, returning the rug to its proper place. She looked at Cookie to move the table to its original position.

"Really? That's all I am to you? A pretty face and some manual labor?"

"Pretty much," she quipped.

With Cookie's help, the room was returned to its original layout, just another storage room holding copy paper, printer ink, cleaning supplies, and the one thing that could guarantee the downfall of the Deltone crime family.

CHAPTER TWENTY-SIX

J AMIE WALKED INTO HEMINGWAY'S WITH Cookie on her six and a drink on her mind. She was buoyed by a small sense of relief, something she'd felt precious little of since Brian had first called for help.

The bar was busy, with most of the stools occupied by a combination of local workers. Fishermen were dressed in button-down shirts that had SPF protection and were stained with the day's work of searching for the top honey holes. More locals were either celebrating being off work or bracing themselves before getting started.

Walking through to the back left of the bar, Jamie was pleased to see that her favorite booth was open, most likely because dirty dishes and glasses covered the majority of the table's surface. It felt good to be back in their corner booth.

Cookie signaled to Marty, his finger making a circular wave around the dishes in an effort to ask, without words, for the bartender to make the dining wear disappear. Marty left his other bartender to tend to the thirsty flock while he walked over with a smile on his face and a large tray in his hands.

"I was going to have to give this table up soon, so it's a good thing you made it here." Marty balanced the tray on the table and used it to transfer the dirty dishes. "A few restaurants in town are without water. Some jackass hit a main line while doing repair work so we're getting the overflow."

"Tricky Dick's one of those places?" Jamie asked, giving him a wink.

"Yep, poor bastard," he said, smiling the entire time. He looked at Cookie. "You want the usual?"

Her friend nodded. "And throw some extra fries in there, will ya? Starving right now."

"You know how Cookie gets when he's hangry," Jamie joked. "He's completely unreasonable until you feed him."

Marty left the pair to their conversation.

Jamie felt a bit lighter, knowing that the journals were in Erin's safekeeping. Still, the reality that they didn't know who had killed Kristen remained something that followed her with every step, every inquiry, and every conversation, regardless of who was on the other end of it.

Jamie leaned in across the booth to Cookie, tapping on the table with her forefinger. "You know the next thing that needs to happen after we eat, right?"

Cookie nodded, ready to respond, but was interrupted by Marty's return with two draft beers. The bartender knew enough to smile, nod, and make himself scarce.

Both Cookie and Jamie took long draws from their beers. Jamie held her own with Cookie, and when the glasses hit the tabletop, the lines were close to even.

He nodded to her glass. "You needed that too?"

"Oh, I could go down that rabbit hole if I'm not careful. You know that."

"I won't let you." The sincerity in Cookie's eyes was evident.

"I know you won't." She reached for her glass but then decided against it for the moment. "As I was saying, you know what we need to do next?"

Cookie took another sip from his beer, swallowed, and smacked his lips. "I know we need to use that burner phone and get Ritchie to meet with us. If he's telling Marissa that he didn't do it, then we need to know more about the last time he saw her."

Marty returned a second time, with burgers and enough fries to feed a Little League team. He had taken Cookie's plea seriously. Certainly, there would be enough left over for Deuce.

Like Cookie, Jamie could manage her pup's mood through food. She took a handful of fries and crammed them into her mouth with all the grace of a truck driver. "We're going to have to hit him heavy, Cookie," she said between chews. "I think you need to be the one on the other end of the line."

Cookie took a bite of his hamburger, the two of them working to squeeze words in between bites. "How do you want to play it?" He wiped his hands on his pants.

Jamie grimaced but said nothing. Her table manners were on par with his, so she had no room to judge. "I think we tell him that we hear he's the one behind Kristen's death, and unless he wants the cops to come around looking for him, he needs to meet with us and tell us what he knows."

"You think there's a chance he'll drop off the grid if we call him?"

Jamie considered that for a moment. "I don't think so, not from the description Marissa gave us. This guy is pretty aggressive, brash. I don't think he'll bolt. I think he'll want to bow up and prove he didn't do anything, especially if he really cared about her."

"Good point." Cookie took another bite from his burger, the ketchup running down the side of the bun as he squeezed it to fit in his mouth. Between chews, he added, "I can get him to show up, but you're going to need to close him. You need to use your relationship with Kristen."

"Relationship is a stretch, don't you think?"

Cookie shook his head. "Not if you count intention. I think you would have been close if you'd had more time, been given a second chance."

Jamie reached for her beer and finished it. "I suppose so, but we don't all get second chances, do we?"

"Maybe not with her, but that doesn't mean you can't get a second chance to do right by her, even if she's gone. It all still matters."

Jamie smiled at him but said nothing as she took a turn at her own fries and wiped her hands on a napkin Marty had left on the table. "I'm thinking if we get him on the line, Perry's Pool Hall is the place to meet him."

Cookie smiled at her suggestion. "Perfect. Let's finish up and get him on the phone. It's time to shake this tree and see what falls."

CHAPTER TWENTY-SEVEN

PERRY'S POOL HALL WAS IN the heart of what locals called Alibi Alley, which was every bit as shady as it sounded. The actual street name, Alene Avenue, had once been a bright spot in the small coastal town—a row of quaint restaurants, bars, and music venues that attracted tourists from all over the Lone Star State. In its heyday, Alene Avenue had fed the town with visitors, and with them came spending money. But once a certain crime element decided to make Alene Avenue its home base, the thriving block of bars and restaurants had quickly crumbled under the weight of new management.

So Alene Avenue had morphed into her seedier sibling, nicknamed Alibi Alley, for the gathering of characters who needed to prove they had been anywhere other than where the cops, disgruntled spouses, and jealous boyfriends claimed. Fifty bucks could easily get a round of drinks and verification that someone was at Alibi Alley for any stretch of hours deemed necessary. It drove the local cops nuts.

It was also the perfect place to meet Ritchie. Being anonymous was expected as soon as one passed through Perry's doors. No one saw anything there. Ever.

Jamie found a parking place toward the back half of the alley, tucked behind a nondescript Ford F150, close to Perry's Pool Hall. Perry was a criminal, but he had personality. In short, Perry possessed a powerful mix of glee and crazy, and it was best to avoid him at all costs.

Jamie kept her attention on the street ahead, dimly lit with one streetlight on each side. She was, however, close enough to spot faces and could identify anyone who darkened Perry's Pool Hall's door. Cookie straightened up in his seat when a red Camaro pulled up into the side parking lot. They watched as the car disappeared from view. A man then emerged from the parking lot into Jamie's line of sight, walking around the corner of the building to the front door.

"That's Bob Baxter," Cookie observed. "I didn't know he was out."

"Maybe he got out early for good behavior."

Cookie snickered. "That guy would pick a fight with his own shadow. I doubt he runs with the likes of Ritchie." He reached over to take a swig from his gigantic Dr. Pepper. Jamie wondered how many of those he drank in a day. She pointed to it. "You know that's the cardinal sin of surveillance, right? You're going to piss like a racehorse later."

Cookie shrugged off her comment. "My bladder's bigger than yours. And besides, we aren't doing long surveillance. We need to go inside because Ritchie doesn't know what we look like. I just told him I was the big one with the Hawaiian shirt."

Jamie sat for a few minutes, spotting several familiar faces coming in and out of Perry's. They were mostly small-time crooks who were known for stealing cars, stealing money, or stealing girlfriends—a collection of guys with friends in low places.

Jamie glanced at her watch. "Okay, let's go inside so Ritchie can find us."

Cookie nodded and opened the car door. Jamie did the same on her side, and the pair slammed doors in unison.

"We really do spend too much time together," Jamie joked.

Cookie led the way, and Jamie was happy to not be first in the door. It was a natural inclination for heads to turn each time someone walked into a place, even if that place was Perry's. She thought it best to let the colorful shirt go first. Besides, Cookie always made a better entrance.

The sign for Perry's Pool Hall was a sad sight to behold. It looked as though it was at least twenty years old, weather-worn, with a dirty, hazy backlight that didn't do much to announce the name of the place. The blue letters were peeling at each end, and it would take just one or two more storms to knock the whole thing over. The truth was that the sign didn't matter. Perry's had no interest in picking up tourist traffic.

Cookie reached for the glass door. The metal bar was dull and gritty, the window tint bubbling from top to bottom. He held the door behind him for his partner, and she slipped in behind him. Once inside, they walked straight to the bar with casual purpose, as if they belonged there. Standing by the front door and surveying the area would have been a rookie mistake.

Unlike many other establishments in Port Alene, Perry's Pool Hall didn't greet guests with a blast of cold air. Perry kept most things in the place running on the cheap. It was cooler inside than out, but not by much, and cigarette smoke hung in the air over the pool tables like a cloud of suspicion. The bar was busy, crowded really, almost exclusively with men well past forty.

They sat on their perches with buddies wedged between seats to claim a sliver of wooden bar rail. Their presence made getting a beer a small obstacle. Fortunately, Cookie's size and presence usually parted bodies.

He moved in closely behind a man dressed in a black concert T-shirt promoting a band name so obscure, it had to be local. His black hair was long and in desperate need of a comb but had likely not seen one since Clinton's first term.

"Excuse me," Cookie said. The man tipped his head to survey Cookie then nodded and leaned to the side to make room. Cookie got that response on the regular, and he knew how to use it. "Two Dos Equis on draft, *por favor*," Cookie said to the bartender, who nodded.

Jamie had her back to her friend, glancing around the room without letting her gaze fall on any one person too long. "I don't think I see him yet." She turned her head so she could speak close to Cookie's ear. "Let's grab a seat in the back. See if there's a table open."

Cookie dropped a ten on the bar and took the two draft beers from the surface, returning a slight nod to the guy on the barstool. Jamie and Cookie walked past the bar to the back room, which showcased over a half dozen pool tables. They appeared to be the best-kept furniture in the entire place. The tables and chairs that lined the walls around the back room looked as though they had survived too many bar fights to count, the wood weathered from the hard living of the patrons who spent their nights there.

Jamie spotted a round table with two chairs crammed in the back corner with no one sitting immediately close by. She gestured to it, a discreet point in the general direction, and Cookie walked over to claim the space. As he placed the glasses on the table, Jamie took the two ashtrays filled with cigarette butts—all the same label, indicating that one guy had smoked an entire pack in a sitting, if that was possible without coughing up a lung on the way out—and moved them to a nearby wall rail.

The two said nothing but, instead, studied the men and women playing pool on the closest tables. Most seemed to have solid shooting skills, with only one couple appearing well on their way to full-blown drunkenness, consistently mishitting the cue ball or popping a target over the side cushion.

Cookie glanced toward a man with a clean-shaven face, dressed in a shiny-patterned black button-down shirt and black pants. "I think that might be our guy." The man seemed more Miami than Port Alene, shorter than average height for a man, maybe five foot eight with a lift. He had a thick head of black, wavy hair, and his green eyes distributed a cool, almost disinterested stare. He carried a draft beer in one hand and reached for a nearby chair with the other then carried it to Jamie and Cookie's table and sat down.

"So," he said to Cookie, ignoring Jamie's presence entirely, "I'm here. What do you want?"

Cookie took a sip from his beer, taking his time, his eyes on Ritchie. "It's in your best interest to be here, Ritchie, because you're the last person to see Kristen alive, and some people already think you killed her."

Jamie closed her eyes when the words "killed her" left Cookie's lips. Hearing it out loud still made her flinch.

Ritchie noticed but didn't acknowledge her reaction. "Sometimes people think I did things I didn't, which doesn't bother me because it helps my reputation without having to do the actual work." His tone wasn't boastful, exactly, but listening to him quickly revealed that he was the kind to take credit whenever he could get it.

Jamie left her beer untouched, her finger tracing a small circle around the base of the glass. "What happened, Ritchie?" Her tone simple, non-accusing. "Kristen was my niece, and I'm not going to stop until we find out what happened. I don't have any interest in pinning it on you—or if you want credit, whatever—but for me, I need to know."

Jamie's approach was to not play games, to appeal to Ritchie's humanity, if he had any. Kristen seemed to care for him, and although Jamie couldn't see why, there had to be something redeeming.

Ritchie appeared to study her face, his demeanor softening only a fraction, his expression transitioning from proud to something more thoughtful. It was strange to witness, but Jamie had seen it before. Sometimes the guys with the most peacock feathers flaring were the ones covering something deeper, their demeanor a hopeful distraction. Cracking this kind was in Jamie's wheelhouse. Cookie had his charm, and Jamie had the ability to read people and sit with silence.

Ritchie drank from his glass, the foam disappearing from the top as he tipped it to his lips then placed it back down. "I thought Kristen and I had something."

"And now you think you didn't?"

He shrugged. "No, I think we did. I think we started out using each other, but it turned into something different toward the end." He took another drink from his beer. "I couldn't hurt her. I can let other people think that, but I didn't do it."

Cookie tended to his own drink and took turns glancing at the pool patrons, letting Jamie continue to take the lead in the conversation. She was making progress, and he knew to keep quiet at those moments.

"When did you last see her?" Jamie asked.

Ritchie leaned in closer to the center of the table. "I dropped her off at that foreclosed house—the one they found her in. She'd been living there for a couple of weeks, keeping it quiet. She liked being alone sometimes."

Jamie checked the people around her, making sure no one was too close. "So you knew about the journals? The ones she was keeping on the Deltones?"

Ritchie couldn't hide his surprise. He sat back in his chair, rubbing his eyes with his right hand, as if he were wiping away the shock. "You know about that?"

Jamie nodded. "Yeah, I know about it. Pretty sure that's what got her in trouble."

Ritchie reached for his glass and took a substantial drink. "Those journals caused a lot of problems, especially for me. Makes it look like I'm giving her information she shouldn't have, you know? She told me about them one night after we were... you know... and she said her father had pushed her to do it. He had made a deal with some guy he wants to work with, but she had changed her mind about it. She was going to give them to me, but..."

"Someone got to her first."

He shrugged, his posture casual, his eyes more serious. "Kristen and I got on pretty good. I liked her. She was fun, lots of energy, real interested in the business." He then added, "Too interested in the business."

Jamie glanced at the pool table. A middle-aged man wearing a plaid button-down and dirty jeans came into their space but stopped at the next table, reaching for pool chalk. He nodded, palmed the chalk, and returned to his table. Jamie waited for him to be out of earshot before continuing the conversation.

"Ritchie, who was this friend of her dad's? Did she say?"

He reached for his beer and finished the remaining amber liquid. "Yeah, something like Boxman?"

"Boxer?"

His face registered recognition. "That's it. Boxer. You know him?"

Jamie and Cookie locked eyes. "Yeah, we know him."

Ritchie straightened up in his seat. "Well, the guy sounds like bad news from what I've heard from… some of my people. Got his eye on Deltone territory, and if it looks like I helped them get in, even if it was just blabbing my mouth to a lady friend, that's bad—bad for business and bad for me. And I'm not letting that happen."

Jamie patted the table. "Boxer's pretty good at making people look bad."

"No offense," he said, "but you don't seem like the type who runs with the rough crowd."

She pointed to Cookie, who said, "That's what I'm for." He winked. "And she's way meaner than she looks. Trust me."

Ritchie stood up and took one last glance around. "You better be, because I may have a reputation, but I'm actually one of the nice ones. It's what got me in trouble in the first place."

"Thanks for telling me what you know," Jamie replied.

He tapped the table with his hand. "Good luck. You're going to need it."

Ritchie departed, leaving Jamie and Cookie at their corner table, quietly sitting with the knowledge Kristen's confidante had shared. They watched barflies play pool, swig cheap beer, and discuss whether or not the Cowboys had a shot at the playoffs this year. Jamie wished she could return to a time when small talk and divorce cases had dominated her time. She couldn't believe she wished for such a thing, but she did. The weight of Kristen's death, and the fact that she couldn't have done anything to prevent it, followed her, a reminder of yet another family failure.

"You okay?" Cookie reached over and touched her forearm. "I know this is hard for you."

The wheels turned in her mind, her thoughts bouncing between

Cookie's concern and what she needed to do next. She reached for her glass and realized it offered no comfort since it was empty.

"That was one of the strangest encounters I've had with anyone. He cared about Kristen, so he says, but he wants to take credit for her death." She shook her head. "The worst thing? I can live with it because I think he's telling the truth. What the hell is wrong with me?"

"We're after the truth, J. You know that how we get there isn't usually very pretty, and we see lots of bad stuff on the way. This hurts more because it's family."

"You realize that Ritchie put Boxer and Brian together? This means not only did Brian know about the journals, he's the reason she began keeping them in the first place."

"I guess I know what happens next."

She reached underneath the table and pulled her phone from her bag. She pulled up Brian's contact information. "I need to make sure he answers me this time."

She opened her text messages.

I have information about the journals. Need to see you ASAP.

She held it up for Cookie to review, and after he nodded his approval, she hit send.

"You think he'll bite?" he asked.

"Oh yeah. That greedy bastard won't be able to help himself."

Her phone pinged.

Where?

Jamie showed the text response to Cookie. "It's time to get some answers."

CHAPTER TWENTY-EIGHT

IT WAS WELL PAST MIDNIGHT, the warm coastal breeze scattering itself between the leaves of the palm and Brazilian pepper trees lining the sidewalks and strips of dry grass that served as the natural lobby entrance for the Jetty. The Jetty, a popular fishing area for locals during the day, found itself largely deserted after dark, the pattern of large granite rock walkway more dangerous to navigate without the benefit of daylight. The huge pink blocks of granite, the patterns blockish and open, permitted—even encouraged—Gulf waters to splash in between their massive squares, requiring proper care to successfully walk across. The patterned granite, transported from the Texas Hill Country in the late 1800s, stood as a reminder that the waters it provided shelter from were both lovely and treacherous. One misstep could mean a broken leg or worse.

Jamie walked with caution, relying upon the moonlight to help her travel from one large granite block to the next. Cookie mimicked her steps, only two feet behind her, each taking care with where they placed their weight.

"I was afraid you were going to choose the Jetty as the meet," Cookie said to Jamie's back.

She craned her head to look over her shoulder and responded to his complaint. "You've done this plenty of times. Besides, you know if you want a private place to meet, this is at the top of the list. Not many partiers or delinquents out here late at night."

"No kidding."

Jamie continued walking, one step in front of the other, head tilted down, watching her feet. Her shoulder bag bounced slightly against her side as she stepped. She could feel the weight of her weapon, reminding her of its presence at the bottom of her bag—not that she would need it, not during this meeting, not with Cookie by her side. As she reached the sign for Mark 22, the metal pole mounted in the water, the sign displaying faded numbers and dents in its surface, she looked up and saw a figure ahead.

Brian.

He wore a jacket that puffed with the wind as it blew. His hands were in his pockets, and his body swayed ever so slightly from one side to the other. She returned her gaze to the ground until she was close enough to address him. She didn't want to look at him any more than necessary. She stopped and glanced behind her at Cookie, who moved to her side.

"You don't need a bodyguard, Jamie. I'm family."

"Kristen was family, and clearly, she needed one." Jamie watched him flinch as the words landed. Cookie remained quiet, watching the exchange between two siblings who were similar only in blood and last name.

"You said you had information about Kristen's journals," Brian said, deflecting the challenge that he had any responsibility for his daughter's demise.

Jamie nodded, taking a moment to look out at the Gulf before returning her attention to him. "I know quite a bit about them. I'm going to give you a chance to tell me what you know first. And remember that whatever question I ask, I already know the answer."

Brian shifted his weight, taking his turn to look at his feet and his surroundings, anything but Jamie and Cookie. He brushed at his face then returned his hands to his pockets. "Kristen was supposed to get information on the Deltones' operation. She had a guy she was seeing who talked too much sometimes and brought her to a few places where things were going down, places she wasn't supposed to be. So she took some notes."

"You never mentioned any of this when you first came to me about her disappearance."

He shrugged. "I wasn't sure this job had anything to do with it. She runs her own scams on the side. I thought maybe she was in trouble that way."

Jamie scoffed at his explanation. "So you thought the real danger wasn't her double-crossing a local crime family but scamming some loser on the side? You really expect me to believe that?"

"I think he does," Cookie chimed in. "Crazy, isn't it?"

Brian looked at Cookie but kept his expression neutral. "I don't care what you think."

"You're an ass, you know that?" Jamie replied.

He ignored her comment. "So, Kristen was going to give me the journals."

"You mean she was going to give Boxer the journals."

Brian's expression changed with the mention of Boxer's name. "Where did you hear—"

"The point is that I know, Brian. I know you're working with Boxer against the Deltones, which means you're trying to get into favor with their biggest rival. The Acuna family is dangerous, Brian. Do you really understand what you're doing? What you're playing with here?"

A break of waves crashed against the rocks where the trio stood, and a small wet spray peppered their bodies. Jamie wiped a few drops from her face, while Cookie remained stoic, not moving, his eyes fixed on Brian.

Jamie's voice was louder now, angrier and incredulous. "How could you do that, Brian? How could you use your daughter that way? Sending Boxer to get the journals from her? Do you have any idea what that man is capable of?" She then said in almost a whisper, "You are so far out of your league here."

At that moment, Brian's façade cracked ever so slightly, his features displaying the fear that he had so carefully covered until now. "Boxer's after me now. When Kristen refused to give him the journals, he…"

"He killed her, Brian. He killed her because you put her up to do your dirty work."

Brian's words came faster now, the panic showing in his plea. "He killed her to send me a signal, Kristen. I'm now on the hook for the journals. I have to deliver them, or he's going to do the same thing to me. You need to get them for me, Jamie."

Cookie scoffed at the comment, while Jamie stood in front of her half brother, considering his plea. "Do you realize that if you had told me the truth up front, maybe we could have found Kristen in time? To protect her from Boxer?"

"I didn't think he would go that far." Brian shook his head. "You've got to help me here, Jamie. He's going to rip through our entire family."

The reality that Boxer would target their family gave her pause. Would Boxer go after them? Her younger sister, Grace? Yet, this was Brian's doing. He was going to have to make it right on his own, come clean or run—run and hide for a good, long time.

Any glint of compassion Jamie might have had for Brian left her when she realized he refused to take any responsibility for Kristen's death, concerned only with his own safety. Like Jamie, Kristen had deserved a far better father than she had been given.

Her anger got the better of her. "Brian, there's no way that I'm giving you the journals." She regretted the words the moment they left her mouth. She had never intended to reveal that she had them in her possession.

Brian's eyes widened, and he raised his voice. "You found them? Where did Kristen hide them? I've looked everywhere."

Jamie could see by his expression that he was considering all the places Kristen might have hidden them.

"You're going to have to fix this without the journals, Brian. You sacrificed your own daughter, so it's up to you to now save yourself."

"How can you do this, Jamie?" Brian's voice was loud and pleading. "You don't understand. He's going to kill me if I don't get them back."

A second gust of wind washed over them as they stood on the granite, and Jamie brushed away sections of hair that had blown in her face. She pulled in a deep breath and took her time before answering. "Let me tell you a few things. First of all, you see this man standing here? The Acunas killed his little brother a couple of years ago. He is one of my closest friends, and there is no way on earth I would help the Acunas just for that reason alone."

He turned to Cookie. "I had no idea."

"It doesn't matter," Cookie replied. "I can tell from watching you here that you wouldn't have cared, anyway. You're just worried about yourself. If you won't protect your family, why would you care about mine?"

Jamie glanced at Cookie, surprised by how calmly he shared his feelings about Manny. She knew him well enough to see a hint of anger underneath the surface, but his response was measured and deliberate. Brian would get no reaction—anger or sympathy—from him.

Even in the darkness, with the moonlight offering only a hint of light, Jamie could see Brian's demeanor change yet again, like flipping a switch. During their short meeting, he had traveled from cool to reserved to panicked and now this—defiant.

"You think this is it, Jamie?" His voice quivered with disbelief. "You think I'm just going to lie down and die? I've got news for you. I'll do *anything* I need to do to get out of this." He jabbed a finger at her. "You hear me?"

"Is that a threat?" Jamie asked. "You going to come after me somehow?"

"I'm done playing, Jamie. Done being nice. You hand over those journals, or it's going to get ugly. You hear me?" He gestured to Cookie. "And I don't care how big your friend is, he won't be able to protect you."

Brian's warning prompted Cookie to move closer to him. The space between them was so slim that light barely passed through. Cookie dwarfed Brian in size, and he used it to his advantage.

"You so much as look at her wrong, and they're going to find you in a ditch somewhere, you hear me?"

Jamie resisted the urge to step in and pull her friend away.

"You don't get it." Brian threw his hands in the air. "I don't care about you or what you might do. I have to make things right with Boxer, or I'm over."

"You're over either way," Jamie said. "You best be careful with your next steps."

Jamie stepped closer to Cookie, her hand reaching over to touch his arm, coaxing him away from the toxic space Brian occupied. He responded by taking his original position back at her side.

"You leave me no choice," Brian warned.

"Likewise." Jamie turned her back on Brian in every way possible.

Cookie followed her through the darkness back across the Jetty. The wind had shifted toward her back, pushing her on the path, away from her sibling, as his warning still stung her ears. He was no longer family, not to her, not anymore. The precarious thread that had once tied them together, Kristen, was gone. All that remained was the battle ahead.

One sibling against the other.

CHAPTER TWENTY-NINE

J AMIE PLACED DEUCE ON THE floor after carrying him down the stairs from her loft to Hemingway's.

"I'm not going to keep carrying you," she said to her pudgy bulldog. He ignored her comments, instead preferring to sniff around the door. As she pushed it open, Deuce bolted like a sailor on weekend leave, not looking behind but scrambling straight to her car, hopping as he waited for her to unlock the door.

"You excited to see Uncle Cookie?" she asked as she opened the door and bent down to lift him into the car. Jamie smiled at him as she got him settled into the back seat, grateful for a small moment of thinking about something other than Kristen, Brian, and what struggle lay ahead.

Traffic was light as she drove to Cookie's apartment, a short ten-minute drive from Hemingway's. Jamie had encouraged the move from his old apartment, which was twice the distance and decades older than his new digs. The new place had several nice amenities, including a weight room he completely ignored and a swimming pool that only Deuce had enjoyed. Still, it wasn't a dump, and it was closer to Hemingway's, so a win all around.

Jamie pulled into the parking lot of Beach Retreats, which sounded more like a retirement home than an apartment complex, and parked in front of Cookie's building.

She sent him a text and, after another two minutes, honked her horn. He soon opened the door, decked out in one of his favorite Hawaiian shirts—hunter green with white hibiscus—as well as khaki cargo shorts and deck shoes. He was dressed as though he was on vacation, as usual.

"Thanks for picking me up," Cookie said as he slid into the passenger's seat and reached back to give Deuce a quick pat. "I think a trip to the beach is a great idea. Deuce needs to get out."

Jamie backed out of the parking space and pulled out the side exit. "I think we all need it. I can't remember the last time I was on the beach."

"Then it's been too long."

Jamie navigated back toward Island Main until she reached the 120-marker turnoff, one of the key entry points to the beach. Once she made the turn, she could see the water. The tires soon hit the sand, and a wave of happiness washed over her. She had missed this, the lightness that came with the surf. Lightness had left her some time ago.

The Tahoe moved slowly, churning sand under the tires, moving past the crowds of summer visitors in search of a space not occupied by strangers and their attention. They finally found their spot, an open space between a family playing horseshoes and a group of college girls sitting in reclining chairs, studying their cell phones.

No sooner had Cookie opened the back passenger's door than Deuce leapt out of the back seat and belly-flopped onto the sand. Snorting out a snout full of white granules, he scampered toward the waves and stopped short before the water hit his paws. He jumped back and forth, chasing the waves then letting the waves pursue him, finally giving in and getting wet up to his belly.

"Your dog is ridiculous." Cookie laughed, his eyes almost watering from watching Deuce play by himself. "Glad he's too heavy to be plucked out of the water by a seagull."

"You better not let him hear you say that." Jamie brushed her hair away from her face, the wind challenging her ponytail to keep her strands in line. "It feels so good out here. Let's stay out here for a week."

"Done."

The two friends stood side by side. The sun strong, the wind equally so, and the sandpipers and seagulls hovered overhead, searching for food. Jamie watched as they circled, dove into the water, and quickly returned to the sky.

"So, what are we going to do about Brian?" Cookie asked, his attention still focused on Deuce's antics, which included chasing a small sandpiper and sticking his muzzle in the sea foam.

"I'm not sure what to do," she said. "I can't just sit and wait for him to do something destructive, but I'm not even sure what that would be at this point. I've got Marty keeping an eye out for anyone trying to access my place, not that he'd find anything, of course." She squatted down and ran her fingers through the sand, drawing a random squiggly line in its surface, her lips tightening in frustration. "I didn't mean to imply that I had the journals. It was a rookie mistake. But now that he knows, I'm afraid he's going to do something drastic."

"Don't beat yourself up, Jamie. This case is all about your family, so you're going to be emotional; you're going to have moments where you react differently than you would in any other case. Be aware but understand that you're human. It's okay."

Jamie glanced up at her friend, grateful for his insight and compassion. She knew he was letting her off the hook, even if she didn't think she deserved it.

"You know my biggest worry right now?"

"Let me guess," Cookie said. "Brian's got Boxer as an enemy, and we now know what that looks like. I still worry that he's going to target Erin since we let Marissa go from her warehouse."

Jamie nodded in agreement. "That's my biggest fear too, but maybe with Brian, Boxer's attention will be focused on him instead. I'm fine with that. Brian doesn't deserve any mercy, especially after the way he treated Kristen like a disposable bargaining chip."

"Waiting it out is painful," Cookie said, standing over Jamie and watching her draw patterns in the sand. "I hate to say this, but whatever he's up to, I hope he shows his hand soon."

She pointed at her pup. "Keep an eye on him for a minute. I'm going to grab a couple of water bottles out of the back of the car. I'm sure Deuce is thirsty."

As Jamie traveled the few steps back to her car, she focused on the sand underneath her feet. The feeling of something comforting and familiar gave her temporary respite from Brian and his threats. She missed those divorce cases she'd once complained about. They were messy and frustrating, sometimes even a bit heartbreaking, but they never sank into her bones the way a case did when it involved family. In the beginning, she thought she'd understood what she was taking on, but it was clear now, after she and Cookie had continued to dig for the truth, that she hadn't had a clue what it had meant to take Kristen's case.

Jamie popped the hatch on the back of her Tahoe and grabbed three water bottles from a large pack wrapped in plastic. Cradling them in the bend of her elbow, she closed the back hatch and walked to the driver's side door to retrieve her cell phone, which she'd left in the cup holder. She reached for it with her free hand and tucked it in her back pocket before walking back to Cookie to make her water delivery.

"Here you go." She handed him a bottle. Deuce was completely disinterested, preferring to spend his time chasing imaginary friends in the surf. She then placed one bottle on the ground while opening the other for herself. She drank almost half of it before taking a break.

"Good thing you don't drink beer like that," Cookie joked. "Oh wait, you do."

She smiled at him.

"Okay, good thing you don't drink beer like that often," he said, correcting himself.

Jamie pulled her phone from her back pocket and checked the screen. She noticed a message from an unknown number, and her chest tightened. She reminded herself not to panic and that she often received messages from unknown numbers in her line of work, but Brian's threat hung fresh in the air, infiltrating every moment.

"What's wrong?" Cookie asked, noticing her staring at her phone.

"I don't know yet." Jamie selected the number to open the text message.

Want to Trade?

Below the message was a photo of Erin, strapped to a chair, much the way Marissa had been back in Erin's warehouse. A white gag split her lips, and while she didn't look directly into the camera, Jamie could see the fear on her friend's face. It looked as though her arms were tied behind her back, her white shirt soiled from a struggle. The image was shot tight to make sure no background information was included and that there was no real way to see where she was being held.

Jamie held the phone up for Cookie. She had witnessed many expressions on her friend's face, but this one was a rarity, and she glimpsed it only for a second. *Fear.* He feared for his friend.

"Okay, so Brian made his move," Cookie said.

"No." Jamie corrected him. "Brian made a mistake."

Jamie texted a response.

She had better be perfect, Brian. If you hurt her, you're dead.

Jamie and Cookie stared at the screen, waiting for a response. It felt as though a day passed, but in reality, it was only mere minutes.

You should have never let my package escape. So now I have a new one.

Boxer.

What do you want?

More waiting, then came his response.

Kristen's Journals. Seems a fair trade.

Jamie stared at the text, her finger hesitating before responding. *I need time to get everything.*

Time is running out, Jamie. For you and your friend. So hurry.

Jamie and Cookie stood side by side, staring at the cell phone screen, taking in Boxer's threat. The fact that Boxer had Erin was far worse than if Brian had been her captor.

Brian was an amateur.

Boxer was a professional.

CHAPTER THIRTY

"HOW DID THIS HAPPEN?" JAMIE asked Cookie. "How could Boxer just grab her like that?"

Jamie reminded herself to remain calm behind the wheel. Her tires churned over the sand as she left their brief beach retreat. Deuce remained pouting in the back seat, unhappy that his frolicking had been cut short. Cookie reached behind his seat to pet him, but Deuce ignored the affection. He had suddenly taken on the disposition of a cat.

"It had to have been when Becky wasn't around or maybe when she was somewhere else," Cookie offered. "I don't have Becky's cell number, do you?"

"No And I don't know that she would be able to call me, either, if she saw this go down. We'll head over to the senior center and see what she knows since we need to get the journals now."

Jamie picked up speed once she was back on proper roads, passing cars whenever possible without driving so fast as to garner a ticket. Her heart rate quickened so much that she felt as if she had been running a race even though her body remained still in the driver's seat. She gripped the steering wheel so tightly that her nails dug into the padding.

Jamie had barely put her car in park before opening the car door. She reached behind the back seat to lift Deuce then placed him on the concrete. Small scatterings of sand fell off his paws. The pup followed Cookie and Jamie inside, where the furry sidekick was promptly greeted by adoring seniors.

"What an adorable dog!" The lady who bent over Deuce had a sweet face and wore a brightly colored caftan. Jamie would have guessed her to be in her mid-seventies. The woman was dressed for lounging.

"Would you mind watching him for a few minutes?" Jamie asked. "I need to speak to Becky real quick."

"Of course, honey. I think she's in the back. What's your dog's name?"

"Deuce."

The lady smiled at learning his name. "Perfect name to be hanging out here with this group of old gamblers."

Jamie left Deuce in good hands and found that Cookie had already walked to Erin's back office. He was standing next to Becky, who leaned against the doorjamb, her hand over her mouth in disbelief.

"I didn't see anything." Becky's voice cracked from panic. "They must have grabbed her from home or while she was out somewhere. I didn't know, Jamie." Becky wasn't one to show her emotions, but Jamie knew how protective she was of Erin.

Jamie worked to calm her down. "This isn't your fault, okay?" She reached her hand toward Becky but didn't touch her. "I just need to know when you saw her last. What time was she supposed to be in?"

Becky took several deep breaths, her eyes studying the ceiling. "I saw her last night after we closed the books. She left here about ten. She said she'd be in tonight so I wasn't worried that she wasn't here today."

"Cookie, can you go ask around out in the lobby? See if any of the seniors saw Erin at all today? Or anyone suspicious?"

"You got it," he said, walking back out toward the main lobby.

"Becky, I need to get something out of the safe. I left something here, and I need your help to get it out. Do you know the code?"

Becky hesitated. "Yes, but..."

"Becky, they want what's inside that safe, and it's mine to give, okay? Erin was just holding it for me, and they'll let her go if I give them what they want."

Becky walked toward Erin's office with Jamie following close behind. With a flip of the switch by the door, light flooded the space. Becky moved toward the lamp on Erin's desk and lifted it, retrieving a key from underneath. She then took the key to the desk, bent down, and unlocked the middle drawer. It was as though Becky didn't want to sit in Erin's chair or occupy the space because she knew Erin should be there.

From inside, Becky retrieved a small green journal. "She changes the codes every so often and writes clues down here," she explained, her voice

184

peppered with a solemnness Jamie had never heard. "She usually leaves clues about what the numbers are—things I would understand. So the book just looks like words and phrases, no numbers. It's her own little security hack."

Jamie could see the worry on Becky's face. "We're going to get her back, Becky. You hear me?"

Becky's expression was one of wanting to have hope but not completely believing Jamie's words. She led Jamie back to the storage room, with Jamie closing the door behind them before the duo worked to move the table, the supplies, and the rug covering the safe's location. Jamie remembered kneeling by Erin not long ago to place the journals there for safekeeping, and now she had to retrieve them to barter for Erin's life.

Jamie stood back, giving Becky privacy while she typed in the code. The lock clicked twice and released. Becky opened the door and signaled to Jamie, who knelt down to take the journals from their secret place. She quickly tucked them inside her bag and stood back to let Becky secure the other contents in the safe. They returned the room to its previous status, neatly stacking the office and cleaning supplies and putting the rug back where it belonged.

The two walked back to the main lobby to find Cookie, who was surrounded by a group of admiring seniors in what appeared to be small talk. Deuce looked to be in a trance of joy, eating up all the affection Erin's patrons offered him.

Jamie walked toward Cookie and inserted herself into the group. "Anything?" she asked simply, not wanting to say too much that would worry the ladies.

"No on both counts," he replied. "Do you have everything?"

She nodded. "We're good." She turned to Becky. "Would you mind looking after Deuce for a bit while we're out? He looks like he's in doggy heaven."

"Sure, but are you sure you don't need me? I can't just sit here and do nothing."

"You won't be doing nothing, Becky," Jamie replied. "You've just given us what we need to get Erin back, and we need you here in case someone shows up." She looked down at her pup. "So, you can keep Deuce?"

Becky smiled for the first time since they had arrived. "Love to. He can keep my mind off of… things."

Jamie left her fur baby surrounded by admirers while she and Cookie slipped out of the lobby and headed to the car. The weight of the journals felt heavy, not in a physical sense but because they were worth Erin's safety. Jamie placed them next to Cookie's feet on the passenger's side of the car.

"Okay, so we have the journals," Cookie said. "Now what do we do?"

"I think we might need some reinforcements." She locked eyes with him, waiting for him to understand her meaning.

When he did, he seemed unconvinced. "You mean get the Deltones involved? Are you kidding me?"

Jamie turned to face Cookie and put her hand on his forearm. "Listen to me, Cookie. We can't do this without help. What if they get the journals and then they kill all of us? Why wouldn't they? Boxer has no honor, and neither does Brian."

"Do you really think Brian would let that happen to you? You're family."

"If he wasn't willing to protect Kristen, why would he protect me?" She inhaled deeply and let out a sigh. "Plus, the Deltones have played straight. We know they weren't responsible for Kristen or Manny's deaths. You believe that, right?"

Cookie begrudgingly nodded but said nothing.

"If that's true, how can we hand over all their secrets to the Acunas? They're the ones who took our family from us, Cookie. You know that. How can we give them the journals after what they've done? So, they don't have to pay for anything? I can't live with that."

Jamie watched Cookie's expression soften. "You're right. I know you're right. I just don't like it."

"I don't, either," she said, "but I don't see any other way." She reached into her bag, touched the journals for comfort, then pulled out her phone. "I'm going to call Marissa's abuela to schedule a meet."

Cookie nodded, while Jamie looked up the retirement home's phone number. Any ideas she'd once had about how such crime families worked went out the window after the meeting in Abuela Deltone's retirement home.

"Mrs. Deltone?" Jamie asked. "I need your help to save a friend."

CHAPTER THIRTY-ONE

"I HAVEN'T BEEN HERE IN AGES." Cookie surveyed the meeting spot that Marissa had chosen. The two stood in an open field overlooking an aging structure. Jamie had no understanding of why anyone would want to hang out in an old park showcasing an old performance stage. The metal stairs leading up to the stage were weathered and peppered with rust spots. The wooden roof hadn't seen glory in some time, the slats home to gaping holes and a section on the end that had collapsed entirely. Clearly, this popular venue was no longer loved.

"Is this where music comes to die?" Jamie asked.

"This place used to be hopping every weekend, many years ago," Cookie explained. "Lots of small-time bands would come and play. There was a huge concession stand over there." He pointed to a shack that no longer had a roof and had likely been raided of any valuable cooking equipment. "I remember coming here as a kid, but it was already at the end of its heyday by then."

Jamie tried to imagine this music venue filled with families eating, drinking, and listening to local bands. Knowing its history made her appreciate the space more, although she wondered who would let such a revered local hotspot slowly devolve into an abandoned field.

Her thoughts were interrupted by the sight of a figure walking toward them, coming from behind the old concession stand. She could see Marissa's confidence in her stride, even from far away. The woman reached the duo in short order, and Jamie could hear her boots crushing the dead grass as she walked.

Jamie waved a hand at the open field. "If you were looking for desolation, you found it."

"You've never been here?" Marissa asked.

"Nope," she said. "Cookie was telling stories of local bands and weekend festivals, but it looks like that was a long time ago."

She smiled at him. "I had some of my best times with my family here."

He nodded, a small smile showing on his lips that quickly disappeared. Jamie could tell he had harbored hate for the Deltone family for so long that he couldn't yet allow himself to feel anything else.

Marissa looked at Jamie. "So, tell me what you need. And what's in it for me."

"Our friend, Erin, the one whose warehouse Boxer kept you in? He's got her. We're not sure how, but he's holding her somewhere, and we need to get her back." Jamie pulled up her phone and showed the photo to Marissa, hoping she would remember what it felt like to be in that same position not long ago.

Cookie straightened his stance. "Boxer has her, but we know he was working with Kristen's father, Brian, because they're both trying to make inroads with the Acuna family."

Marissa's eyes narrowed at the utterance of her rival's name. "Boxer's been making inroads with them and what? Brian was trying to do the same thing?"

Jamie nodded. "Boxer wants Kristen's journals—the ones that outline what she knew about Deltone business. He's willing to trade Erin for them."

Marissa took a step back and crossed her arms in front of her chest. "So why would I help you with this?"

"We know where the journals are now," Jamie said, not revealing that she actually had them in the trunk of her Tahoe. "If you can help us get Erin from Boxer and his thugs, we'll give you the journals instead."

Marissa's arms relaxed, as did her expression. She put her hand over her mouth, tapping her finger on her lips. "So we need to figure out how to convince Boxer that you're going to hand over the journals. He will need to have them in his possession for you to get Erin. We then need to get Erin to safety"—she looked at Cookie—"all of you to safety, before we can do anything."

"We can't give him fakes, either," Jamie explained. "One of the books she used is a travel guide from long ago. I actually gave it to her when she was in high school, and he's going to recognize it. This won't be easy."

Cookie and Jamie exchanged a quick glance as they watched Marissa's wheels turn, considering how they could leave Boxer on the losing side of the negotiation.

"He's going to want to meet somewhere deserted, like this, but he has a reputation for doing business at Drake's Den. If we get that lucky, I can figure out some logistics ahead of time."

Jamie's instinct of calling in Marissa's crew had proven to be on point. What they needed to do was not only a bait-and-switch but also a rescue mission. In both of those areas, she and Cookie could claim zero experience, whereas Marissa's family had likely negotiated many hostage exchanges and even double crosses in their line of business.

"Give me your phone," Marissa commanded.

Jamie hesitated but then unlocked the screen and handed it to her. Marissa typed on the screen and handed it back to her. "My number is in there. It's under Sophia. That's my abuela's first name."

Jamie sent a quick text to the number with only her name in the text line. "Now you have mine, too."

"You let me know the moment you hear from Boxer," Marissa said. "The where, the when. We'll work out something and be ready."

"What if we don't have time to discuss the plan ahead of time?"

"I'm not going to discuss the plan with you ahead of time," Marissa said. "If this is going to work, the less you know, the better. You don't want to be anticipating anything. He'll be able to sense if you're worried or holding something back. All you're going to do is follow Boxer's instructions. We'll take it from there when the time is right."

"So I need to trust you?"

Marissa looked at Cookie and nodded. "Yes, you do."

"This is new for me," Cookie said.

"I'm sure it is," she replied. "And I can't guarantee that no one will get hurt. I'm confident we can get what we want and also keep Erin safe, but Boxer is a wild card here so you need to know that going in. My guys are the best but each extraction has risks."

"Extraction?" Jamie asked. "So you've got some experience here?"

"You don't want to know that." She held her hand up and waved. "You text me the minute you hear from Boxer, and we'll take it from there."

Marissa turned and walked away, leaving Jamie and Cookie standing together, watching her figure get smaller as she traveled across the open field. Once she was gone, Jamie turned to her friend. "You okay with this?"

"You're right. It's the best chance we have at getting Erin back safely. I don't trust Boxer—or Brian—to just let her go once we give her the journals. I can't say my conscience is clear making deals with the Deltones. My grandfather, rest his soul, would be rolling in his grave if he knew."

"What choice do we have?" Jamie asked.

"None," Cookie replied. "This needs to work, for Erin."

"This needs to work for all of us."

CHAPTER THIRTY-TWO

WE HAVE THE JOURNALS.

Jamie hit "send" on the text to Boxer and held her breath. She had let half an hour pass to allow Marissa a head start to coordinate with her people, and she also wanted Boxer to believe that she'd needed to work hard to get them in her possession. She shuddered to think what might have happened if he'd realized the journals had been in Erin's safe all along. There would have been no leverage, and no telling if Boxer would've been willing to leave Erin in good health after getting what he wanted. That remained the biggest concern.

They were in limbo, waiting. They needed a small distraction, anything, to keep their minds off the fact that Boxer held their friend and that she remained in danger as long as she was under his control.

"Let's get out of this field," Jamie said. "It's a bit creepy standing out here."

Cookie nodded, and the two returned to her car. Jamie placed her cell phone back in her cup holder with the screen facing her in case any other communication came in regarding Erin's condition.

After meeting with Marissa, the two floundered directionless, not sure where to go or what to do next, so they drove down Highway 361 with no destination in mind. Cookie's jokes fell flat, and Jamie had little to say at all. In past difficult situations, the pair's sarcastic banter had always helped them manage any anxiety in the moment. But with Erin in danger, they found no comfort in their usual coping mechanisms.

Jamie turned into the Save-N-Go parking lot and pulled up to the gas pump. She hadn't realized she was close to driving on fumes, as her attention was focused on bigger things. The convenience store was busy with what Jamie surmised were twenty-somethings stocking up on beer, cigarettes, and packaged snack cakes. She witnessed two middle-aged men, dressed in T-shirts, cargo shorts, and flip-flops, leaving the store, eating hot dogs. She shuddered at the thought. All the great food on the island, and they eat that crap?

She turned off the ignition, not that Cookie noticed. He remained looking straight ahead, lost in his thoughts. Jamie gave his meaty arm a small poke. "Why don't you go inside and get some sodas? I could use some caffeine right now."

"You got it." He opened the door and stepped out. Jamie watched him as he walked into the store, hunched forward, his posture not tall and strong as usual. He wore his worry in his stance; the weight of Erin's safety sat square on his shoulders. Jamie knew the feeling all too well.

After swiping her credit card and filling her tank with gas, she closed her gas tank and glanced toward the store's front entrance. Cookie was coming her way, a plastic bag swinging from his right hand. He slipped inside the passenger's seat and moved Jamie's phone to the small divider between their seats so he could put the drinks in the cup holders.

"You know what we need with this?" she asked.

"What?"

"Taqueria San Juan tacos, bean and cheese for sure," she said, trying to get a smile from him.

"I don't really feel like eating," he replied. "Just not in the mood."

"Let's hit the drive-through while we wait, and maybe you'll change your mind once you get a whiff of that intoxicating smell from the drive-through window."

Traffic picked up now that evening had come, and Jamie caught glimpses of groups of college girls walking down Island Main, dressed in appropriately beachy summer dresses in colorful patterns. They wore beaded sandals, and crocheted, fabric-print handbags swung from their shoulders.

Taqueria San Juan's was hopping already, the parking lot packed with cars and the drive-through busy with people uninterested in table dining. In truth, San Juan's delivered food less than ten minutes after ordering because their cooks were faster than most track stars. But Jamie knew sitting down to a meal was something neither of them found appealing at the moment. If they had to wait, they would wait in the car like they did during long surveillance jobs. It was comforting, somehow, knowing they were ready to bolt at any minute.

Jamie bought eight bean-and-cheese tacos with the understanding that she and Cookie might be hungry later, something they often did when working surveillance. Still in the parking lot, Jamie unwrapped one and began eating. Cookie glanced over at her, and after a few minutes, reached for the bag and retrieved one for himself.

"Sometimes it's good to eat your feelings," Jamie joked.

Cookie couldn't help but smile. "My feelings are delicious." He grinned, and the taco disappeared in short order. They each cleared two before taking a break. They sat in the parking lot, watching groups of people enter and leave San Juan's, and Jamie realized how much she enjoyed being part of Port Alene. She liked having favorite local restaurants, knowing the latest town gossip, and helping neighbors when they didn't know where else to turn. For the first time in her life, Port Alene had given her a sense of belonging. She was no longer a drifter, but a member... with roots.

Jamie's phone pinged, alerting her to a text. She and Cookie shared a glance, then she reached for her phone, which was resting face down in between them on the center console. She held the phone for Cookie to see. Boxer had finally replied.

Drake's Den. Come alone. One Hour.

Cookie shook his head at this command. "There's no way you're doing this solo. No way. It's dangerous enough with the two of us."

Cookie comes. Not negotiable.

The duo waited, staring at the phone for several minutes before a response came through.

Jamie's heart pounded in her chest, the sound loud in her ears, as she wondered if she had pushed too far in the negotiation for Erin's life.

Fine. No weapons.

Done.

Jamie took a deep breath and exhaled with the force of a strong wind. "I'm surprised he agreed to that," she said.

"Better to negotiate it up front because I would have come anyway, and that could have been a problem. Besides, if we can't pack, how much of a threat could we be?"

"I hate going in that way; no way to protect ourselves."

"I know." His brow furrowed with worry. "We're going to have to trust that Marissa can protect us."

"How do you feel about that?"

Cookie cocked his chin to the side, shrugging his shoulders. "Nothing we can do, right? We have to have faith."

Jamie texted Marissa the details of the meeting, and the woman replied immediately.

Got it. See you then.

"I hope we're doing the right thing," Cookie said, reading Marissa's text message.

"Me too, Cookie. Me too."

"You ready?"

Jamie nodded and put her car in drive. "Let's go get our girl back."

CHAPTER THIRTY-THREE

Drake's Den wasn't the kind of destination most people chose to visit willingly. Located on the other side of the island, it required a ferry ride to Arlington Pass, followed by a twenty-mile drive on the other side of TSR 361, through the center of town, and into the desolate emptiness that resided on the far side. Drake's Den had history and lore, the kind of history that made people think twice about checking it out to see if the stories were true.

Lancaster Drake had been powerful in his time, back in the sixties, when his illegal empire had ruled the stretches from Port Alene well into parts of Corpus Christi. His ventures were many, as were his loyalists, and he spread his favor to those who abided by his commands. Known for giving back to the community, he had parceled out some of his ill-gotten gains to local families who had lost husbands in his command and had given anonymous donations for parks and playgrounds. Supposedly, local leaders had known the money they received was tarnished, but they'd been all too happy to take it as long as its origins weren't revealed. On both sides of the law, the lines blurred to the point of seeping into the ground, the ends not justifying the means but ignoring them instead.

Jamie pulled into the ferry line and took the road that wound down one side of the nearby park then hooked around the other. The view from Cookie's passenger's side window was the Corpus Christi channel. The moon offered its own soft light, and the waves crashed into the rocks with force. The regular run of the ferry disturbed the surf with its regular trips back and forth across the channel.

Cookie rolled down his window as he always did when they approached the ferry. The humid evening air rolled through the interior, and he leaned his head outside, his hair flickering back and forth with the whim of the winds.

During the summer months, the ferry line could take an hour or longer, with each ferry capable of transporting twenty vehicles at a time across the water. Jamie was pleased to find the ferry line relatively short, consisting of only a few cars. She drove slowly toward the ramp, the ferry director waving her through and directing her to pull into the right lane, behind a silver Dodge Ram with two black Labradors sticking their heads out the back window.

Cookie took note of the dogs in front of them. "Deuce is going to be pretty pissed if he finds out we rode the ferry without him. You know how much he loves it."

"I thought the same thing, but you know, scary danger and hostage negotiations ahead, so maybe we can wait 'til next time."

"Good point."

The remaining cars lined up in rows behind them, and Jamie felt the strong thump of the ferry locking its back ramps, then the director handled the chains and secured everything. She turned the ignition off and stepped outside, with Cookie exiting as well. The two stood together, their arms resting on the side of the ferry, taking in the salt air and the pelicans and sandpipers perched on nearby wooden stumps alongside the gate entry.

"I wonder where the rest of these folks are going tonight," Jamie observed, glancing around at the other cars parked on the ferry. They were moving at a steady clip now, the ferry's motor rolling in a low hum, the water churning beneath it.

"I can tell you where they aren't going," Cookie said. "I can't imagine anyone wanting to go there if they didn't have to."

"Have you ever been?" Jamie asked.

"Once, when I was a teenager, and it scared the crap out of me. Really, it was just the stories about how many bodies had decomposed in the bay nearby, all courtesy of Lancaster Drake. It was like his personal burial ground, according to the old folks around here."

"Sounds lovely," Jamie replied sarcastically. "So, what does it look like?"

Cookie stuck his face forward a bit into the sea air as the ferry continued to travel across the channel. He reminded her of Deuce, who she was certain was still enjoying the lavish attention from Erin's senior patrons. "I have no idea now, but there used to be a couple of buildings there. One was a restaurant he owned and was also a gambling hall that the cops seemed happy to ignore because of the money he sent their way. And another building was just a shack. My friends said that was where Drake used to interrogate his enemies before killing them and dumping them in the bay. They told me that there's an inlet there that feeds out into the channel so the bodies would just get carried off with the tide."

Jamie shuddered at the idea of how many bodies had actually been carried off due to Drake's dealings, but a small part of her wondered if the story, like most of Port Alene lore, had been embellished as the tales were shared from one person to the next, each generation adding another layer of macabre mystery. Fishermen were known liars, after all, and most of the islanders enjoyed fishing.

When the ferry was a few short minutes from reaching Arlington Pass, Jamie signaled Cookie to get back in the car. As she slipped into the driver's seat, he remained standing on the ferry's side, taking in the last few moments of island breeze and the freedom it offered. They would soon trade that feeling of lightness for containment. Jamie reached for her cell phone, checking to make sure she hadn't missed any texts from Boxer, Marissa, or Becky.

Nothing.

She then sent a quick text to Becky to let her know they were all okay and working on Erin's safe return. Cookie returned to his seat and pulled the car door shut. He glanced at Jamie, who was typing on her screen. "Is this really the best time to be doing your online shopping?" he deadpanned.

"I have an idea for a bit more leverage since, you know, we have to walk in there like sitting ducks with no weapons."

"I'm not completely on board with the 'no weapons so Boxer can gun us down' rule, okay?"

"I agree, but if we do anything to set him off, there's no telling what will happen."

Cookie grimaced, not in agreement but as if he understood her position. His eyes shifted as though he were considering where to hide his Glock 22.

"You know, if you switched to a Glock 19 like I did, it would be easier to hide."

"How did you know what I was thinking?" Cookie asked.

She finished typing on her phone. "Because I'm thinking the same thing."

"We still have time to decide what to do when we get there. The drive is a good half hour once we get off the ferry." Cookie looked out the window. "I don't want to be a sitting duck, Jamie."

"Right there with you," she replied.

The ferry arrived at the Arlington Pass landing, and Jamie waited as the director, sharply dressed in a reflective vest and jeans, released the chains and signaled the drivers to exit, pointing at each car specifically, letting them know to follow in order. Jamie knew better than to make those guys angry. It was best to follow their instructions and get off the ferry.

Her Tahoe drove over the metal incline with a small thump, then she found herself back on paved road. They traveled down TSR 361, taking note of the growing town and the increase in restaurants and convenience stores on each side of the road.

"Last chance to yell for help," Cookie joked, pointing to a couple walking hand in hand inside a convenience store.

"You're a sick puppy, you know that?"

The drive felt like an eternity. As each mile passed, Jamie made sure to stay at the speed limit, not wanting to attract any attention from local law enforcement, although she wondered if that might actually be a good thing. *Excuse me, officer, could you please hide in the back seat of my car and have your weapon ready?* Going to law enforcement for help would have been Jamie's first choice. Unfortunately, such an act would almost guarantee Erin's end.

The road had turned from small town to open land, with little more than trees and small bodies of water bordering it at any given time. The darkness was stronger, inkier, and deeper, like the waters that surrounded them. If an area could have claimed a mood, the land leading to Drake's Den would have been ominous.

"Keep following this road, and there's a small sign that says 461 on the left. Take that," Cookie instructed. "You're going to go for a couple of miles."

Jamie turned onto the gravel road marked 461 and felt as though she were driving straight into a field. No markers, and nothing to look at save for some trees and brush in the distance. She continued until her headlights fell upon a building in the distance.

"Is this it?" she asked.

Cookie nodded. "Yep, that's the old restaurant. Creepy, right?"

Creepy was an understatement. The restaurant sign was little more than a frame; no lettering or other indication of its name was visible. The building itself could have been salvaged if someone cared enough, although Jamie was betting the idea of a restaurant this remote held little appeal to anyone with common sense. One side of the roof had collapsed from decades of weather and neglect, the rot a reminder of what happened to things that were no longer loved. Jamie kept her car running and her lights on as she drove slowly toward the building. In the distance, she saw the shack.

"Is that it?" she asked Cookie, pointing to it.

He nodded. "Yep. Afraid of the stories those walls could tell."

Jamie parked her car by the shack's nearby field and turned the lights off but left the engine running. A car pulled in from behind the dilapidated restaurant and faced away from Jamie's car on the opposite side. Each car shone a strong light in the center field in front of the restaurant and shack.

"Look over there." Jamie pointed to the door of the shack, which was opening.

Erin stepped outside, squinting in the light. She took a few steps forward, revealing a second figure—Brian.

Brian pushed her to walk forward.

Behind him, one more person followed—Boxer.

Jamie felt a knot in her stomach, and her throat tightened at the image of Erin at the hands of two such cruel and careless men. Cookie reached his hand to hers and gave it a small squeeze before letting go.

From the distance, Jamie could see Brian was holding something at Erin's back—most likely a gun—keeping her in line and letting Jamie know that he was in charge.

"Here we go." Jamie gave Cookie a nod. "Let's get our girl out of here safely."

CHAPTER THIRTY-FOUR

"N O GUN, OKAY?" JAMIE WHISPERED to Cookie.

He nodded, seeming to realize that they were in no position to hide any sort of defense. Such an act might trigger a domino effect guaranteed to end things badly. He took his 22, wrapped it in an old foil wrapper from the tacos, then bundled it up like trash and tucked it underneath the back seat.

Jamie stepped out of the car, as did Cookie. Both had their hands in the air. Jamie's bag was on her shoulder, and the journals were inside. As they stepped out, three more men emerged from the restaurant, all looking like hired henchmen—tall, bulky, dressed in black, and armed. Jamie and Cookie walked slowly to the middle, as did Erin, Brian, and Boxer, each working to reach middle ground.

"Check the car," Boxer commanded his men. They walked swiftly to her vehicle and rifled through the interior, popping the trunk. She couldn't see what they were doing but could hear the shuffling sounds of her belongings being invaded and dispersed.

"Clear," they called back, moving to where Jamie and Cookie stood. Jamie kept her expression solemn, not wanting to show a hint of relief that Cookie's weapon remained undiscovered in the car. The lead henchman, his size comparable to Cookie's, said, "No sudden movements. Going to check you for weapons."

Jamie held her arms out from her sides, her eyes taking in her surroundings, as he made sure she had kept her word. His hands ran over her shirt and jeans then down to her ankles and tennis shoes. Cookie stiffened up for a second when the henchman came to him. His body language clearly communicated that he didn't like this one bit.

"Don't worry." The guy's expression was casual, relaxed. "You're not my type."

"Glad to hear it," Cookie said as the man conducted a quick but thorough pat-down.

Jamie looked at Erin. Her face was dirty, her hair tangled, with strands in her face. She couldn't move due to her hands being bound behind her back.

"You doing okay?" Jamie asked.

"She's fine," Boxer interjected.

"Let her answer me herself," Jamie snapped. She kept her eyes on Erin's. "Erin, you okay?"

"I'm fine," she said, her voice softer than usual. Jamie couldn't imagine what terror her friend had felt during her short time in Boxer's custody.

"Take the cuffs off her," Jamie said. "Please."

"Let me see the journals," Boxer replied. "Your brother needs to verify their authenticity. Nice to see he's good for something after all."

Brian winced at the words but said nothing. He held his hand out to receive the journals.

"Erin first. Hands free, then I'll take them out and show them to you."

Boxer's lips tightened, and his eyes shifted around to his lead henchman, who remained at attention. Pulling a large pocketknife from his pants, Boxer flipped the blade and cut away the duct tape securing Erin's wrists together. She leaned forward a bit, her features scrunched tight as the tape broke free. She massaged one wrist with the other hand, making small circles with her fist.

Jamie pulled the journals out for Brian to inspect. She made sure to put Kristen's travel book on top so he would be able to identify it. "Here," she said, holding them up in front of her.

Brian stepped toward her and snatched the journals from her possession. She watched as he leafed through the travel book then the black composition book, nodding. A self-satisfied smile crossed his lips.

"This is all of it," Brian said. "You'll be able to do real damage to the Deltones' operation with this." He handed the books to Boxer. The two smiled at each other, triumphant in their mission, convinced they would now take over Deltone territory.

Jamie reached for Erin's hand and pulled her friend to her side. The three now faced Boxer, Brian, and their henchmen. Jamie kept holding her friend's hand, so tightly that it almost hurt. It would hurt more to let go. Cookie also moved closer to Erin, the two friends forming tight bookends, keeping Erin in their center.

"You have what you want; we have what we want. So it's over now," Jamie said. She turned to Brian. "Good luck surviving in this world. You're in so far over your head, you don't realize that you're already drowning."

Brian's smirk slid from his lips. "I think I've proven my worth here." He looked at Boxer, his expression a bit more conciliatory.

"You've kept your word, even though it took longer than it should have," Boxer quipped.

Jamie's eyes narrowed from sheer hate. "Cost you a daughter, but hey, I guess it's worth it to you."

"It might also cost me a sister if you keep it up," Brian replied, his message sharply delivered.

Boxer watched with amusement the exchange between two siblings on opposite sides of the law. "Maybe we should just get rid of them. They've been trouble in the past, and you know, we've got them out here. Maybe we can just add to Drake's legacy by putting a few more bodies in the water."

"I don't think that's a good idea," Jamie said. "It's in your best interest that we get out alive."

"I doubt that," Brian scoffed, checking Boxer to gauge his response.

Boxer held his hand up, his eyes locked on Jamie's. "I'm listening."

"Before we came out here, I wrote a detailed email about you," she said, pointing to Boxer. "And you." She pointed to Brian. "Along with all the details about Kristen's death, the journals, this meeting, everything. And I set it on a delayed delivery. So if I'm not back to delete the draft, Detective Herrera will be looking for you tomorrow."

Jamie and Boxer stared at each other, her expression stoic as he considered her words. Jamie could almost see the wheels turning in his head, weighing the risk of having a possible trail out there should anything happen to her or her crew.

"I tell you what," Boxer said. "We're going to call this even. I don't like unnecessary violence, and we both have what we want here. Extra bodies are bad for business, so we can call it even."

Jamie nodded and said nothing more, hesitating to make eye contact, even with Cookie. The negotiation was between her and Boxer. And with a successful exchange under her belt, Jamie wanted nothing more than to get away from Drake's Den as quickly as possible.

Jamie was about to take a step back when the sound of gravel crunching pulled her attention. Jamie and Cookie each turned to the side to look, keeping Erin between them as they watched Boxer witness two SUVs drive toward them. Boxer's three henchmen all drew their weapons, watching, eyes darting between the vehicles and back to Boxer.

Boxer drew his own weapon and commanded, "Take the tires!" Boxer's fire took the front two in short order, and the approaching SUV swerved from the hit. Boxer's backup shooters remained stoic, unmoving.

"What the hell is wrong with you?" Boxer barked, clearly angry his backup had failed to do just that. Instead, the three men rested their weapons at their sides. Boxer, a mixture of confusion and anger on his face, returned his attention to the wounded vehicle, waiting for the unwanted guests to appear. "I'll deal with you later," he said over his shoulder.

The back passenger door opened, and Marissa Deltone stepped out, no weapon pointing, just her arms at her sides. Her driver, tall enough to rival a professional basketball player, and two other men stepped out of the car. All four walked toward the group in standoff, Marissa at the lead. The doors on the second car opened, and four more men emerged, walking to the opposite side of the group. Jamie could see they had weapons on their belts, though no one was pointing them at anyone.

"Well, things just got interesting, didn't they?" Marissa asked, looking at Boxer. "Did you really think I would let you have one scrap of information related to my business? It isn't yours to claim."

For the first time, Jamie could swear she saw a hint of fear in Boxer's eyes, another reminder of how much power the Deltone family wielded. Boxer fidgeted as he shifted his weight, his eyes surveying the number of men Marissa had under her command. His posture straightened, and he answered her. "You may have more men, but I'll make sure I aim for you first. Are you willing to go that far?"

Brian watched the exchange between the two rivals. Kristen's journals were still in his possession, and he looked more worried as the seconds passed. Jamie watched his fearful expression as he finally realized he had risen above his pay grade. He would never be on par with the likes of the Deltone family.

Marissa looked at Boxer's lead henchman and winked at him. He and his two assistants promptly turned their weapons on Brian and Boxer.

Jamie pulled Erin back several steps, and Cookie followed her lead.

Boxer's mouth fell open, his eyes registering that his own men had turned on him. "What the hell is wrong with you, Antonio?" he barked at his armed help, who had seemingly switched sides.

"She pays really well," Antonio offered. The man then looked at Jamie. "And don't think I didn't see the gun wrapped in foil."

Jamie smiled. "I thought you would be better than that."

"I am," he replied.

Marissa walked toward Brian and held her hands out. "The journals, please. I'm going to give you a chance to give them to me nicely so I don't have to humiliate you in front of all these people."

Brian handed Marissa the journals, and Jamie could see that his hands shook as he released them from his grasp. Then he stood there, his hands free of the one thing he'd sacrificed everything for, and his fingers twitched by his sides.

Despite his size, Antonio demonstrated his stealth, quickly moving behind Boxer. His muscular left arm wrapped around Boxer's neck, and his right hand quickly disarmed his former boss. Boxer struggled for only a moment before releasing his grip on the weapon, Antonio's sheer strength too much to overcome. Although unarmed, Boxer's stance remained confident, as though he still commanded the group.

Marissa then moved slowly toward Boxer. "You have a reputation for having no code, right? So here's a lesson for you. When you have that reputation, your people won't be loyal to you because you give them no reason." She pointed at Boxer's men. "You have to earn their loyalty so they will return it. Fear alone doesn't work for long. Someone like me comes along—someone willing to pay very well—and that's all it takes. Your men are now my men."

Jamie had no desire to witness anything that might happen to Boxer and Brian now that Erin's safety had been secured. "We're going to leave you so you all can finish your business," she interjected. "Erin's been through enough."

Marissa nodded. "Yes, go. We still have some loose ends to handle."

Jamie looked at Brian. Fear claimed his features, from his wide eyes to his parted lips, and his body trembled visibly. Jamie left him to fend for himself, just as he had done with Kristen. He began bargaining for his safety, stuttering and making promises, the words running together as he rambled.

Jamie almost felt sorry for him. Almost.

She led Erin to the car and opened the back passenger's door. Erin slid inside the car, while Jamie and Cookie took their seats in the front. Once safely inside, they all breathed a sigh of unified relief.

Jamie paused before putting her car in reverse, watching as Boxer and Brian walked to the shack with Marissa's crew of men behind them. Marissa looked over her shoulder, squinting at Jamie's headlights.

"Go," she mouthed, waving them off.

Jamie put her Tahoe in reverse. Her tires ground the gravel, and clouds of dust billowed below her car.

Erin sat upright and inhaled deeply. She tapped Jamie on the shoulder. "Did you go to Taqueria San Juan without me?"

Jamie smiled at her friend. "Nice to have you back."

Cookie reached down, grabbed a foil-wrapped taco, and handed it to her. "We saved you one."

Jamie drove away from Drake's Den and considered looking back one more time but thought better of it. She was done living in the past, and Brian was part of what she ached to leave behind.

She glanced at Cookie, who was watching Erin, and knew she had enough.

She had everything she needed.

CHAPTER THIRTY-FIVE

J AMIE WAITED TWO FULL DAYS before contacting Marissa to ask for a meeting. She wanted one more favor and wasn't sure Marissa would oblige. When Marissa replied, she directed Jamie to an old pier down by the ferry landing. Jamie wasn't sure she was ready to travel in the direction of Drake's Den, but this time, she would stay on Port Alene's shores.

She arrived a few minutes early and followed the sidewalk path running parallel to the ferry line, noting how many trucks with fishing racks, coolers, and other related tools patiently waited to travel to Arlington Pass. While she loved taking the ferry, she knew it would be some time before she did it again, especially with the knowledge of that small pocket of darkness nestled on the other side.

She walked slowly but with purpose, observing the people around her. The park by the ferry was busy, even though it was barely noon. The sun, normally unforgiving, had hidden behind a wide stretch of clouds, causing the temperature to decline from burning to merely roasting. It was downright brisk by South Texas standards.

Three little girls swung from monkey bars at a children's park on the other side. A man in his thirties held his arms up in case they needed to be caught. Jamie smiled at his gesture. He was there even if they didn't need him at the moment. *More little girls should have that.*

Jamie continued on, the breeze blowing the hair sticking out of her Corpus Christi Hooks baseball cap. She'd pulled it low, to the point of almost grazing her sunglasses. Looking around, she noticed things she'd somehow missed in previous trips to the ferry landing—the formations of decorative rocks around the edge of the park, how many benches were available for visitors to sit and enjoy the water, the little things that made the area a haven to visitors and locals alike.

Jamie came upon the pier and traveled to the far side. The weathered wood creaked underneath her feet, each step making itself known. She was alone on the pier with no one else to share the space or overhear any conversation. It was solitary in the way Jamie loved. Once at the end, she rested her forearms on the pier's ledge, letting tiny wooden fragments poke her skin.

She waited.

Jamie checked her watch. Marissa was almost a half hour late. She reached inside her bag to retrieve her phone, when she heard the creak of footsteps. Turning around, she spotted Marissa walking toward her with the same confidence that had carried her at Drake's Den. She didn't smile exactly, but her lips considered it, offering a small hint of a grin.

"How are you doing?" Marissa asked, moving next to Jamie to take in the view from the pier's edge. She slipped a small sling pack from her shoulder and placed it on the ground next to her.

"I'm alive, Erin's alive, Cookie's alive, so it's good," Jamie replied. "How are you?"

Marissa avoided eye contact. "I'm fine. I don't particularly enjoy every part of my… work, but it's necessary. The family is strong. My abuela says hello, by the way."

Jamie smiled. "I really like your abuela."

"She has that effect on people."

"I can tell." Jamie leaned a bit more toward the water, her body over the pier's ledge, letting the breeze blow stronger on her face. "So, how much should I know about what happened after we left?"

Marissa turned to look at Jamie. "The less, the better. Better for you, better for me."

Jamie held Marissa's gaze. "Is Brian alive?"

Marissa stared into Jamie's eyes for several seconds, expressionless. "Yes, he's alive, but getting around will be difficult for some time. And I have a feeling he's going to be picked up on a big bust in the near future. Definite jail time, no question. He won't see it coming."

Jamie grinned at the idea of Brian finally paying for some of his sins. "I shouldn't be smiling. That's awful."

Marissa held her hands up, and there was definitely a small smile on her lips. "Not judging." She then reached for her sling pack and placed it on the top of the ledge. She pulled open the drawstring top and reached inside. Jamie watched as Marissa pulled out the contents of the bag.

"You wanted this?" she asked, handing Jamie the travel book Kristen had used as part of her coding system.

Jamie reached for it carefully, then ran her hand over the cover, admiring its battered beauty and the memories it held for her. "Thank you."

"I took the liberty of pulling a few pages out," Marissa explained. "Safety concerns."

"The books are only valuable when used together, but I see your point."

Marissa shrugged. "Call me paranoid."

Jamie slid the book into her shoulder bag, the weight of it now a comfort rather than a burden. She was grateful to have some small reminder of her niece.

"Do I want to know about Boxer?" Jamie asked.

Marissa made a clicking sound with her tongue. "You definitely don't want to know anything about Boxer. You can tell Erin he will no longer be a problem for her and we are now square on my debt to her." She brushed her hands together as though she were wiping away the debt. "We're even."

Jamie extended her hand to Marissa. "So this is it? I guess I'll see you around."

"I hope not," Marissa said. "You're all too much trouble." Her smile returned.

Jamie smiled back. "Say hello to your abuela for me."

Marissa pushed her body from the pier's ledge. "Say hello to Cookie for me."

Jamie nodded and watched Marissa walk across the pier. The sound of her steps grew faint as she made it back to the sidewalk, and her long black hair blew to one side, revealing the silhouette of her face. She never looked back.

Another thing the two women had in common.

CHAPTER THIRTY-SIX

A MONTH HAD PASSED SINCE THE Drake's Den incident, and Jamie had since thrown herself back into the dull comfort of divorce cases and surveillance work. She sat at Hemingway's bar, waiting for Cookie and watching Marty sling drinks as he egged patrons on to share their latest stories. She signaled to Marty, touching her empty glass with the top of her forefinger. "Uno mas, por favor."

Deuce sat next to her on a high-backed barstool, a padded cushion providing enough stability for the stocky bulldog to stay balanced. Marty had placed a bowl of water on the bar for him, which he largely ignored. The pup would settle for nothing less than jalapeno poppers.

"I've got you covered, don't worry," Marty called from across the bar as he reached for a clean beer glass. As Jamie turned to look toward the door, Cookie walked in. He claimed the empty seat next to Deuce. Jamie had saved it for him by placing her satchel on the stool. He put the bag on the floor, prompting a scolding. "Give me that." She wrapped the strap around her leg before letting it fall to the floor. "No one's going to lift this bag without taking my leg with it."

"Must be one of those girl tricks I'm glad I don't have to deal with." Cookie signaled to Marty for a drink. Marty navigated his way through two other bartenders and brought them matching beer glasses. "Another blonde ale for the lady and a Fireman's Four for the gentleman."

"We are definitely in the wrong place," Cookie joked. "Do you see a lady?" His jab at Jamie resulted in a mock stink-eyed stare.

"Be nice," Jamie said.

"I love you, you know that."

Jamie grabbed a handful of peanuts from a nearby bowl, causing

Deuce to take note. "Marty," she called, "can we get some chicken strips for Deuce?"

He nodded at her and tended to the other waiting patrons piling up at the bar. Cookie held his glass up for Jamie to toast. "Cheers."

The clinking of the vessels almost caused beer to spill over the top, foam threatening to escape down the sides of the glasses. The two friends drained their glasses like stranded sailors on an island, prompting Jamie to signal to Marty by circling her finger in the air to bring another round.

At that moment, Erin walked through the door and waved to her friends. "Bring me whatever they're having," she called to Marty as she pulled up a barstool and sat next to Cookie.

Cookie reached over and gave Erin a side hug, while Jamie offered her friend a wave from a few stools over.

"How are things at Silver Sands?" Jamie asked.

Erin reached for the bowl of stale snack mix and popped some of the salted concoction in her mouth. "Business is great. I think I'm going to start needing Deuce at least once a week for appearances. All my regulars love him."

Deuce turned his face in her direction at the mention of his name, but when no food was offered, he quickly lost interest. Jamie gave his head a pat and reminded him that food was on the way.

"So, you want to take the Carter case?" Cookie asked, leaning over Deuce so Jamie could hear him above the conversations of nearby patrons.

She nodded. "Absolutely. I'm ready for some good old-fashioned domestic drama that pays well." She took a long draw from her beer glass. "I can't believe I just said that."

Cookie placed his hand on Deuce's head, giving him a solid behind-the-ear rub. "I agree. It's kind of nice to have some boring, basic cases for a bit."

Jamie felt her phone vibrating in her back pocket. She reached behind her, retrieved it, and glanced at the screen. She recognized the number as Huntsville Prison. Brian had been trying to reach her since his unfortunate drug bust down in the Valley.

After a few seconds of deliberation, she turned the phone off and placed it face down on the bar. She knew who her family was now.

ACKNOWLEDGMENTS

Although Port Alene is a fictional place, it was largely inspired by Port Aransas, Texas, which is our family's favorite vacation spot. Port Aransas is much more of a family town than its imaginary counterpart, and this special place has recently endured the wrath of Hurricane Harvey. While it has been devastated by this storm, I have no doubt that the wonderful people of Port Aransas will rebuild their homes and it will soon return to being one of our state's most loved holiday destinations. One special place, the William R. Bill Ellis Public Library, experienced substantial loss. So if you are a library lover in search of a good cause, please consider supporting this jewel of a community library.

A special thank-you to the Port Aransas Police Department and to the many local businesses that answered questions and allowed me a glimpse into their daily lives.

Writing is often a solitary pursuit, but by no means was I alone while writing this book. I'm so thankful to have had the support of my fellow Austin Mystery Writers members—Elizabeth Buhmann, Valerie Chandler, Kaye George, Scott Montgomery, Manfred Reimann, and Kathy Waller—as this book evolved from characters in my head to a finished novel. I'm fortunate to be among a group of such supportive and talented people.

I would like to extend a special thanks to Gretchen Archer and Wendy Tyson, who, in addition to being extremely talented and successful authors, are also wonderful friends. Thanks for helping me get through the bumps in the road.

And finally, a very special thanks to my family, who have supported me while I have juggled writing projects with work, family, and community commitments. David, Rachel, Ryan, and William—you are my world. To my mom and John David, thank you for your support and your faith. And to Henry and Marian—well, everyone should be so lucky to have such fantastic in-laws.

ABOUT THE AUTHOR

Laura Oles is a photo industry journalist who spent twenty years covering tech and trends before turning to crime fiction. She has been widely published in numerous photography magazines and has served as a columnist for several trade and consumer publications.

Growing up in a military family, Laura discovered the frequent travels were made more enjoyable with the company of Nancy Drew. She has been an avid reader and writer of mysteries ever since.

Laura is a Writers' League of Texas Award Finalist and is a member of Sisters in Crime and Austin Mystery Writers. She lives in the Texas Hill Country with her husband, daughter and twin sons.

CPSIA information can be obtained
at www.ICGtesting.com
Printed in the USA
LVOW10s0305160518
577269LV00001B/48/P

9 780615 816319